W. Parker

Wandering Thoughts and Wandering Steps

Volume 1

W. Parker

Wandering Thoughts and Wandering Steps
Volume 1

ISBN/EAN: 9783337194178

Printed in Europe, USA, Canada, Australia, Japan

Cover: Foto ©Andreas Hilbeck / pixelio.de

More available books at **www.hansebooks.com**

WANDERING THOUGHTS

AND

WANDERING STEPS.

BY

A PHILADELPHIA LADY.

"Go, little book, from this my solitude!
I cast thee on the waters,—go thy ways!
And if, as I believe, thy vein be good,"
A few "will find thee after many days."

PHILADELPHIA:
J. B. LIPPINCOTT & CO.
1880.

PREFACE.

FAR away toward the rising sun is our Mecca, the Old World. Toward its shrines, pilgrim-like, our steps wander. We put on our sandals, prepare our scrip, take up our staff, and turn to seek a companion with whom to cull sweet flowers by the wayside, and to chat on subjects "grave and gay, pleasant and severe."

Will you, kind reader, be our companion while we thus beguile the way and *peep—only peep*—into a few interesting places? If so, when arrayed in a vesture of that gentle "charity which believeth all things, hopeth all things," and forgiveth all imperfections, we shall recognize in you the sympathetic friend and reader whom we seek.

Our first literary venture is a very modest one. We launch our little bark on the tide of public opinion, conscious that it will be buffeted by many waves, but trusting that it will not be utterly wrecked through harsh criticism.

" Be to its virtues very kind,
Be to its faults a little blind."

CONTENTS.

WANDERING THOUGHTS AND WANDERING STEPS.

CHAPTER I.

PARIS—VERSAILLES.

PARIS.

WE consider it a happy fact that our first introduction to Paris is by gaslight; for so dazzlingly brilliant are the scenes that meet our delighted gaze as we ride through the grand boulevards, that we think their splendors must pale under the light of a mid-day sun; probably remembering that those physical charms that are often bewildering under the gaslit chandelier wane under the prosaic, disenchanting light of day. Of no luxury is Paris more prodigal than that of gas; the streets at night are ablaze with it, and when the hundreds of jets are arranged, as on the Champs Elysées, in fanciful designs, the effect is resplendent beyond description; we need not look up into the firmament above, for stars of scintillating ray are shining around us, making the air quivering and bright with their twinkling light.

The boulevards are swarming with the most animated life; for French life is an out-door one, and it is here that the cream of society floats on the surface, while the less attractive phase of human existence is so far below that one seldom meets with it. We think that the distinguishing peculiarity of Paris street-life is that nothing repulsive ever obtrudes itself; all is glamour, brightness, and exuberance, with no suggestion of sickness, cloud, sorrow, or death.

As we ride through boulevards, each of marvellous width, allowing "ample room and verge enough" for the gay, good-humored crowds, numberless concert-gardens glittering with illuminated lights; "the night filled with music;" laughter refined, often feminine, mingling joyously on the air; the hundreds of seats on the broad avenue filled with elegance and fashion; military accoutrements flashing in the light; clashing swords giving a martial ring to the gay sounds, we repeat our felicitations that this brilliant phase of human life—the brightest we have ever seen—should be our introductory experience to this, the most brilliant city of the world. Imagining that the next morning the streets, like deserted banqueting halls, will show only the traces of a past revelry, seeming in the whitish glare of day comparatively unattractive.

A cup of nectar, as we think, but called by the ordinary name of coffee; rolls, white, crisp, and toothsome, with tiny moulds of unsalted butter, form the dainty repast brought to our room next morning. A leisurely, luxurious toilet, a wandering through the salons, and we are summoned to the eleven o'clock French breakfast, *déjeûner à la fourchette,* after which our first day in Paris begins.

We feel sure that the sun loves Paris; it seems always to hover in its sky, shedding upon the glorious city its most beaming rays. On one of the brightest of days we take a carriage and give ourselves up to enjoyment, for this is a lesson quickly learned of the people. We have no recollection of any experience more delightsome than a ride through the boulevards of Paris. Their surface being as smooth as glass, one is never rocked or jostled, but borne on gently and swiftly through scenes fascinatingly animated and bright. As we glide by stores, magnificent in display and decoration; buildings suggestive of affluence, grandeur, and old-time royalty; fashion rampant; women piquant and sparkling; men the pink of elegance and the very synonyme of polish and grace; fountains whose waters seem to shower diamonds; statues world-famed; towers and monuments of rare historic interest, and parterres gleaming on every side with a luxuriant growth of shrubs and flowers; the air, mellowed by a grateful warmth, seeming perfumed in its deliciousness; music floating dreamily on the air, we feel that this world is full of beauty, joy, and charm.

The Seine, which divides the city into two parts, is crossed by twenty-seven bridges, and its pretty banks, as we approach the rural suburbs of the city, during an excursion to St. Cloud, form a most picturesque feature. Some of its bridges are of grand construction, and are graced with fine statuary.

Passing through the magnificent Place de la Concorde, where colossal statues, representing the principal cities of France, surround two mammoth fountains, we enter the Champs Elysées, an avenue that has no rival in Europe and is the centre of the social world. It presents a scene gorgeous and dazzling; it seems to be an epitome of all the varied delights that can greet the senses. Many beautiful kiosks and chalets; fanciful cafés embowered in green and gay with music; sumptuous equipages in showy liveries dashing by the grand arch which crowns the summit; equestrians superbly mounted; gay crowds composed of the representatives of every nation, it would seem, Orientals often in their national garb; even peasants giving quaint charm to the picture by their unique, bright costume; fountains playing; trees o'ershadowing; flowers blooming; men wooing; women flirting; nature and mechanical skill contributing from their deep-est resources to form a scene of perfect beauty and human felicity. Dull care is exiled; ennui unknown; poverty a stranger; and the thought of death banished from the mind.

We cannot imagine a scene more impregnated with all the elements of joyous life, where the most phleg-matic must be moved to vivacious expression and the most stolid won from their habitual apathy. Paris seems to be the city counterpart of the country Eden of our first parents, offering all the delights possible to a town residence.

Beyond the Arc de Triomphe lies the Bois de Bou-logne, with its rural attractions, which, however, were much despoiled by the rude touch of the late war. We remember with pleasure taking this famous drive many years since, when royalty gave *éclat* to a scene as brilliant as the human imagination could conceive. A coach and four, with outriders, announced the fact that the emperor, Napoleon III., was approaching. There he sat impassive, silent and self-absorbed, accompanied by several august-looking personages. Catching his eye, we bowed, and he, probably recognizing the courtesy as from those whose country was always kindly re-membered by him, doffed his hat graciously to us. It was the last time that we met the man who, then at the pinnacle of human power and greatness, was, ere long, to die in ignominious exile, shorn of all that had made life to him a brilliant victory.

Alas! what tragedies do human experiences often afford! How little thought she—Eugenie—whose queenly appearance suggested the title; whose graceful form, regal air, and charming beauty so well became royal attire and dignity, that before a decade had passed she would be an object of such pitiable commiseration as to win tears from all womanly eyes!

At the hotels and in most of the stores on the Continent there is always some one to be found who understands and can speak English, but the drivers are all most provokingly tenacious of their own idiom, and will neither understand our native tongue nor its substitute,—pantomime. There are, however, so many English and American travellers who speak French, that there is almost always some good Samaritan among them who will step forward and create an understanding between perplexed parties; so that one does not often experience painfully the need of the accomplishment, although the ability to speak the French is convenient, and adds materially to the pleasure of foreign travel.

The experience of an American lady whom we met in Paris is a representative one, and we will endeavor to " tell the tale as 'twas told to us."

Mrs. C. was theoretically acquainted with the French

language, but had never been made familiar with its
verbal practice, her ear and tongue being alike uneducated to its use. Her husband's knowledge consisted
of a heterogeneous collection of words which lacked
linguistical cement, if we may use the expression, to
connect into intelligible sentences. Imagine the pair,
then, during their first afternoon in Paris, as having
the courage to enter a voiture, utterly unable to pro-
nounce the names of the streets in a comprehensible
manner, and trusting to that good genius—luck—which
had so far befriended them. To find the address of a
certain friend was their first object; congratulating
themselves upon the driver's evident understanding of
their maiden attempts at his own language, they gave
themselves up to an enjoyment of the fleeting panorama as they drove through the gorgeous streets of
the wonderful city. But, unhappily, their pleasure
was soon at an end: the carriage halted at the entrance
to a mean court, and Mr. C. jumping boldly out and
knocking at the first door, was met by a bland, smiling
Frenchwoman who, alas! could not understand a word
of his query. On he passed from door to door, and
before many moments was surrounded by vociferating
women, each trying to explain and inquire, until he
was wellnigh deafened and distracted by their futile
attempts to relieve his perplexity. Mrs. C. rushed
forward, followed by the driver, only increasing the

Babel by the addition of their tongues. At length, struck by a happy thought, one woman, with beaming face and earnest gesture, motioned them toward a door which they had not seen. In response to her rap a pleasant, handsome man made his appearance, who, upon reading the ill-fated address on the card they handed him, spoke a few magic words to the puzzled driver, and, with true French grace and politeness, with many a smile and bow, received their cordial thanks. All looked relieved; the crowd dispersed; Mr. and Mrs. C. re-entered the voiture and drove off with lightened hearts.

Their next halt was at the desired haven; but when that business was accomplished their troubles were renewed. Mrs. C. sat in the voiture, while her husband, facing the driver, endeavored by pantomime to explain that they would like to drive up and down the splendid boulevards. Giving a wide sweep with his hand, he was startled to find it had come into contact with a man's hat. The man, a peaceable citizen walking the street, was staggered by the blow, which had wellnigh struck him in the face, and turning to inquire angrily into the matter, was met by such profuse apologies from the driver, who sought to explain the inadvertence, and by such gesticulations of regret from the unlucky stranger, that his rising choler was appeased, and he passed on. Here Mr. C., wellnigh discouraged, stood with corrugated brow, striving to root out from his memory the desired words to explain his wishes, when suddenly his face brightened and his thought blossomed into the words " *Allez à les belles femmes,*" as he jumped with satisfied air into the voiture.

This was more than Mrs. C.'s equanimity could bear, and, catching the driver's sympathizing glance at her and his horrified gaze upon her husband, she hastily explained, " *Non, non, il veut dire les beaux magasins,*" and, leaning back in the carriage, yielded to a hearty burst of laughter. Up scrambled the driver, and, cracking his whip, off he drove. "Do you suppose," said Mrs. C., after they had ridden some time, "that he finally understood?"

"I know not," said her husband, in despairing tones. "Let him take us where he will, *I* shall not try again;" and, applauding the wisdom of the resolve, she followed his example.

A prominent and popular institution in Paris is its hotel-life, delightfully represented in "The Continental," which is capable of accommodating fifteen hundred guests; and happy guests they should be, with every comfort provided and luxuries abounding. Its banqueting-hall of mammoth proportions and regal in its appointments is worthy in fresco, carving, architectural finish, gorgeous draperies, paintings, superb furniture, and crystal to be famed as an appropriate appendage to any palace in Europe. This apartment is reserved for unusual occasions, and for an extra *table-d'hôte* on the Sabbath, when its immense tables are crowded with a brilliant company, mostly from Paris circles.

We live, indeed, in a luxurious age, when, for a few dollars per day, we may, by registering our names at such a hotel, enjoy the luxuries afforded by the rarest cuisine; well-trained attendance and a wealth of beauty displayed in chambers and salons; without effort fancying ourselves legitimate incumbents of a palace; with the added blessing of security, which such do not always enjoy; going out and coming in without fear of the assassinating knife or traitorous gunpowder.

After a day spent, as can be nowhere outside of Paris, we make as elaborate a toilet as is possible for tourists, and descending, enter the brilliant salons, now dazzling with artificial light and charming with human grace and beauty. Having previously procured the tickets to be presented at the door of the *salle à manger*, we join the crowd, and find ourselves soon seated at one of the many large tables. We look around us. The scene is an impressive one, and would be if the apartment itself were the only object of interest. It is immense, with very lofty ceiling, which repays one for the effort of upward gazing, as it glitters in the flood of gaslight with brilliant, artistic

beauty; mirrors sparkle everywhere; fine frescoed
pictures filling intermediate spaces, while the tables
are made bright and alluring by a profusion of rare
plants and flowers, silver and white and colored crystal.

But the human is an important element of attraction,
and the rustling of silks and the flashing of diamonds
invite the wondering gaze to women whose beauty
gladdens not only masculine eyes, but those of their
less-favored sisters, however incredulous men may be
of the fact. Some radiant in natural charms, and all
in those of elegant dress, their finer sensibilities exhil-
arated by the splendor, brightness, and glow around
them; men in studied toilets, their gallantry appearing
in gracious form, with faces expressing content with
the prospect before them.

The tables are of great width, permitting one, if
inclined, to comment upon a *vis-à-vis* without detec-
tion. No bustling, obtrusive service to annoy; the
quick, noiseless tread of attendants adding animation
to the scene. No clatter of dishes, only the faint
sound of glass and china, which is pleasantly suggestive
to the waiting appetite. We have it proved to us that
the French are masters of the gastronomic art; dainties of wondrous concoction, which defy analysis, must
be partaken of with a simplicity of faith which is
rewarded through the palate.

The scene gathers interest. The feast of appetite

induces a " flow of soul ;" faces brighten under stimulating influences, and, although voices are modulated by refined instinct, yet there is a livelier ring in their notes as the talk flows on the crimson tide of wine. It is an inspiriting scene of elegance, display, and animated enjoyment, which all, whatever the temperament, must recognize and respond to.

We are all more or less sybarites by nature; even those endowed with natural energy, if necessity did not urge its exertion, or some other impelling motive did not prompt its exercise, would soon be found drifting on some sunny, sluggish stream of life, ready to anchor in any inviting harbor.

The love of luxurious ease is natural, and, however antagonistic it may be to the previous habits of a man's life, it is astonishing how quickly he becomes enamored of the seductive charms of an elegant leisure.

After the dinner, which has occupied an hour and a half, we saunter into the salons, one of which in all its details is a perfect imitation of a Turkish apartment. The effect is delightful, heightened by soft music, mellow lights, and gliding forms in rich array; and as, through satisfaction of appetite, an impetus is given to the social nature, a pleasing hum of voices makes a flowing undercurrent of sound.

Donning our overgarments, we are soon on our way to probably the grandest opera-house in the world.   It was a pet creation of Napoleon III., and in every particular testifies to its exceeding cost and magnificence. Indeed, it would be difficult to distract one's attention from the elaborate architectural and artistic beauties of the building to concentrate it upon the stage and the players. The entrance and the corridors, which form a grand promenade between the acts, are majestic and splendidly imposing. The situation of the opera-house is well chosen, as it is in the vicinity of several fine boulevards, for which also we are indebted to the late emperor, who imprinted upon the city, which it was his ambition to embellish and glorify, his own elegant and, it would seem, classical taste. Whatever his weaknesses and even faults, we will not withhold the admiring commendation due his laudable and successful efforts to make Paris *the* city of the world, a city " whose light cannot be hid." May it continue to enliven and gladden the world with its gayety and wondrous brilliancy !

Paris in its brightness and magnificence is as indescribable as it is unrivalled; its boulevards, avenues, and principal streets are truly wonderful; their great distances, colossal statues, abundance of verdure and foliage, and fine stores, in the windows of which the elegant fabrics are arranged with all the skill, fancy, and taste which distinguish the French, produce such an effect as dazzles and fascinates the beholder.

We draw a deep sigh as we turn our backs upon the seductive delights of a city where gloom seems a stranger, and where, unlike any other known spot on the globe, no lurking shadows hover. Charm is something so subtile in its nature that it eludes verbal or written description, so that we can never hope to analyze the attraction which Paris has for all who have walked in its sunshine and mingled in its gay, brilliant scenes.

Very many have explored the *heart* of a city, but how few comparatively have penetrated to its very *bowels*. This we do in visiting the *intestine*-like sewerage of Paris. They are one of the most astonishing features of this remarkable city, and are a triumph of engineering skill; the prose of Paris life, while its poetry rises higher, having rare illustrations in the art-galleries and even in some phases of street-life.

The most singular excursion we have ever made is through these sewers. So great is the demand for entrance that is extremely difficult to obtain a *permis*, and it can only be accomplished through the influence of our resident minister.

A friend, with "power at court," procuring admission for himself and family, includes us in the novel experience. A party of a dozen sallying out at midday find themselves standing around a flat grating on the sidewalk, under the very shadow of the beautiful

Church of the Madeleine. Presently the square grating is uplifted, revealing a stone flight of winding stairs, narrow, dark, and uninviting.

> " Deep was the cave, and downward as it went
> From the wide mouth a rocky, rough descent ;
> And there . . . th' lake extends
> O'er whose unhappy waters, void of light,
> No bird presumes to steer his airy flight."

Arriving at the base we look instinctively around for the old boatman, Charon, for it seems to our excited imagination that the river Styx flows sluggishly by at our feet. What we do see is a turgid stream, whose dark waters betray its impurity, and on it, awaiting our entrance, a boat resembling an ordinary row-boat. Attached to it by ropes are two men, who are to pull it forward. On each side of this murky river is a narrow tow-path, wide enough for a single man. We look aloft and around us to find our vision bounded by the colossal iron sewers through which we could travel three hundred miles under the city. The sombre gloom of this subterranean passage is relieved by lamps such as are used to light the streets above. They emit a lurid flame that adds to the weirdness of the scene, and as the eye glances forward to an apparently interminable distance the effect is very peculiar. The sullen waters purged of palpable impurities are yet impregnated with their essences, and fail to reflect clearly the ruddy lights which strive to brighten them.

They are like many souls which, clouded by the darkness of sin, repel Heaven's light and refuse to open their recesses to its healing beams. On and on we speed, drawn by the two fleet human steeds mile after mile, knowing always our location, as the lamp-posts bear the names of the streets under which we are floating. Peering into the dim distance the immense sewer seems to narrow to impassable limits, and yet when we reach that horizon, we find ourselves still in apparently unrestrained liberty.

At the expiration of perhaps half an hour we are disembarked and transferred to an open car, which runs on rails and spans a narrower stream. The car is drawn, as was the boat, by men, and so rapidly do they bear us along that we are surprised, on reaching the terminus of our ride, to find that they are not breathless, but all standing quietly by in their harness with no appearance of weariness. To our great relief we find no dog Cerberus guarding the portal as we emerge from the Stygian gloom.

Mounting the stone steps, we are once more denizens of the upper regions. Surely we have been in the lower long enough, and are glad now to inflate our lungs with the pure air and feast our eyes with the bright sunlight, which seems to gladly greet us once again.

VERSAILLES.

The ride by rail to Versailles is an interesting one, not only from its natural picturesqueness, but because it introduces us to that portion of the country made memorable by being the site of many battles fought between Germany and France. Here, as in Paris, all traces of devastation are being obliterated, it seeming to be the policy of the republic—a policy well conceived—to teach the people forgetfulness by removing all vestiges of an experience harrowing and fermenting to the thought and disturbing to the peace.

Reaching Versailles, once a populous city, but long since dwindled to the insignificance of a sluggish town, we find an omnibus awaiting the arrival of the train. With dismay we are compelled to the necessity of mounting a narrow flight of steps to occupy seats on the top. To what strange expedients does travel restrict one! Having many times before experienced its arbitrary power, we are the better prepared now to accommodate ourselves to the unfeminine situation. So "screwing our courage to the sticking-point" we scale the ladder, conscious that we are attentively watched by masculine eyes from within; for whoever knew a Frenchman to turn them away at such a time? although his inborn politeness would forbid the nearest

approach to a smile, a restraint which our awkwardness must make painful.

The Palace is an architectural marvel, probably the
finest royal residence in the world; it is more than
eight hundred feet long, and contains, beside eight
magnificent salons of paintings and statuary, a gallery
two hundred and thirty-two feet long, thirty broad, and
thirty-seven high, and is lighted by seventeen immense
windows. It is unsurpassed in magnificence by any
in Europe, being an enduring monument to the fame
of Lebrun, to whom it is indebted for its architectural
perfection. We look in upon the chamber in which
Louis XIV. closed his brilliant reign: the bed on
which he died has been restored to its original condition; and, as if to present a marked contrast, the next
room shown is where Louis XVI. used to dine in
public on Sundays with his queen, Marie Antoinette.
Among the salons is the card-room where Madame de
Montespan is said to have lost in one night four hundred thousand pistoles. The effect of all this display
of immensity, grandeur, beauty of decoration, of furniture, and of artistic treasure upon those whose tastes
and associations are of republican simplicity is almost
overwhelming. We experience actual relief when introduced into that part of the Palace containing the
petites appartements de Marie Antoinette, for they are
marked by an even uninviting degree of plainness,

singularly destitute of the luxurious embellishments which abound elsewhere.

Within the boundaries of the park are the two villas called the Grand and the Petit Trianons. The first was built by Louis XIV. for Madame Maintenon. It is in Italian style, and consists of but one story with two wings, and is handsomely ornamented with paintings and statuary. The Petit Trianon is small and of simple construction, built by Louis XV. for Madame Du Barry, and afterwards appropriated by Marie Antoinette as the nucleus of a little Swiss village, composed of a few rustic houses, a mill, and a dairy. 'Tis said that, surfeited with the splendors of the great Palace and ennuied with the cold formalities of court-life, she delighted to escape from them, seeking with her husband this rural retreat for a while to play the rôle of pastoral queen. A part of the romance was to go to the dairy, and there skim the milk with queenly hands and pat the butter into pretty forms between her delicate royal palms. Indeed, she might well be pleased with her novel task, for the dairy, situated in a lovely, sylvan spot, secluded from courtly or rustic gaze, amid sweet growth of shrub and tree, furnished with white marble shelves, a crystal stream running through, forms a graceful little temple for the royal worshipper of pastoral life.

It is affirmed that this pretty conceit of the romantic

queen cost her the respect of her subjects, who, loving display and magnificence in the royal estate, had no sympathy with this unqueenly whim. Believing, too, that courtly dignity was forfeited thereby, the prejudice already springing up against her was increased by this really harmless indulgence.

As we saunter through the pleasant woods back to the Petit Trianon we are filled with sad, regretful thought, that this innocent, pure-minded woman, with such a yearning for the simple joys of life, weary of the burdensome obligations of royal rank, should, by courting happiness in its simplest forms, have incurred denunciation. We should think that womanly sympathy and chivalric admiration and approval would have been her meed, instead of condemnation for this and for the other frivolous offences which culminated in her terrible fate. In the Petit Trianon we stand in the small room which the queen and the king occupied; the furniture, even to the simple bed, standing as they did one hundred years ago, when this pretty farce of country life was enacted. The dressing-table is mounted with a glass exceedingly small, but large enough to reflect the sweet face and the delicate neck which were to be sacrificed to the guillotine by the cruel mandate of an infuriated people. Not satisfied with the blood of the weak-minded king, they thirsted for that of the woman whose dignified mien, courageous bearing, and gentle patience, during the last months of her life, proved her to have been a woman of character and of magnanimous soul.

The park pertaining to the Palace is fifty miles in circumference, and offers the most diversified attraction of temples, pavilions, artificial lakes, groves, parterres, and shrubbery, with a prodigal display of exquisite statuary. The fountains are numerous, and when playing present the most extraordinary spectacle of the kind in the world. The magnificence of the park and gardens accords with that of the grand structure to which they belong. They are most surely the creation of great talent, the more marked as nature lent no aid, the grounds being originally peculiarly uninviting, offering obstacles even difficult to conquer, "genius being obliged to struggle against nature." But what a victory did it achieve!

The Coach-House, situated between the two Trianons, contains great curiosities in the way of royal equipages. The finest was constructed for the coronation of Charles X., and was used also at the baptism of the Prince Imperial. Here, too, is the coach used by Napoleon I. when First Consul; his wedding-coach also, with others of inferior beauty, but all of fabulous cost and elegance. Heavily gilt, and displaying the most exquisite paintings on their panels, they seem like moving thrones for mighty gods, or at least for the most august sovereigns.

The Republic will scarce employ these wonderful chariots, for ostentatious display ill comports with Republicanism, which is rooted in simplicity, and if losing this distinguishing characteristic becomes a misnomer. How astounding has been the result of this republican sentiment in France! A people naturally volatile; remarkably susceptible to outward impressions; born and bred amid monarchical scenes; their national vanity and pride pampered by its dazzling display; their diversions secured through the ministry of ephemeral pleasure,—for it has ever been the policy of the French government to amuse the people, thus diverting their active minds from serious thought. They have witnessed monarchy dethroned, and pomp, upon which they once fed, fade out. Martial music no longer fills constantly the ear, nor does military presence obtrusively make brilliant every promenade in Paris, the *éclat* of royalty being superseded by the unostentatious *régime* of a republic.

And yet this people, with an adaptation that has astonished the waiting world, have so quietly and determinedly returned to the prosaic industries of life that national prosperity is assured, its sun already rising in the horizon with a brightness that is an augury of a brilliant Future. A Future whose dawning greatness shall prove more permanent than any past, because founded upon the solid rock of Republicanism, whose crystallized elements are *literal* Liberty, Equality, and Progress.

A *self*-governing people is the most reliable and substantial, because to feel that the reputation and stability of the government *depend* upon its own sobriety, dignity, and fidelity, is to develop all that inherent force and nobility which is the germ of national as well as of individual character, and the responsibility of self-government evokes it all.

Long life to our young sister Republic of France! May her characteristic enthusiasm lead her to continue, and to rejoice, in her new liberties; through her wonderful ingenuity and skill replenishing her lately exhausted treasury, and losing the reputation of a character governed by impulse and inflammable passion, win one for self-control and national stability! And now that the country is no longer under the influence of a feminine fanatical papistry, may she become a " nation whose God is the Lord!"

Endowed by nature as the French are with a skill and fancy that assume beautiful forms; a grace and polish that make them an elegant and attractive people; a politeness and urbanity of manner that win the admiration of the world,—gifts of such universal bestowment that the humblest class seem "to the manor born," —they are eminently qualified to hold a brilliant and prominent place in the family of nations.

CHAPTER II.

NICE—GENOA.

NICE.

NICE, open to a fine view of the Mediterranean, is half encircled by hills, whose rugged sides afford sites for many villas. The old portions of the city are dirty and dilapidated, its streets dark, narrow, and crooked; while the new, through the influx of visitors, has been made very elegant by the erection of fine buildings and the opening of grand boulevards.

A curious feature of the view from our window is that of a walk on the flat roofs of some low-built houses, and as we write we see many passing to and fro on the strange thoroughfare. Our eye wanders beyond to the swelling sea, which is reflecting with dazzling brilliancy the glare of a meridian sun. The scene is an interesting and animated one, and presents characteristic features of lowly life in this olden town. The fishermen and their wives are mingling together, engaged in their respective avocations; the men disentangling their nets and arranging fishing-tackle, or in

32

their little rocking boats catching sardines; women in groups, talking and washing; the beach covered with clothing spread out to dry; the waves fringed with white foam dashing up against the shore. And little children toying with the white sand, stopping at times to cast wondering glances over the surging sea, by their careless grace and bright movements add completeness to a scene worthy the eye and pencil of an artist.

Not far beyond is a walk lined with trees and called the " Promenade des Anglais," built by the subscription of some English, who wished in a time of great destitution to give employment to the poor of the town. It is the fashionable resort during an hour or two at noon, when the scene is enlivened by music from a band in the Jardin Publique at the extremity of the Promenade. Gay bevies of ladies in fascinating toilets and gentlemen in exquisite array are standing exchanging morning greetings or walking up and down; moving models of fashion and style; some cluster around a little carriage drawn by a man, in which an invalid is seated, for this climate so salubrious, and its air so pure, bright, and healthful, is found to be healing to irritated lungs and reviving to enfeebled frames. We have seldom witnessed such a scene; for although our American watering-places present such a panorama of elegance, yet here, the winter's resort of Europe, one may meet the representatives of every nation, and this infinite variety is very refreshing.

The suburbs of Nice present very delightful views, for here nature has lavished her treasures of sea and mountain, blossom and foliage. A drive on the banks of the Mediterranean affords a rare combination of loveliness and of European luxury. Fields of living green dotted with trees, some in full bloom, others weighed down with their rich burden of golden fruit in beautiful contrast with the dark green of the foliage; the dappled skies of silvery clouds, golden lights, and azure; the profusion of flowers, cacti, geraniums, and blossoming vines; the ever-changing sea, with the Italian villas on its borders and the protecting hills which crown the landscape.

In the rear of our hotel is a high hill, which forms by terraces a fine garden; its gravel walks are bordered with the luxuriant growth of flowers indigenous to this clime and a great variety of fruitful trees, the olive, date, pepper, orange, and lemon. Mounting several terraces we come to an old tower and fortress, enjoying a view whose wide sweep embraces the town, the sea, and the mountain ranges, and we wonder not to learn that this romantic ruin was the chosen spot of Meyerbeer while writing his opera "Robert Le Diable."

Not far distant, within a grove redolent with the

perfume of rare plants, and amid a wealth of bloom, is a mausoleum erected to the memory of the eldest son of the Emperor of Russia. The Czarowitz, who was twenty-two years of age when he died, had come from his own northern home to seek in this balmy clime relief from his sufferings; and perhaps he even dreamed that its soft southern breezes would bear health on their wings; but, alas! the dread fiat, which comes alike to prince and peasant, had gone forth, and he died here, in a house which stood on the spot where his parents have erected this costly and elegant memorial. Its entrance is of marble and stained glass, and within are exquisite paintings in niches on the wall. As we enter the eye first falls upon an altar which is entirely covered with richly decorated cloth, in front of which is a rug beautifully embroidered by his mother; on this a bouquet of natural flowers had been placed the day before by a sister of the deceased.

Surrounding this altar are three fine paintings, the first representing the baptism of the Czarowitz immediately after his birth; the next, the centre one, the patron saint; the third, the death-scene, with angels hovering near. The dome is very high and gorgeously ornamented in gold and fresco. Three times a year the Greek service is performed within this miniature chapel.

Remembering that Nice is the birthplace of Garibaldi, we seek out the home of his early years, finding it in an humble house, poor and dirty. At the head of the stone stairs a marble slab has been inserted in the wall, on which are inscribed his name and the year of his birth, 1807. The room in which the mother bore the embryo patriot is very small, with floor of red tile; the only article of furniture is the bed standing in an alcove. A very aged woman, soiled and grotesque in appearance, shows us his picture, below which he had written his name, with the words, "To the friend of my childhood." She had known him when, as a child, he had played on that very floor, and is proud and happy to find that we Americans have come to do honor to the patriot.

A ride over the Corniche Road, one of the most beautiful in Europe, introduces us to nature's grandest forms of beauty. The sea on one side and "Alps piled on Alps" on the other. Never have our eyes rested upon views more sublime at times, and at others more picturesque and lovely. We ascend to a height of twenty-two hundred feet above the level of the sea, looking down upon towns with their towering steeples, which seem dwarfed in the distance; upon valleys fertile and pastoral, suggestive of peace, quiet, and plenty; and upon the Mediterranean Sea, the white-crested waves gleaming like silver spangles, and the variety of colors blending as in an exquisite painting; ships, like toys, on its mirrored surface; the sunlight shedding a halo of light upon the distant hill-tops. Leafy dales and glens, filled with soft shadows, nestling in the lap of huge mountains; stupendous rocks mounting toward heaven, with a crown of snow upon their lofty brows. Billowy Alpine hills assuming majestic forms, the rays of the setting sun seeming to deck, as with rubies, their coronets and breast-plates of snow; some of them dotted to their summits with cottages and hamlets. Many ruins of buildings supposed to have been built before the Christian era; dilapidated villages; gigantic crosses; mules with panniers, such as we have seen in pictures; peasantry with their bright-colored, picturesque costume; vegetation rich and abounding; shrubbery in full blossom, all conspire to form a view worthy of the original divine benediction, "And God saw everything that he had made, and behold it was *very* good."

An hour's ride by rail brings us to Monaco, the capital of the smallest monarchy in Europe. It is composed of fifteen hundred souls; boasts of a little fleet, two cannons, a few soldiers, a palace, and a Casino, whose gorgeous salons are the attraction which allures many strangers. Introduced for the first time to a place of this character, we see much to interest, to astonish, and to shock.

The spacious salons into which we are ushered are

dazzling in display and regal in all their appointments.
Art has contributed in many forms to make the scene
beguiling and fascinating. The breath of exotics burdens the air with its oppressive sweetness, their bloom
delighting the eye with brilliant hues; music in stirring
strains, and in the softest and most subtile, excite, stimulate, and inflame. The light of day, too prosaic for
such a scene, is excluded, and gas-light, which can be
made tributary to the producing of certain influences,
is mellowed and subdued; a suppressed quiet, yet vital
with the germ of intense feeling, marks the occasion;
while rich color, potent in effect, pervades the air.
The very atmosphere and all the surroundings conspire to beguile the senses and to pander to the lower
feelings of human nature.

In each salon there are several large tables covered
with green cloth, a revolving wheel set in the centre of
each. In arm-chairs, seated as closely as possible, are
the absorbed players, a crowd of attentive spectators surrounding them. The study of their faces is a singular
one. Some, as they stretch forth their polished wooden
rakes and draw in their gains, look delighted, while
the unfortunate ones, in many cases, fail to conceal their
chagrin. At one table stands a young American of
about twenty, whose evident pleasure as the money he
has won is handed him attracts our attention. He hesi-
tatingly lays on the table another coin, and as he sees

it swept away, with heightened color and anxious eye repeats the act and re-repeats it, only to lose again and again, until in disgust he turns away.

As we look aloft at the magnificent ceiling, and around us upon the gorgeous display of art, decoration, and dress, and watch the faces which, in many instances, express the most evil passions of our nature; seeing women without a blush of shame lay down their money, and hoary heads, even, bowing low over their gains; we feel that we have a glimpse of a gilded hell, a painted sepulchre, full of corruption and moral death.

At one of the tables sits the Countess of Homburg, a very large lady, painfully lame and *very aged*, who is raking in her gains with great rapidity, wearing an expression of almost satanic glee. After playing for some time her luck changes, and she rises, declaring that she has lost all, declining the suggestion of one of the officials, who advises her to try another table. We learn that she is an *habitué* of the Casino.

Turning away, we saunter out into the open square, where are many pretty shops. While looking at some jewelry in one of them, a woman of about forty-five, dressed in deep mourning, with even a crape veil, comes in, and beckoning the proprietor into a recess, shows him a ring which she wishes to pawn. Following her back to the gaming-table, where, with purse replenished, she stakes at first cautiously and with varied results, we scan her closely; her cheek becomes deeply flushed, her eye feverish, and her manner painfully eager. To see her, a woman, leaning over the men's shoulders, and with delicately-gloved hand push her money to the position she wishes, and then watch with absorbed attention for the result of the throw, turning with a despairing look to the manager when she loses, and then with a gleam of unholy light in her eye when she wins, is at once disgusting and pitiable. At length, gathering and clutching her hoard, she starts away, counting it as she goes.

GENOA.

On leaving Nice for Genoa we take a row-boat to convey us to the small steamer lying out in the stream. Such vociferation and gesticulation we have never before heard or seen, but at length we are safely aboard, enjoying extremely the seven hours' trip, which is one of great beauty; for, as we " hug the shore," the Corniche Road, winding through the mountains, and every town and city on their sunny slopes are in plain view. The sunlight is brilliant, the water like a mirror, and as calm as a summer's sea.

As we approach Genoa we are delighted with the view which opens before us, the port being considered one of the finest in Europe. The city, called La Superba, from the beauty of its situation, is like an amphitheatre on the sea, with mountains towering above it. Genoa, although making a grand appearance as it is approached by water, is not beautiful in itself, as many of its streets are dirty, narrow, and steep also, the city being built upon a declivity. It was a splendid city in former days, and retaining vestiges of mediæval beauty in its numerous palaces, is interesting to the stranger. Some of the churches, five and six hundred years old, are replete with beauty of fresco, marble, and paintings. Huge forms of marble and bronze, all hewn from solid blocks of the same, and some of the altars inlaid with rare jewels, are among the curiosities. Many of the churches were built by noble families, and are of great value and interest. The Church of the Annunciation is the most magnificent in Genoa. The twelve pillars of black marble richly inlaid with brilliant colors, the rich gilding of the dome and vault, and valuable paintings form some of its attractions.

In the Municipal Palace we are shown some of the original manuscripts of Columbus, drawn up in the Spanish language, and also the leather bag which he used during his first voyage to America to preserve the book which contained his diary giving an account of his discovery of the New World. The guide telling us that all good Americans kiss the bag, we take the hint and press it to our lips, lingering long over the sacred relics. Columbus was born in Genoa, and although he found in his native land no sympathy with his views and aspirations, yet his memory is now cherished with pride by his countrymen.

In an adjoining room, on the ceiling, is a fresco painting of the interview between Columbus and his royal Spanish supporters after his return from America. Two Indians, whom he has brought with him, are standing by his side; while pigeons, birds, and North American animals are at his feet. The expression of astonishment and delight is very apparent on the faces of his illustrious auditors as they listen to the thrilling narrative of their immortalized protégé. In the same building, in a closet lined with pink wadded silk, hangs Paganini's violin and its case. The instrument which had breathed forth such marvellous strains in the hands of its almost inspired master is further protected in glass.

Perhaps the most ancient curiosity yet shown us is a bronze tablet, strongly resembling iron, covered with written Roman characters, which are almost obliterated; this dates back to one hundred and eighty-seven years before Christ. It records the decision of the Roman commissioners in a dispute which had arisen between the ancient Genoese and their neighbors, the Vitturi, in relation to the proper boundary of their respective territories.

We ride to the suburbs of the city to visit the Albergo de' Poveri; this is a very fine, large building, capable of accommodating two thousand two hundred persons. It is devoted, as its name implies, to the interests of the poor. It stands on an elevated position, from which we enjoy a delightful view of the city, and being brightened by beds of flowers, tastefully arranged, is a most attractive spot. We are ushered into immense halls lined on each side with colossal statues of the founders and other celebrities, but the chief attraction, and that which allures us to the spot, is a bas-relief, by Michael Angelo, of the "Dead Christ." It is hung over one of the altars in the chapel, and is framed in gilt, which seems out of taste and incongruous. It is the finest piece of sculpture in Genoa, and should, we think, be placed in one of the great cathedrals, where it would secure the attention and admiration of every stranger. It represents the Virgin, with head draped in a· veil hanging in graceful folds around the face, which wears the most saintly expression of tender pity that we ever saw in marble, painting, or even in the "human face divine." Infolded in her arm, with the head reposing on her bosom, is the form of her Adorable Son. The pallor of death rests upon the features, the eyes closed, and the mouth slightly open, the long hair falling back, kept in position by one finger of her hand. Oh, what a heavenly face it is! Divine peace and glory seem stamped upon it; the bitterness of death is passed, and "Heaven is won!" We all stand in awe, feeling our spiritual natures thrilled and stimulated by the almost inspired symbol.

In a palace occupied by the daughter of the Marquis Pallavicini, the richest noble of the city, we are delighted by paintings of the best masters and many elegant and curious works of art. One painting represents the noble Roman maiden nourishing at her breast her imprisoned father, who had been doomed to the lingering, torturing death of starvation. But the devoted daughter, with an ingenuity born of love, conceived this novel and touching expedient of succoring her beloved parent. The judges, who from a satanic malignity had consigned her father to an agonizing death, wondering at the continued strength and life of their victim, enjoined upon his jailers a stricter vigilance, which resulted in the discovery of love's stratagem. Amazed and touched by this pathetic manifestation of human affection, the judges restored to liberty the parent so rich in filial devotion. Ah, love hath its victories!

The mosaic floors and tables in this palace are very fine, and the ceilings glitter with fine frescoes. One of the salons is hung with the richest flowered silk, some with damask, and others with Gobelin tapestry. On a table stands a marble cushion covered with wrought flowers, on which rest the sculptured hands of the lady of this palatial home. They were modelled from life, and are exquisitely small, plump, and tapering.

Seven miles from the city is a villa belonging to the lady's father, whose only child she is. He is fabulously rich, and owns in Spain one of its finest estates, which he has never yet seen. The villa we visit is one of many belonging to him, costing many millions of dollars. It is made ground, much of the soil, it is said, having been brought from the Holy Land and huge rocks from the neighboring mountains. There is a grotto of stalactites, artificially made, in which is a pond with boats upon it. We walk through the meandering paths of the grotto,—it is a perfect labyrinth,— and row out on the pond. As we emerge from the fairy spot we see before us in the midst of the water a marble temple of Diana. Scattered through the grounds are Turkish kiosks and little summer-houses, in which concealed jets are made to play suddenly by a sly touch of the guide, and a spring, around which are arranged the same unseen and dreaded fountains.

In this interesting park are curious trees,—the camphor, whose green leaf, if tasted, suggests its character, and the cork-tree, which presents a singularly rough, gnarled appearance; also the banana, date, fig, together with the cedar of Lebanon, which was transplanted from its original sacred soil. The designer of this interesting place, which is too full of curiosities to describe in detail, is the owner himself.

We visited other palaces curious in their crumbling decay and marks of antiquity.

The ladies of Genoa a few years since wore no hats or bonnets in the street, but a broad, long breadth of white muslin of delicate texture; this was arranged becomingly on the head and allowed to flow behind to the bottom of the skirt. The lower classes wore a head-covering of the same form, but of colored and coarser material. In our recent visit to Genoa we find that this unique head-dress has been superseded by a black lace veil.

CHAPTER III.

PISA—FLORENCE.

PISA.

WE are astonished to find that many of the streets in this once great city are grass-grown; a fact which, added to that of the brooding silence and comparative absence of human life, gives it the appearance of an almost deserted city. How has its greatness fallen! Formerly a powerful city of one hundred and fifty thousand inhabitants, now numbering scarcely seventeen thousand. Pisa has been blessed with a brilliant prosperity, and has also had an active, warlike experience; but gradually sinking into its present sluggish insignificance, presents the counterpart of human life when it has dwindled into the " lean and slippered pantaloon,—mere oblivion, sans everything."

All that is of interest to the traveller is concentrated around a square where cluster the Cathedral, the Baptistery, the Leaning Tower, and the Cemetery. The grand Cathedral is the most ancient; it is built in the form of a cross, and contains fine statuary, many rare

47

paintings by Andrea del Sarto and others, and remarkable old monuments. Over the altar is a colossal mosaic figure representing Christ, looking like a gigantic Chinese, singular in its grotesqueness. The altar is covered with silver tablets, which cost thirty-six thousand dollars. Suspended in the nave is the chandelier whose oscillations suggested to Galileo—whose birthplace was Pisa—the principle of the pendulum.

The Baptistery is a large, rotund building of elaborate architecture externally, but plain within, containing only a large marble baptismal font, and a pulpit supported by pillars of rare marble, and covered with exquisitely wrought ivory tablets representing our Saviour's nativity and crucifixion. But the marvel of all is the echo which the guide produces, by his voice raised and lowered in a graduated scale. This effort is rewarded by a response, in its first notes, as powerful as the deepest sounds which an organ gives forth; a harmony profound and soul-thrilling, reverberating from the lofty dome and from all sides of the building; then, with a melody exquisite, heavenly in its sweetness, seeming to be wafted from some distant world and from a divine source, it lingeringly melts away on the soft air. An awe, like a spell, descends upon us; all that we can do is to whisper, "More, more;" and again the guide evokes from vast, far-away realms, it would seem, the seraphic harmony.

This echo, so wonderful, is deservedly considered one of the greatest enjoyments of a visit to Pisa.

Opposite the Baptistery stands the Leaning Tower, so justly celebrated. It is very beautiful externally; of white marble, consisting of eight rows of pillars, one above another, and is one hundred and sixty-eight feet high. Built in the twelfth century, all knowledge of its origin is obscure, and it is not known whether its inclination of fifteen feet from the perpendicular is the result of design or of the sinking of the soft soil; the latter is a reasonable supposition, as two public buildings in the neighborhood show a slight obliquity on the same side. This peculiarity imparts great interest to the Tower, and as it has stood thus six hundred years, no apprehension is felt in ascending it or in loitering within its shadow. Its interior is bare and rough; the stone staircase, much worn, is enclosed within the wall and lit by loopholes. The gentlemen of the party ascend to the dizzy apex, wishing to enjoy the extended view to be obtained at such a height; the guide first requiring the assurance that they had not indulged in the " inebriating cup" at dinner. The ladies are compelled to be satisfied with sitting midway on the stairs, awaiting the return of their more venturesome companions.

The Campo Santo—the Cemetery—abounds in relics of antiquity, among which are many Roman urns and sarcophagi. It is an old church-yard, the soil of nine

feet having been brought by the Pisans from Jerusalem.   Surrounded by halls built in the Gothic style,
it seems to have been the school of the early painters,
who covered the walls within the enclosed arches with
curious frescoes, many of them being partially effaced.
There is a painting of the Inferno, into which a man,
bound hand and foot, is being thrust headlong.   The
guide laughingly calls our attention to the resemblance
the unfortunate man's face bears to Bonaparte, inti-
mating that there is also a similarity in their fate.
Let us, however, exercise charity and believe this idea
to be merely imaginary.

We walk by the graves of the ancient nobility, who
have grand memorials of sculpture to mark their final
resting-place, ruminating upon the contrast presented
between these defunct patricians and the modern re-
publicans who are treading upon their dust, most of
which had slumbered centuries in these graves before
our Republican Land was discovered.

We represent one of the political and commercial
powers of the world, while *their* glory has culminated,
individually, in these graves at our feet,—a death which
symbolizes that of the national glory of their country :
its present decadence presenting, at least, a sad contrast
to its former grandeur.   What a commentary upon
the changes wrought by Time ! So " He putteth down
one and setteth up another."

While walking in one of the solitary streets of Pisa, a man enveloped in blue gown, and mask of the same, with eyes gleaming through small apertures, steps towards us, holding out a box to solicit charity for some benevolent institution. It is a startling apparition for unaccustomed eyes. We are surprised to find that the suppliant is probably a nobleman in disguise; this humiliating ordeal being often imposed upon the rich and proud as a penance for the commission of some heinous sin.

FLORENCE.

Florence is said to be the fairest city of the world, and we, on visiting it a second time, are not disposed to question its claim to so enviable a reputation. It is situated in a fertile valley. The surrounding hills, their sunny slopes studded with picturesque villas, give beauty to the landscape. The Arno, which divides the city into two unequal parts, might have added beauty to the portions through which it flows, but it is robbed of it by being enclosed within walls. Those who have dreamed of its peaceful flow between green and flowery banks are disappointed on first seeing it. Nature seems to resent its artificial restrictions, and withholds the beauty until later, when its course becomes bolder and freer, and it gracefully meanders between sunny banks, on which villages nestle, creat-

ing a picturesque charm that has inspired many a
poet's song. The river, as it flows through the city,
is spanned by several bridges, one of which is covered,
and is lined on both sides with cheap jewelry-shops,
whose stocks are principally exposed in glass cases outside. One can readily imagine the competition existing between the many merchants whose traffic is in
like commodity.

The chief architectural ornament of the city is the
Duomo, or Cathedral; its grand cupola, the largest in
the world, designed by Brunelleschi, was so admired
by Michael Angelo that he adopted it as his model for
that of St. Peter's at Rome. The floor within the
Cathedral, and its walls without, are formed of black
and white marble. The paintings, the frescoes, and
the statuary are masterpieces of the most eminent
artists and sculptors; but one is not easily tempted
from the contemplation of the beautiful *exterior* of
this stately structure, for we have stood spell-bound,
lost in admiration of its immensity and elaborate
adornment. We have in this enjoyment an ancient
and illustrious precedent in the poet Dante; the stone
upon which he was wont to sit contemplating the
grand creation of genius is now inserted in a building
opposite, with an inscription commemorating the fact.
The stained glass of the windows is pronounced the perfection of the art, dating back to the fifteenth century.

Very near the Cathedral is the "Campanile," or belfry, which is so graceful and beautiful as to deserve the praise of Charles V., when he declared it to be "worthy of being enclosed in a glass case."

Opposite the Cathedral is the Baptistery, whose many granite pillars supporting the dome are relieved by the brilliancy of the mosaic. The three large doors of sculptured bronze are miracles of art, Michael Angelo declaring them worthy of being the gates of Paradise. The designs, representing the most important events of biblical history, require a long time to discover and to digest their full meaning and beauty. It is here that, according to law, all the infants are brought when two days old to be baptized. Two priests are constantly officiating, and dirty enough they are. While gazing around upon the marble walls of the Baptistery and upon its paintings, all of which have reference to the ordinance of baptism, we are startled by a sound which always awakens interest in the feminine heart,—the cry of a babe. We turn to witness the ceremony. The father with proud air— do we imagine it?—first appears, his youthful look surprising us. Then come several lady friends, followed by a white-capped nurse, with a closely swaddled atom of humanity in her arms, its long robe of richest lace falling to the floor. We stand awhile, instinctively dreaming of the happiness that had been born with the little brown head, which we can faintly discern, when a lusty scream breaks rudely upon our revery. We scan the priest more closely; he is putting salt (!) in the mouth of the little stranger, who must imagine, if its powers are sufficiently developed, that it has been ushered into a harsh, disagreeable world. A few hastily-mumbled prayers, the priest is openly paid, and the ceremony, so trying to the tiny novitiate, is completed.

While walking in the street we are startled by encountering a procession of about a dozen men robed in black paper-muslin gowns, wearing masks of the same color and material, having slits for the eyes. Four of these sepulchral beings bear upon their shoulders a bier, covered also with black. Seeing them enter an adjoining building we follow, and are surprised to find ourselves being locked in with the men, who lay down their burden. Each man unmasks, and, divesting himself of his robe, answers to the roll-call. Observing a man lifting the black cover from the bier we step forward, and see that it contains a mattress and pillow and bears the impression of a body. Realizing the danger of coming into such close contact with what we learn has conveyed a patient to the hospital, we fly from the building.

The Church of " St. Croce" reminds one of Westminster Abbey, inasmuch as it contains the tombs of many illustrious men. It proudly claims the remains of Michael Angelo, Galileo, Machiavelli, Alfieri, and a sculptured tribute to the fame of Dante, whose body reposes elsewhere. The tomb of Michael Angelo is worthy of the perhaps unequalled brain and hand which it encloses; colossal marble statues bend weeping over it, representing Painting, Sculpture, and Architecture, of which three arts he was the marvellous exponent. Over these is a bas-relief of the great dead. Dead, truly, in bodily presence, but if "reputation is the immortal part of ourselves," he is alive to-day, and will be evermore, in the thoughts and minds of all those who find in chiselled forms of power and grace, in glowing color, and in those grand conceptions of beauty which we call architecture, delight for the eye. Nay, more, for whatever, through refined sensibilities, brings pleasure to the outward sense ministers to the soul.

The exterior of this church is remarkably beautiful, and it is the only one in Florence, excepting the Cathedral, whose front is complete. The interior of many of the churches of the Italian cities are marvels of beauty, but some of them present rather dilapidated exteriors.

One of the wonders of the city consists in a chapel, as it is called, although it contains no altar, or arrangement for religious service. It is built in the rear of

the Church San Lorenzo, and is connected with it.
The frescoes on its dome are as fine as any we have
seen. In shape, octagon; the walls of the chapel are
composed of the rarest marbles, in which are inserted
the most precious stones,—lapis-lazuli, agate, jasper,
emeralds, pearls, and corals. Some are of very large
size, with the arms of the Medici family and Tus-
can towns in mosaic. The floor of this wonderful
room is very ordinary, but the lofty dome and the
walls reflect a novel beauty not to be equalled, we
imagine, for the cost of this one small chapel is es-
timated at twenty-two millions of lire, or nine hundred
thousand pounds. It is the mausoleum of many of
the Medici family, and contains the sarcophagi of dukes
and kings. Its frescoes represent several of the principal episodes in our Saviour's life, and the marble
mosaics are made to form most beautiful designs.

The wealth of many of these churches is almost
incalculable, and it makes one's heart sink to see it
thus invested, while the masses of this Roman Catholic land are so degraded and suffering.

The two world-famed galleries of the Uffizi and
Pitti are burdened with art-treasures of sculpture and
painting. Repeated visits are necessary to see and
"inwardly digest" their contents.

An octagon hall called the "Tribune," in the Uffizi,
contains several of the finest specimens of ancient

sculpture in the world. The Venus de Medici, found in the sixteenth century in Hadrian's villa, the Young Apollo, the "Grinder," the "Wrestlers," and a satyr, or "Dancing Faun."

We visit the house in which Michael Angelo lived. It is preserved intact by his worshipping countrymen. Although appearing plain to us, it was probably considered fine in his day. We wander through the salon, the dining-room, and library, penetrating with keen pleasure to the little sanctum, only large enough to hold his desk and the wooden seat before it. We look upon his manuscripts and autograph; handle his little slippers,—almost incredibly small for a man's use,— his brushes and cane, and see many of his rough sketches and clay models, delighted to come in such close contact with the life of one of the most gifted men of olden time. The floors are all tiled, the wood-work dark and rich, and the doors very narrow, all bearing the stamp of ancient style and customs.

Dante's house is very high and narrow, and in a narrow street. An inscription on the house declares it to have been the home of the "divine poet."

How strange that two of the most gifted men, representing the genius of Italy,—Petrarch and Michael Angelo,—should have lived lives of celibacy! We who believe that domestic happiness—the highest form of all—is a grand inspirer of all that is good and great;

that a happy love is wonderfully developing to the
whole nature of its subject; that it enkindles every
laudable ambition; heightens every noble desire; is
suggestive to genius; awaking *talent* often in the
slumbering mind; elevating and ennobling every sentiment of the heart; creating beauty even in the barren
soul, cannot but think that every life would be enriched and made more fruitful of grand results were
it crowned with wedded joy and family ties. As we
wander through the suite of Michael Angelo's bachelor
apartments we think with regret that they have never
resounded with the tuneful voices of children, or to
the musical accompaniment of a wife's tender tones.
With such mellowing influences permeating his life
might it not have been richer even, or, at least, more
serenely happy?

We enjoy exceedingly a drive on the Cascine, the
fashionable park of the city, bordered on one side by
a luxuriant flowering hedge which grows to a great
height; the Arno, here unfettered, gliding by, and
gleaming through the rich green foliage. The park is
beautifully diversified by little copses of woodland;
romantic and sheltered foot-paths; meadows of living
green, of such shades as nature alone can produce;
gigantic trees vine-clad to their tips; sequestered paths
where only coquettish sunbeams can peep through the
vine-trellised branches; the graceful river; the bold

line of Apennines, on which the deep rich shadows love
to linger, relieved by bright gleams of sunlight, make
this drive a continued delight.

We can always associate with this sweet spot a
pleasure never before enjoyed. It is later, when "twilight gray is with her sober livery all things" clothing;
a delicious hour; flowers and verdure are exhaling
their richest odors; a dewy sweetness fills the air;
deep shadows born in the valley, gathering gloom, are
creeping up the hill-sides to be soon lost in the embrace
of the clouds that crown the summits. Our very souls
are silently absorbing the beauty and charm, when the
softest trillings, swelling to airy flights and fuller
melody, reach our ears and touch our hearts. Although
strangers to these sweet warblings, we exclaim, "'Tis the
nightingale unburdening his rich throat of its flood of
wonderful song."

We remember during a drive in this same park some
years since to have met Victor Emmanuel on the broad,
smooth road. Youth, beauty, and fashion glittered in
open carriages, on horseback, and on the promenades;
but the king was passing, and we were eager attention.
What a face! Of figure quite imposing and military
in its bearing; but his features, his expression! Had
angels ever moulded such? No; vice had worked the
materials into their present form. His face was of a
purplish hue; his eyes were bleared, and being the out-

look of a soul given up to voluptuous indulgence, were such as a pure woman would shrink from encountering. His face was full of brute force, instinct with animal propensities, and as a woman's intuition is "neither wayward nor blind," we were not surprised to find that the story of a life of sinful license confirmed the record indelibly stamped upon his features.

CHAPTER IV.

ROME.

WITH what eager desire does the traveller turn his eyes toward Rome, the "Eternal City;" for what a blending of interest is there, of the historian, the ecclesiastic, and the artistic! There is so much of majesty and dignity in its history, that when we trace its epochs down the long line of centuries through the enduring mementos of its brilliant achievements; its indestructible monuments of art; the splendor of its artistic accumulations, and the power ecclesiastic once dominant, and still active and world-wide in its influence; with its sacred association with the apostles of our own Protestant faith, we move amid its modern scenes filled with a solemn reverence. What could be more august in its crippled strength than the ruins of the Coliseum? Built by Vespasian, it still attests its pristine solidity, and although much of its material has contributed to the building of palaces, yet it presents a grand, formidable appearance to an admiring world. Indeed, it teaches one to appreciate a colossal ruin shorn of many ornamentations, dismantled and hoary, much more than many a grand structure which has retained its original perfection. Even as we are often more attracted towards the gray head and drooping form, which has assumed the quieter grace of age, winning admiring respect through its very venerableness, than towards the athletic figure, instinct with youthful vigor.

We stand in the unvaulted arena of the Coliseum imaging with horror the frightful scenes once enacted here; for we read that during the inaugurative festivities, which continued through many days, ten thousand lives were sacrificed to the brutal tastes of a populace who thirsted for blood and gloated upon its flow as do the wild beasts of the forest. According to custom, after the gladiator had felled his antagonist, with foot upon his prostrate victim, he would look aloft to the tiers upon which sat the ladies—wild with enthusiasm —to learn the fate of the vanquished. Should their dormant sympathies, by chance, be aroused and they willed that the life of the unfortunate wretch be spared, they *elevated their thumbs;* but if they would further pander to a vitiated appetite for the horrible, craving a sight of writhing physical torments and a freer flow of human blood, a *turning down of the thumb* intimated their desire. We would fain believe that *our* sex were not represented at these scenes of wilful carnage, but history forbids the indulgence of the hope. Nor can we doubt that the feminine element was the most rapacious and eager, as we believe that a woman when she unsexes herself goes to the extreme of possibility.

What acclamations rent the air as the spectators, maddened by brutal passion, watched the successful thrust of the fatal spear into the infuriated beast or, worse still, into the throbbing heart of the human martyr! Did not those cries pierce the Divine ear? and was it not through Divine justice that this imperial city, the capital of Christendom, the arbiter of monarchies, and even the conqueror of the world, became one of the least of its powers? Its national glory and prestige departed; its splendor paled by time; its grandeur faded out; its papal tyranny, which once set its heel upon crowned heads, now dethroned, humiliated; its once unrestricted sway limited to an ecclesiastical rule, and that *greatly* enfeebled. So does time avenge the wrongs of truth and justice.

We look down into the passages through which the beasts emerged for the slaughter, some five thousand being prepared for the inaugurating festivities, and think of the soil being further enriched by the blood of slaves and of martyrs innumerable.

The ruins of Rome, its stately Forum; its graceful arches; its gigantic Coliseum; revered Pantheon and unique little Temple of Vesta; with the fragmentary splendor of the Public Baths, are all so full of thrilling interest that one loves to linger in their midst. Those of the Coliseum and Caracalla Baths we visit on a sunshiny day, when the heavens are filled with a radiant light, and when azure clouds hover over its broad surface, reflecting beauty upon every hill and dale of the landscape. The masses of ruin are covered with a rich verdure sprinkled with wild-flowers, among which nature's sweet choir, feathered songsters, carol so gladly, so blithely, that one would think they ·sang amid luxurious haunts and would tell some glad tale, instead of warbling amid the ruins of a former grandeur, whose story of great achievements, pomp, and glory they might now sadly tell.

Ah, there is a great charm in this old city! A quaint, quiet, meditative charm, which seeks for its indulgence a dreamy contemplation of spots sacred in religious association, or memorable through historic events, brilliant and impressive. The very air seems burdened with the weighty secrets of a power so great as to have controlled the fate of nations, which later it ruled with ecclesiastical despotism. Where are the glittering pageants whose description gives such brilliant coloring to the pages of history, and those scenes of festivity which, with the general abandonment to sensuous luxury, helped to culminate in the utter enervation of the people? And those royal entries into Rome of the returning conqueror, attended with such Oriental, barbaric magnificence as to make it necessary for a slave to stand beside the idolized victor and exclaim at intervals, " Remember thou art a *man*," lest amid an adoring, worshipping populace and pomp overwhelming he should be beguiled into the belief that he was in very truth a *god !*

We walk the same streets, in which life is now sluggishly represented, that once were swarming with a warlike people, and after, with those who were rich in all the arts and wealth of a pampered race; but what a contrast does the present age present,—the arts lost, wealth decayed! We cannot be merry in Rome, our minds are busy with conjuring such scenes as were once enacted in this grand theatre of the world's action, and in recalling to memory those pictures we have seen and descriptions we have read of Babylonish-like luxury, ease, and sumptuousness of days whose twilight has long since faded into night. But the glow of .its national sunset seems still faintly to linger around the city of such dazzling memories.

Grand, imperial Rome, with its glorious, rich past, must fascinate the traveller. Its ruins of centuries are full of intense power, and in its very decay is its charm. There is so much that breathes of the eventful history of the centuries past that we learn to dissociate ourselves from the present, and live only in the

scenes of those early times when the apostles trod
these places, and when contemporary and succeeding
heroes left upon their age the stamp of great genius
and renown.

St. Peter's, the grandest church in the world, is almost, through the combined skill of the architect and
artist, an inspiration. Entering the door, before which
hangs a thickly-wadded leather curtain so encrusted
with dirt that one shrinks from its contact, even with
gloved hands, we suddenly find ourselves in a vast
space, so magnificent in dimensions, in mammoth statuary and superb mosaic, that we are fairly dazed, and
feel, with the Queen of Sheba, " that the half was not
told us." It is impossible to form permanent impressions of so wonderful a fabric on first inspection, for
St. Peter's grows upon one. We find ourselves more
delighted with its artistic beauty and more amazed at
its immensity and grandeur on each succeeding visit.
Its perfection of proportions is such as prevents the
realization, at first, of its vastness. The extreme length
of the church, within the walls, is six hundred and
seven feet, its width four hundred and forty-five feet,
while its height, from the pavement to the cross, is four
hundred and fifty-eight feet.

When walking through its broad naves one realizes
his own physical insignificance, for the vault above
seems heaven-high, and the space surrounding one

illimitable. Indeed, even large persons and objects at a short distance seem pigmy-like and dwarfed.

The high altar, under a canopy, is all in bronze gilt, supported by four twisted columns ninety feet high. Here is placed the great chair, which the Pope only occupies on his coronation and upon certain festive days. Under the high altar is seen the chapel of the "Confession," where are preserved, 'tis said, the remains of St. Peter. One hundred and forty-two lamps are always kept burning here. Pius IV. is interred in this chapel, and his kneeling statue by Canova is very fine. At the bottom of the Tribune, in the middle nave of the church, under a canopy, is a bronze statue of St. Peter; seated on a bronze chair, which encloses the wooden one said to have been used by St. Peter and his successors. This is an object of special devotion, all Catholics who pass it stopping to kiss the foot which projects from the pedestal, touching it with their forehead, some kneeling before it to pray. The toe is really much worn and the foot is burnished from constant friction. It is curious to watch the throng as they pass this shrine; the lowliest, filthiest beggar often preceding the most elegant, refined men and women; the latter touching with their dainty lips the toe which the polluted mouth of the dirty pauper has just pressed.

Learning that there are to be unusual ceremonies at

St. Peter's on Ascension Day, we gladly avail ourselves
of the opportunity to witness what must prove to be a
curious and novel scene. We arrive early at the church,
and as no seats are provided, we wander from pictures
to monuments, and from chapel to chapel, of those
that open out of St. Peter's, until the services begin.
These are all choral, the choir being composed of male
voices, conducted by one of Italy's great musical artists.
What voices! A grand medium to chant the Creator's
praise. The crowd gathers around in silence, all ears
intent upon the concord of sweet majestic sounds that
are worthy of the superb cathedral in which we stand.
The hour approaches for the singular ceremony of
lowering the sheet, which we are to believe was the
veritable one in which our blessed Saviour was en-
folded while lying in the sepulchre during his three
days' entombment! The grand music strengthens in
volume, and, we think, gains in sweetness too; the
afternoon is waning, and long shadows creep through
the wonderful dome down into the church, filling it
with a subdued light in keeping with the sombre
memories evoked by the ceremonies. All eyes wander
to a lofty gallery, and the gaze is riveted there, as a
sheet, bordered with wide strips of red velvet, is gradually lowered, until its full dimensions are displayed.
The devout, or we should say the superstitious, fall
upon their knees, cross themselves, and apparently

pray fervently. To our eyes the sheet seems marvellously preserved, and very white and fresh to have attained the age claimed for it. And in the kneeling devotees who surround us the credulity of the Romish faith is abundantly proved.

"St. John Lateran" is probably the second church to St. Peter's in splendor. It is rich in art and in marbles; indeed, the marbles which form the finest churches are many of them very rare, and almost as beautiful as gems we often think, as we trace the veined lines and note the varied colors which form pictures in themselves.

Under a portico near this church is the "Santa Scala," a marble staircase of twenty-eight steps, which, it is alleged, belonged to the house of Pontius Pilate, and to be those on which our Saviour descended from the judgment-hall. No one is allowed to mount these except on their hands and knees, saying an ave or a paternoster at each step, and descending by another flight of steps at the side. So great are the crowds of all ranks and conditions who attempt to ascend the sacred steps in the prescribed awkward manner, that to insure their preservation they have been enclosed in wood. We have reason to realize the veneration in which these stairs are held. A gentleman of our party being ignorant of the conditions of their ascension starts to mount them by foot, when he is seized by

several men, who handle him somewhat roughly before
being convinced that his politeness alone would have
insured his compliance with their rules; or, at least,
an avoidance of all disrespect to their religious prejudices.

The Church of St. Clement we find is always visited,
as it offers the singular attraction of two churches, one
above another and a third structure beneath them.
The upper church is ancient, dating back to the ninth
century; beneath this is a lower and more ancient one,
discovered in 1857, in which we see curious frescoes
and some marble pillars. Beneath these are the remains of what is supposed to be the house of the
saint whose name the church bears. The Pantheon is
another prominent monument of ancient times. Built
by Agrippa, it has been despoiled of many of its original ornaments, yet still presents a noble appearance.
The portico is embellished with sixteen Corinthian
columns. The interior, a perfect circle, is lighted by a
central opening in the vault above. Originally a pagan
temple, it was converted by Pope Boniface IV. into
a Christian church in the year 608. It is a fitting
sepulchre for Raphael, who is buried here.

In visiting the Church of the Capuchins, we found
a monastery connected with it, which is supported by
charity. The monks are extremely poor and dirty, and
are said to wear their clothing, which consists of a

brown gown, hood, and wooden sandals, without change
until they are worn out. The most peculiar feature of
the establishment is the sepulchre beneath the church.
A startling sight greets us as we enter the close, musty
aisles. There is a long, narrow passage lined on one
side by small recesses, in each of which stand the skeletons of the most distinguished of the deceased monks
in their customary habiliments, with crucifixes tightly
clenched in their fleshless fingers. The variety of ex-
pressions upon the faces of these gaping skeletons is a
curious study; some seem to be grinning at their fate,
while others, with dolorous and sometimes frightful
countenances, to be bewailing theirs, and as if they
would warn the spectators to avoid the same. The
ceiling of this singular sepulchre is ornamented—if we
may use the term—by the bones of the numerous dead,
most fantastically arranged with marvellous ingenuity
in odd designs. At the sides are heaps of the heavier
bones of the human body, showing that many hundreds, if not thousands, of monks have contributed
towards the collection. We learn from the attending
guide, who is himself a monk of the order, that when
a member of the fraternity dies he is buried in the
ground of these recesses, and after three years is exhumed, and if he had been unusually distinguished for
saintly qualities, is dressed in the robe which was laid
aside at his death, and is assigned a niche; or he is dis-

sected, his bones aiding in the general ornamentation. Pointing to a grave at our feet, the cicerone informs us that the last candidate for these sepulchral honors was buried there about a fortnight before. Overcome by emotions of awe, horror, and disgust, we turn and hastily flee from the place apparently haunted by the spirits of the deceased friars.

The grand steps on the Piazza di Spagna, leading to the Trinità de' Monti, is the spot chosen by those who would be engaged by artists and sculptors as models. Here they are to be seen at all hours in characteristically indolent attitudes, lounging gracefully on the steps. The little cherubs, not with the proverbially sunny hair and blue eyes, but those of raven blackness, their eyes gleaming with most mischievous sparkling light. The peasantry of the country form, in many instances, its most picturesque feature. They are dressed coarsely, and yet so fancifully with their scarlet bodice, white neckerchief, graceful coiffure, and sandalled shoes, that the effect is extremely pretty and unique. The dancing black eyes and rich heavy hair of the little urchins often tempts us to stop and admire these gifts, of which nature is here so prodigal, and which many of nobler blood might envy them.

The Vatican, the palace-home of the Pope, contains a vast number of salons and galleries in which are collected some of the richest gems of art. Its museum is considered the finest in the world, while its library contains twenty-three thousand manuscripts and thirty thousand printed volumes. Years might be consumed in the investigation and study of the vast collection of art-treasures and ancient relics of these galleries, for there are several objects of such unfailing interest that one would never exhaust their suggestive meaning. ·The most prominent of these are two of the most celebrated pictures in the world, "The Transfiguration" by Raphael, and the "Communion of St. Jerome" by Domenichino, standing near each other. What a marvellous conception of the infinite must Raphael have had to give such beauty to the Saviour's visage and such inspiration to His whole figure! We find some new beauty blossoming out under our warm, rapt gaze each moment. Celestial glory, through the rifted clouds, is irradiating the uplifted, Divine countenance of the Saviour as He stands on the mount surrounded by the three prostrate apostles. What a blending of adoring love, sweetness, and majesty as He raises His eyes towards the beloved Father, whose presence is manifested by an ineffable light in the cloud, as He says, "This is my beloved Son; hear ye Him!" And then the speechless awe of the crowd below! among whom is the powerful representation of the demoniac boy whose restoration had baffled the skill of the disciples, but which was afterwards effected by the Saviour.

Certainly the spiritual nature of the artist must have been quickened, and his pencil touched with inspiration as this wondrous revelation of divine grace, glory, and power was made through his magic touch. We cannot associate any such success with Murillo or Rubens, as their colors are marked by a sensuous warmth, and their outlines and figures are so invariably suggestive of voluptuousness,—of the earth, earthy. But Raphael's conceptions, coloring, and touches are refined, subdued, and chastened by a purer thought and taste. · What a fitting crown for his head as he laid in state was this expiring effort of his genius! for it was previous to the completion of the painting of the " Transfiguration" that he sickened and died, having reached the zenith of his fame. Let us hope that he was admitted to an abundant entrance into the heavenly kingdom whose celestial light and glory he had—although with the in-evitable imperfection of human effort, yet with an un-equalled skill—striven to portray on the Divine features.

The " Communion of St. Jerome," by Domenichino, is of lowlier aspiration, as it is *human* features that are there depicted. And yet what absorption and earnest-ness in spiritual emotion are delineated in the expres-sion of the dying saint, as in a condition of frightful emaciation his frame is supported in a kneeling posture while he partakes of the last sacraments!

The Villa Borghese and its park, although not

healthily situated, are very inviting from their beauty
and the fine artistic collection within the palace. Its
chef-d'œuvre is the full-length reclining statue of the
fair and frail Pauline, sister of Napoleon Bonaparte,
and the faithless wife of the Duc de Borghese, whose
palatial estate this once was. The symmetry of her
form, and indeed every feature of this dissolute
woman, was pronounced absolutely faultless, with the
exception of her ears, which, we are told, "were two
flat, thin pieces of cartilage," deformingly ugly. An
envious beauty remarked, in Pauline's presence, that
were her ears similarly deformed she would cut them
off; the mortified subject of the insult burst into tears
and fled from the room. She afterwards avenged herself by calling her fair enemy, who was very tall, "a
May-pole."

The statue, by Canova, was modelled from life, a fact
which so shocked and displeased the Duc that he banished it to a more secluded palace in Genoa, where it re-
mained until after his death, when it was replaced here
in its original position. A lady inquired of Pauline how
she could have submitted to so trying an ordeal. "Oh,"
exclaimed the shameless beauty, "there was a fire in
the room;" utterly ignoring the indelicacy of the experience but presuming a prosaic meaning to the lady's
question. The statue represents the original as half
reclining; one hand holds the apple of Paris, from

which circumstance the statue derives its name of
" Venus Victrix." So exquisite is the beauty and
grace of feature and form, that had it wings we should
consider it a sublime conception of angelic beauty.

Judging from Pauline's antecedents, it is not surprising that she wearied of even the great natural
beauty of this famed estate and of the wealth of its
artistic collection, but separating from her husband she
repaired to her brother's court, where, in a dissolute
throng, she "out-Heroded Herod."

Several years since when in Rome we stumbled into
a studio where we were fairly entangled, for the exceeding beauty of a sculptured gem threatened to keep
us prisoners by its side.

On a marble couch lay two cherub boys, the head of
each crowned with flowing curls; they had been indulging in a joyous frolic; pillows were awry and sheets
displaced; the short dress revealing the beauty of
chubby infant limbs. Sleep had stolen upon them
with such sudden, irresistible power, that one hand had
been arrested in its attempt to grasp a stray curl of the
little brother, and the smile of mischief had not died
out from the half-parted lips. All was in sweet dis-
array, presenting such a picture as, we thought, would
awaken the maternal instinct *even in a maiden's breast.*

Involuntarily paying the sweetest tribute that genius
can receive,—tears,—we turned and met the pleased

expression of the artist, who had approached us. "Who," we inquired in covetous tones, "is to possess this exquisite gem?"

"This, the sixth copy, has been ordered by a bachelor in Chicago," was the answer.

"And why," exclaimed we, "should he reject the reality and seek the semblance of a joy?"

"Perhaps this may convert him," was the merry response of the bachelor artist.

Upon further conversation we found that he whose work we were so enthusiastically admiring was none other than the late Mr. Rhinehart, the gifted Baltimorean, who, although dying young, lived long enough to fairly earn the laurel wreath of fame.

While in Rome during the pontificate of Pius IX., we found that his receptions were one of the social features, and as most strangers sought the opportunity of an introduction to him we decided to follow suit. On learning, however, that one must submit to the rule of bowing the knee to "His Holiness," we declined to go. It seemed to us sacrilegious to assume a worshipful attitude towards one who demanded it as a spiritual right, and whose claims to infallibility were shocking the Protestant world. There surely is but *One* "to whom all knees shall bow," and His "kingdom is not of this world."

When expressing our sentiments in the parlor of our

hotel, a young Englishman heartily endorsed them, and, while declaring his intention of joining the party at that evening's reception, said he was equally determined to parry the obligation and escape with a low bow.

"Well," said we, "we will await the result of your experience and act accordingly." He went to the Vatican that evening with many others, and the next morning was eagerly questioned by us as to the denouement.

With some chagrin he related his experience. Advancing in his turn to be presented to the Pope, he made a profound bow, when "His Holiness," detecting his attempt to evade the customary ceremonial, laid his hands on the two shoulders of the young reprobate—as he probably considered him—and pressed him down on his knees.

We did not go !

While standing on the steps of St. Peter's one day, the Pope's carriage issued from the grand portal of the Vatican grounds and slowly passed by us, so closely that we could have shaken hands with its occupant. We looked with interest upon the face, which, although 'twas furrowed by age, and his eye was dimmed by time and the sorrows it had brought him, yet was beautiful to look upon, beaming as it was with benevolence, a very "love-letter to all mankind." He stretched forth his hands as if in benediction, and we bowed in grateful acknowledgment of an old man's blessing.

He looked much more deserving of his title, Innocent, than were some of his predecessors who incongruously bore that name.

We turn with sadness from this old city, and feeling unwilling to believe that we have threaded its narrow streets; driven over the famed Appian Way; wandered through its endless galleries; lingered in its vast churches; stimulated our æsthetic tastes and indulged contemplative moods, through its classic resources, for the last time, we bethink us of the fabled fountain of Trevi,—the most remarkable of the Roman fountains, —whose waters are said to possess the magic power, if drank, of insuring one's return to Rome. Accordingly the last evening of our stay we drink at its brink, throwing in a petty coin,—one of the conditions,—and so, merely with an *au revoir*, turn from the delights of Rome to seek "fresh woods and pastures new."

CHAPTER V.

NAPLES.

NAPLES is most beautifully situated upon the Bay of Naples, and forms a semicircle on its shores. But, however attractive it may be to the eye, the stranger is impatient to digest its beauties and flee to some Northern Zoar; for, having a very defective system of drainage, its air is often burdened with impurity, and its scents are so unsavory as to be at times unbearable.

To obtain a fine view of the city and its delightful environs we ride to the Church of San Martino, one of the most beautiful in Italy. It is built upon an eminence of one thousand feet above the level of the sea. As we ride higher and higher the view widens, and when we reach the church a beautiful panorama lies before us. Below, and stretching out on every side, is Naples, with its labyrinth of narrow streets, with their passing throng. The hum of voices and the din of city life have become so blended and modulated before the waves of the air have rolled them to our ear that

80

they greet us with really mellifluous sound; fields, whose surface is burdened with grain, are wooing the sun's rays to unfold their wealth; while vines are wreathing every stalwart tree, fairly concealing saplings with their riotous growth. Beyond, the rippling waters of the majestic bay gleam in the sunlight, the islands of Capri and Ischia rising boldly from their surface; while Vesuvius, apparently peaceful, but with torrents of wrath foaming in her bosom, rises dangerously near. Such views as these, we believe, nourish the soul, allaying its fretful, restless passions; giving its aspirations larger breadth and more elevated tone; impressing it with a profounder appreciation of the Infinite, through the revelation of His power, as manifested in these works of His hands. It was a rare treat and well worthy of the two hours' ride.

The church is a perfect gem in marble and rich decoration. There is much wooden mosaic curiously wrought by the monks, who occupy an adjoining monastery. One of the order, physically a noble specimen of manhood,—probably chosen on that account,—is kneeling upon the steps of the altar, mumbling his prayers and manipulating his beads, while an artist includes his figure in a sketch of the interior of the church.

Visiting another church one day we are surprised, nay, more, astounded, on approaching the altar, to

see the several priests who are kneeling around it, and
are apparently absorbed in their devotions, suddenly rise
and confront us with faces expressive of consternation.
That we are the cause of their perturbation is evident;
but why? For many years we have been mingling
in the society of their sex without, alas! ever having
created a sensation. Can it be possible that our mature
life is to be crowned with a social success denied our
youth? Doubting, and much mystified, we turn inquiringly to our intelligent guide. "I don't understand
it myself," he says; "but I will inquire."

Advancing towards the priests, he speaks a few
words, when several of them, with earnest gesticulation
and significant nods towards us, relieve their minds,
but remain standing, as if awaiting our movements.

The guide returns and says that they assure him it
is impossible to continue their devotions while in the
presence of a woman, as it is the anniversary of the
beheading of John the Baptist, whose head, we remember, was the price of a woman's smile and favor.

Indignantly we turn away, regretting that the guide
is too good a Catholic to repeat to them our remon-
strance, based upon the fact that, as they are addressing
their prayers to one of our sex,—the Virgin Mary,—we
see no objection to the visible presence of another; and
that had they the chivalric regard for us entertained
by the noble of their own sex, they would find inspira-

tion while indulging the finest feelings of their spiritual natures, in the living presence of a good woman.

The streets of the old portions of these Italian cities are so narrow that when a vehicle is passing through them foot-passengers must seek refuge in a doorway or hug the wall closely, and even then their toes may project a little *too* far and be trampled upon. One peculiarity of Neapolitan life is that the lower class of people live out-doors all day, seeming only to enter their houses at night. Every morning the dwellings are turned inside out, as it were, the people performing many of their domestic duties in the streets, seeking the sunshine in winter and early spring for the warmth it gives. This custom gives the streets a constantly crowded appearance, men, women, and children swarming in every direction, their houses but burrowing-holes, dark, filthy, and crowded. The open air of the street, although impure, is preferable, at least, to that of their dens, and it must be to this fact that they owe their health and their life even. And here let us interpolate that if any are endowed, or afflicted, perhaps we might say, with an unusual degree of refinement of feeling, particularly if they are of morbidly delicate sensibilities, we advise them to avoid Naples in their travels. Such repulsive phases of domestic life could scarcely be thrust more openly upon the stranger's notice than here. Domestic life in its finer types pre-

sents naught but charm, but in its lower it is a conglomeration of coarseness and vulgarity. Filth and
squalor being prominent phases of Neapolitan life,
they could hardly be ignored in its portrayal.

Donkeys are universally used in this country, as they
are strong, hardy, capable of great endurance, and eat
little. They are exceedingly small, some of them not
much larger than a large dog, and one feels inclined
to fondle them as they would a canine favorite. We
have never seen but one instance of the obstinacy which
is thought to be characteristic of the species; it was
while at Genoa, when walking through one of the narrow streets we saw some men striving first to induce
and then to force a donkey to turn around and be
attached to a cart. The little fellow held his own well;
he was pushed, pulled, beaten, kicked, and sworn at,
to no purpose. At length in despair, and probably in
remembrance of some past experience, the men left the
wagon and the mule standing *mulishly* beside it, and
sat down awaiting a change in his mood. We have
repeatedly seen little donkeys with immense quantities
of wood strapped on and around them, or with masses
of divers vegetables, which so completely covered them
that one would suppose a small forest or market-garden
had become animate and was marching forth to supply
the needs of the cold and hungry; until impressed by
curious doubts, a closer inspection would be made, and

with some difficulty a little head would be found protruding at one end and the swaying stump of a tail at
the other.

While in Naples we visit the Museum, and although
it contains masterpieces of sculpture, we are most interested in the apartment devoted to Pompeian relics.
There are blackened, charred loaves of bread and
cake as found in the ovens, perfect, and resembling
the modern in form; nuts, figs, coffee, and olives, all
retaining their shape, but black as ink; cameo sets,
rings, bracelets, articles of clothing and of housekeep-
ing, among others a pan still full of a kind of polenta
for a repast, and a purse found in the grasp of an exhumed skeleton.

" Thou hast made of a city an heap; of a defenced
city a ruin; a palace of strangers to be no city; it shall
never be built."—Isaiah xxv. 2.

We visit Pompeii, its ruins being one of the most
interesting sights in Europe. Many walls of houses
remain, some of them covered with frescoes of well-
preserved colors; many fountains and statues still
stand, and recesses covered with the most elaborate
mosaics. The streets are in regular order, their curb-
stones and pavements perfect, the marks of the car-
riage-wheels being in deeply-worn ruts. The character
of the stores is easily defined, not only by the signs,
some of which are yet traceable, but by their relics, as

ovens in the bakers' shops, wheels to grind the grain, immense jars in the oil and liquor stores, and in the barber's shop the stone seat for the customers and the niches for the pomades. In the theatre are the seats of stone, the Forum also being easily identified by its grand columns, standing as a monument of the skill and opulence of former days.

But the most thrilling sight in this excavated city is in a certain little room, where in glass cases are preserved the different members of one family, all encrusted in a kind of lava, and in positions strikingly natural, as death suddenly overtook them. Two children lie together, adhering in one portion of their bodies, the feet of one towards the head of the other. The father is partially turned, as if striving to free himself from the inexorable grasp of the destroyer, while the mother is stretched upon her back, with her head on one side and one limb raised. The lavarous crust upon the bodies leaves their forms defined, but in a measure enlarges their proportions.

There is a skeleton standing in the corner grinning apparently at the spectators, showing a set of teeth of faultless color and shape. The guide rather grimly remarks that they must have done good execution with the macaroni.

We are shown the impression, clearly defined, on the wall of a subterranean passage, of the faces and figures of several persons, who were discovered pressed against it; one of them is clutching a handful of jewels, which she had caught up and sought to fly with on the first note of warning. But, alas! they were doomed to find in this subterranean refuge their death and sepulchre.

The impression made upon one is very peculiar in wandering through streets where beauty and fashion once displayed their charms; through the once busy marts of trade, where the relics of art still remain; in the salons of dancing and revelry, which are still gorgeous in their richly-colored frescoes, the echoes of youthful gayety and mirth seeming still to linger in the air; through the majestic halls of the Forum, where Philosophy and Logic held the pagan ear; and in the Theatre, in whose seats we could fancy the assemblage of Pompeian beauty and strength, all alike delighted with the crude representation of dramatic art.

We cannot realize that this is the partial resurrection of a city that for eighteen hundred years has been dead and buried, but it seems more like a recently deserted village, and as if by the renovating effects of mechanical skill it could soon be rendered habitable and echo again with the sounds of busy life.

Herculaneum is far less interesting than Pompeii. We are led down a flight of steps and are introduced into a series of intricate, dark, subterranean passages, which are lined by walls of intensely hard lava. The Theatre, with many of its seats and some other features, are to be seen, and this is all. It reminds us of the Catacombs of Rome. Herculaneum was buried by masses of lava, which, mixed with rain, formed a thick conglomeration very difficult to penetrate; but Pompeii was destroyed by a storm of dry ashes and *débris* which is easily removed, even with its accumulation of centuries, revealing the treasures of Pompeian wealth and art.

We have often read, heard, and dreamed of Italian skies as being unrivalled for beauty and glory, but never have we seen any to equal many of ours until the day we travel by rail from Naples to Rome. The landscape is smiling and green; the olive-trees clothed with vines; the green verdure of the fields picturesquely relieved by the gay, bright costumes of the peasantry as they turn the soil with their rake and hoe; the graceful slopes and the bold promontories of the Apennines, with their deep, lingering shadows; and, above all, the most heavenly skies that one could imagine. Light, fleecy clouds, with banks of deep gold and crimson, relieved by the more sombre hues, until the broad expanse above us seems a sea of glory.

VESUVIUS.

A most adventurous undertaking is that of the ascent of Mount Vesuvius. Taking a carriage at Naples we ride to the Hermitage, which is situated some distance up the mountain-side. As we wind up the gentle slope we are surrounded by a troop of infantry, which, although they have not been drilled in military tactics, are expert at the "double-quick" movement and in " presenting" hands if not " arms." A crowd of these youthful beggars besieges us until we arrive at the Hermitage, where we enjoy the lunch we have brought with us. After it we take horses, which are provided for the short ride to the base of the cone.

During an eruption the crater breathes forth a fiery destruction that blasts all nature within reach of its exhalations, vomiting lava, which pours down the mountain-sides congealing, and forming billow-like irregularities, black, unsightly, and forbidding, rendering most of the region round about sterile and uninviting. And yet occasionally there appear tiny oases of a thin superficial coating of arable soil, where simple wild-flowers, as if in pity, offer their tribute towards redeeming the scene from utter desolation. It is said that during an eruption, or immediately subsequent to it, " there is such an abundance of rain, owing to the mass of vapors ejected into the atmos-

5*

phere, that it precipitates itself along the sides of the
cone in actual torrents, charged with a fine, impalpable,
volcanic dust, which, carrying with them a fine ashes,
acquires a consistence to justify the name given to
them of ' aqueous lavas.' "

Alighting from the horses which have brought us
from the Hermitage to the foot of the cone, we each
engage two guides and attempt the task. A herculean
one it proves, although with one man alternately to
pull and support, and another following in the rear to
push gently but firmly. The soil to a great depth is of
a loamy, yielding, crumbling nature, that gives way
under the pressure of the foot, seeming to give impetus
to a backward movement instead of allowing an advance. An hour and a half are consumed in the wearisome climbing, which, singularly enough, is more exhausting during the first part than the last. Being
novices, and not having learned the necessity of reserv-
ing one's powers, we put forth our entire strength at
the outset, soon succumbing to a fatigue attended by a
painful difficulty in breathing, which threatens to inca-
pacitate us for further effort. After resting, however,
on the large stones which nature seems to have provided for an occasional seat, and by paying strict heed
to the guides' admonitory advice, we pluck up our courage, and bearing more heavily upon our wooden and
human staffs, " taking it easy," we make slow but steady

progress. When half-way one of the ladies accepts
an earnestly proffered seat on the shoulders of two
guides, who unfalteringly but pantingly bear their
precious burden up the " Hill Difficulty." Had Bun-
yan had this mount in his mind he could not have
more vividly portrayed the difficulties and dangers to
be encountered in its ascent. Not the gates of the
heavenly city loom up before our view, however, but
rather, as we near the goal, volumes of smoke impregnated with sulphurous fumes warn us of a nearer
approach to what seems more like the mouth of the
Inferno. Indeed, the illusion is the more complete
when, on reaching the summit, we look down into the
pit-like crater of brimstone and fire, into the very
jaws of death. Shall we descend into this threatening
abyss whose under-currents are in perpetual ferment?
being an intense fire, whose lurid flames occasionally
shoot their fiery tongues through forced fissures. As
we look down into the seething basin, waves of black
lava, here and there, suddenly redden, dissolve, and
boil over as if from a surcharged cauldron. But the
American spirit of dashing enterprise and reckless
venture determines the question, and with tremulous
excitement, clinging to our trusty guides, we descend
into the literal fiery furnace. The heat is intense and
feels scorching as its breath sweeps our cheeks, while
our feet must be kept in constant motion, skipping

from point to point, to avoid the burning sensation produced by a momentary lingering in any one spot.

Indeed, we must have watchful eyes, too, as without other warning than a faint trembling beneath our feet the lavarous crust opens, and through the gaping fissure flows the boiling fluid, which, as it cools, becomes a hardened billow of blackened lava.

In a distant corner is a large mass of congealed sulphur, through whose occasional apertures issue sulphurous fumes of the deepest orange, blended with 'red, green, and mingled colors, beautiful to the eye, but, as we find on timidly approaching, are *almost* suffocating, and would be overwhelmingly so in the *midst* of its variegated cloud and vapor. We remember that the death of Pliny the Elder was attributable to this cause.

We begin the descent, gathering many specimens of lava, with colors as numerous as those in a paint-box, but which change by keeping to dingy hues. Finding at each step our limbs embedded in the soft, yielding soil, we complain that the effort is even more laborious than that required in the ascent. The guides exclaim, "If you all would run down fast, letting us support you under your arms, you would not find difficulty." And so, withholding all personal exertion, but yielding ourselves entirely to the control of the strong men at each side, we are assisted easily and rapidly over the surface of the precipitous mountain slope. Indeed, so exhilarating is the experience, and so swiftly are we guided, that amid exceeding mirth and merry laughter, with occasional halts "to catch breath," we accomplish the descent in ten minutes.

A visit to the Observatory is made very interesting by a critical inspection of the exceedingly delicate instrument through which, by detecting and calculating the vibrations of the earth, science is enabled to predict the coming of an eruption.

A PICNIC AT PÆSTUM.

We almost hesitate to write the words, so incongruous seems any feasting, but that of the soul, amid some of the most venerable ruins in the world. Arrived at Salerno, we find it a fine old town, situated on the Bay of Salerno, half encircled by the Alban Mountains, which protect it from "the rough winds of Heaven" on one side, the swelling bosom of the blue sea ever pulsating before it. The principal street, which follows the shore, is very long and full of lively scenes, presenting a picture of Italian life only to be seen in its completeness in a town of Southern Italy. Almost every phase of life is represented as we drive through the town at eventide. Human life swarms; and it is only by the repeated cracking of the postilion's whip that a passage can be effected.

Groups of picturesquely-dressed peasants, their gay

colors giving brilliancy to the scene; tables surrounded
by gesticulating men, with their bottle and convivial
glasses before them; women with tightly-swaddled
babes in their arms; beggars in every form of decrep-
itude, and in a squalor almost inconceivable; rickety
wagons, absolutely loaded with human beings, dashing
through the crowds, the poor, attenuated beasts goaded
on by the loud and dissonant cries of their drivers; and
young fops with swinging canes and eyes glancing constantly up to the balconies above, over which lean their
bright-eyed friends; women of the better class, their
heads covered by black lace veils, which are a becoming setting to the bronzed faces and black, sparkling
eyes of the wearers, who invariably possess a fine set
of pearly teeth ever gleaming from ripe lips,—charms
which are foiled by the strangely-wizened faces of the
aged in this country. What a scene! and how often
repeated in this sunny land, where houses are always
deserted and the streets filled with gay, merry throngs
at this twilight hour!

Early in the morning we take a carriage for Pæstum,
twenty-four miles distant, driving through a country
very sterile and uninteresting, reaching the grand ruins
about mid-day. Not with frivolity, but with deep
thoughtfulness, do we approach some of the most ancient
as well as magnificent ruins of the past. They con-
sist of three Doric temples, the most imposing of which

is the Temple of Neptune. The situation is admirably adapted to the imposing structure, for grandeur is heightened by isolation. Nature herself seems a worshipper at this ancient shrine; deep, ay, profound silence reigns, only broken by the unequalled music of nature's orchestra, the birds seeming to revel in the beauty around them, and if their sweet warblings break upon the solemnity it is a relief to the oppressive influences of the scene.

We enter the Temple with slow and reverent step; its only roof is the vault of heaven; its pillars, honeycombed by time, enclose us in their quiet majesty; and so we stand in rapt communion with the great Past, so eloquently represented by this architectural conception. Three continuous stone steps surround the Temple, from these arise the six columns of the front and the fourteen of the sides. They are fluted and conical, their circumference being smaller at the top than at the base, and this delicate graduation is very effective and pleasing to the eye. The architectural merit is unsurpassed, the genius of Greece finding expression in this marvellous structure. Looking aloft from the interior of the Temple upon the upper blocks of stone, we witness the union of modern Flora with old Neptune. Closely entwined is he by the graceful tendrils of a sweetly flowering vine, which, being a spontaneous tribute of the goddess to the hoary old god, is the more effective.

Seating ourselves on the reverend stones within the Temple, we spread our meal and prepare to dine under circumstances more novel than ever before, not forgetting in the wine of the country to drink a libation to the old god whose temple we seem to be desecrating.

As we look above and around us and see how nobly this grand monument has withstood the buffetings of storms; the fury of tempests; the " peltings of pitiless rains;" the fervid heat of summers; and all the combined effects of time and the elements, we resolve that we, with our human souls, will strive to endure the shocks of fate and the sorrow which sometimes rains upon us: resisting all the adverse influences, which often undermine the foundations of character, just as these great, grand forms have conquered the effects of ages, retaining not only their pristine strength, but their beauty as well. We leave the sacred spot knowing that never again will our eyes rest upon its wonders, and feeling that somewhat of its grandeur and beauty are reflected upon our moral nature.

CHAPTER VI.

VENICE.

"Thy borders are in the midst of the seas, thy builders have perfected thy beauty."—EZEKIEL xxvii. 4.

FAIR, lovely Venice, the queen of the Adriatic, is the most remarkable city we have visited, its very name suggesting all that is unique, poetical, and dreamy. How surprising to eyes which look for the first time upon buildings rising magic-like from the sea, instead of gazing upon rolling meadows and flowering gardens, or even streets where rumbling wheels weary the ear; to look ever upon the rippling tide and the dropping and lifting of the active oar as it dips into the water and rises vocal with sound! Nor does the interest of the novel experience wane during the traveller's sojourn here, as some fresh form of loveliness, some new feature of the singular scene, constantly greets the eyes that are on the alert, and ministers to the mind that is receptive to new delights, through new sensations.

Venice is built upon a cluster of seventy or eighty

islands, connected with one another by four hundred
and fifty bridges, of which the Rialto is the grandest,
consisting of a single arch one hundred and eighty-
seven feet long and forty-three wide. The effect
of this fine structure, however, is marred, if not destroyed, by its two rows of rude booths or shops,
whose stocks are adapted only to the trade of the lower
classes.

Instead of streets there are canals, boats instead of
carts, gondolas instead of coaches. In the rear of
many houses there are passages, but too narrow for a
carriage, no horse being in the city. The doors of the
buildings open upon the canals, with steps leading to
the boats. According to an ancient law, still enforced,
all gondolas are painted black. The law was made
necessary by the unbridled extravagance that the nobility displayed in the embellishment of their water
equipages. Each gondola has a tiny cabin in its centre,
its cushions and all its appointments being of the same
sombre hue, and only needing a recumbent figure to
look, for all the world, like one of our occupied biers.
The gondola resembles our row-boats, is somewhat
longer, and is ornamented at one end by a shining steel
prow. This flashing in the sunlight on a crowded
canal, where the gondolas are floating side by side, or
are skimming by one another with rapid motion, adds
much to the beauty of the scene. The gondolier stands

on the narrow edge of the boat at one end, and with a
graceful bend and swaying movement of the body
sends his little craft lightly over the water, turning the
corner from one canal into another deftly and with
consummate skill. Each gondolier as he makes these
turns with his noiseless boat utters a cry of warning,
which is made by the melodious Italian voice so welcome to the ear that it forms one of the delights of our
ride.

There are many churches rich in mosaics, paintings,
and statuary, but the most remarkable in Venice, and,
indeed, one of the most so in the world, is St. Mark's,
that conglomeration of many types of architecture, but
chiefly perhaps Byzantine. The exterior of the church
is very Oriental in its style, the roof being covered
with what appear to be little mosques, making the
tout ensemble very striking. The interior is brilliant
with mosaic, the groundwork of the ceiling being in
gold. The marbles which compose the columns are of
various colors, and are wonderfully beautiful. The
altar is inlaid with precious stones, and so profuse is
the whole building in the display of gorgeous color
and rich material, and so pronounced are the traces
of its antiquity, that one may well stand in wondering
admiration before this relic of the magnificence of the
old-time *régime.* In the "Square of St. Mark," which
is five hundred and seventy-six feet long and two hun-

dred and sixty-nine in greatest width, and near the venerable church, stands the Campanile, from whose summit we have a fine view, and opposite is the "Torre dell' Orologio," with a large clock, two bronze figures striking the hours upon the bell.

St. Mark's Church, with all its mosque-like cupolas; its many arches one above another; its famous bronze horses, which stand outside the portico, the ancient Campanile rearing its majestic height near by; the arcade enclosing the paved square; gay throngs filling the many cafés, and sauntering along the broad promenade, while on the smooth stones of the centre are the pigeons, whose variegated plumage is made brilliant by the rays of the noonday sun. So gentle, domestic, and tame have these city pets become through regular feeding that they will voluntarily perch upon the extended hand or upon the shoulder of a stranger and partake of the crumbs or corn offered them. The pigeons flock in such numbers that they almost cover the square, forming a bright picturesque feature of a mid-day scene in this famous spot; indeed, one of the curious sights of Venice is the feeding of them at two o'clock every day. Many years ago an old lady died leaving a legacy to be appropriated to their support. Some ten years since we witnessed the pretty scene enacted each day. And again during a recent visit we find the custom still in vogue, much to the amusement of strangers, who seldom fail to be present at the accustomed hour, lightening the official's task by their personal aid.

The Doge's Palace stands at one side of the church, and is full of historical and artistic interest. On ascending the imposing staircase, we are shown many apartments whose associations with the political history of Venice make them very attractive. Their walls are lined by large allegorical pictures by the old masters, portraying the glory and power of the Republic. Proceeding to the upper story, our eyes fall upon the aperture, on one side of the door, leading into the Inquisitor's chamber, where letters of secret denunciation were formerly deposited. The lion's head, in whose mouth the letters were dropped, has disappeared. Here again are series of salons, whose paintings and carved ornamentation, particularly that which surrounds the mammoth fireplaces, testify to the former opulence of a government which provided for its rulers such palatial luxury and wealth of art. We are ushered into a room which in olden times was hung in black, and was the scene of the secret tribunal of the Council of Ten. Through a narrow passage the condemned was led forth to a death, to be effected with the same secrecy and expedition that had characterized his mock trial.

We are invited to explore the recesses of the prison,

connected with the Palace by the " Bridge of Sighs,"
whose commemorative verses by Byron,

" I stood in Venice, on the bridge of sighs,"

are as familiar as household words.   It is even frightful to inspect these dungeons, which, we are happy to
learn, have not been occupied since the seventeenth
century.   Small, dark, dank cells, with only an inclined
board to supply, in cruel mockery, the place of a bed.
The cell of the condemned often proved, tradition
tells us, the scene of the death of the criminal, for,
from its immediate juxtaposition to the waters below,
the dampness, almost palpable, engendered disease
which in mercy deprived the executioner of his victim.
Outside of this cell, in one of the thickly-walled passages, is the dread spot where the condemned, did he
chance to survive his fearful incarceration, was hung ;
and when dead, was easily slipped down an inclined
plane into the dark, silent waters below.   So all traces
of these judicial murders were buried secretly from the
sight of the outside world.   No wonder that the establishment of this satanic Council of Ten was one of the
causes of the downfall of the aristocratic power of the
imposing Republic of Venice.   Indeed, what government can be permanent, however brilliant its success,
reaching even the zenith of a mid-day splendor, whose
building is not of a righteous foundation and its laws

based upon justice and equity? And so, with other adverse circumstances, this demoniac power subtilely undermined a prosperous nationality; a glory which knew few peers sinking beneath the waves of time.

A row on the Grand Canal presents to our view a series of palaces with which there are connected many pleasant reminiscences. The Palace Morodin falling into the possession of the Moro family is said to have given one Doge to the Republic. He is thought by some to have been the hapless lover of Desdemona. The Palace Mocenigo is where Byron, in the society of the beautiful Countess G., wrote the first cantos of "Don Juan" and some other poems. In the Palace Barbarigo Titian once lived, to whose memory a noble monument has been erected in one of the churches. It is embellished with statues and with bas-reliefs of his works. The last picture painted by this wonderful artist, "The Entombment," is in the same salon with his famous painting of "The Assumption." With what tremulous hand must he have wrought upon this last work! and how appropriate the subject, as it prefigured his own rapidly approaching dissolution! Although ninety-nine years of age his "right hand had not forgot its cunning," for upon this celebrated picture was he working when death arrested his hand.

Upon a neighboring island is the famed Armenian monastery where the unhappy Byron sought refuge temporarily from his worst enemy,—himself.   But, alas! his restless spirit, grown morbid through sensibilities painfully acute, and goaded by a conscience too delicately organized to become deadened by his life of unholy license, failed to secure the peace it sought.

Although his sins were chiefly the outgrowth of an entire absence of respect for woman,—and we believe that reverence for her is the rudder which helps to steer a man's soul into the heavenly port,—yet what woman can refuse her pity to him whose naturally warm, generous impulses might by a fond, judicious, maternal hand have been early directed, and pruned of all riotous growth?   Warmed by a mother's sunny smile, watered by her tender tears, they might have grown into noble traits, which, through their very elements, if subdued and modified, would have enriched his own and others' lives.

This man of brilliant genius, but with an undisciplined moral character, with tendencies belonging to rich emotional natures, right in themselves, only unfortunate in their rank luxuriance and criminal in their unrestrained indulgence, was forced to exclaim, in bitterness of spirit,—

" I am eating the fruit of the tree I planted."

He sought the quiet asylum of a monastic life, within

sight of lovely Venice and within the sound of her pleasant waters, but

> " The mind is its own place, and in itself
> Can make a Heaven of Hell, a Hell of Heaven."

So amid scenes of apparently holy calm, with naught in outside influences to ruffle the spirit's serenity, he found that the tempest of passion in his soul was only allayed, and after a temporary lull threatened to break forth into thunder and storm. The monks tell now how earnestly he strove to adopt their habits, and through these external influences to minister peace and consolation "to a mind diseased." After a few months' retirement within the shade of this secluded life, discouraged, he returned to the glare and heat of a dissipated career.

Venice and moonlight should be inseparable in reality, as they are in imagination. How chaste its light as it beams upon the wondrous city! How beautiful are the queenly palaces rearing their tall forms against the evening sky, the classic towers standing out in bold relief, graceful minarets piercing the air, noble churches throwing their shadows on the moonlit waters! How exquisite the silvery sheen, mingling with the blue of the waves, all things below seeming to reflect the beauty of night's grand illuminator! How soft and mellow the voices of the serenaders who constantly float by, or linger beneath the casements to win their well-earned reward, which, while the ear is ravished by their rich tones and sweet airs, is not grudgingly given! We leave the window out of which we have leaned, our very senses beguiled, and, slipping out of the rear door of our hotel, emerge into the narrow street. In all directions there are little alley-like passages, whose every house is sending forth its inmates, all wending their way to the grand Venetian rendezvous, St. Mark's Square. We enter it with the crowd of pleasure-seekers. It is enclosed on three sides by fine buildings, the upper portions of which, connected, form the residence of the king, occupied by him when he visits the city, the lowest story being a series of stores, which make a brilliant display of jewelry and other tempting articles.

The chairs of the numerous cafés are mostly occupied, and we find some difficulty in obtaining several, with a table, where we may sit and, with toothsome ices before us, enjoy the brilliant scene. In the midst is a fine regimental band, pouring from the mouths of many brass instruments the soul-stirring strains of martial music. Ladies with black lace veils, picturesquely arranged on their dark hair, fastened with showy arrow or bright flower; the gaudily-dressed flower-girl with very high-heeled slipper, which peeps forth from the short skirt, her hair elaborately coiffured, her

cheeks ruddy with paint, her eyes brightened with desire to captivate, her basket of tiny nosegays swung
coquettishly on her arm, tripping here and there, followed by many a jest from her masculine customers;
the brilliant uniform of gay officers; the clatter of their
trailing swords; the eager voices of the vehement for-
eigners, which, with their accompanying gesticulations,
give life and vivacity to the occasion.

Although delighted with this phase of Venetian life
we shift the scene, by walking through the neighboring Piazetta to the waiting boats, and stepping into an
open one, for the night is serene and all the influences
inexpressibly lovely, we yield ourselves up to a sensuous delight, the more intense because of its novelty.
The experience is one of unequalled enchantment.
The twinkling gaslights of the buildings which border
our course are doubled by their quivering reflections
in the waters below; gondolas with their red and blue
lights glancing here and there in every direction give
a brilliant, variegated hue to the atmosphere, and indeed to the element beneath us. Many parties glide
by; the air is rich with melodious song, which seems
re-echoed in the refrain of voices wafted dreamily to
us from a distance.

We recline, and lazily watch the swaying of the
oarsmen, who, bending low, rise with grace, seeming
never to weary, always sustaining the poetry of mo-

tion; the green festoons of seaweed clinging to the lifted oar, sparkling with liquid pearls or diamonds; the churches rising from the waves; palaces looming up above the waters; and pretty young faces leaning over balconies that are green and bright with many-hued flowers. So we float insensibly down the tide, the splash of the dipping oars like "drops of music" to the enchanted senses; the soft notes of warning breaking upon the sweet evening air.

We seem in a delicious dream, gliding noiselessly on, propelled by some unseen power; for our boatman stands in the rear and so guides our long, narrow bark unseen. It moves as if by magic, adding to the illusion that we are in fairy-land, all the surroundings contributing to the births of fancy.

CHAPTER VII.

MILAN—LAKE COMO.

MILAN.

MILAN, a large, prosperous, and affluent city, its buildings fine, modern, and spacious, giving elegance to streets broad and light, impresses one with its cleanliness, brightness, air of comfort, and opulence. Although containing much of exceeding value in souvenirs of ancient and modern art, and although the course for driving and promenading, and the public gardens for lounging, are unusually attractive, yet the magnet which draws the world hither is the famed Duomo, or Cathedral. As we stand before it we think it must be a crystallized dream, for the magic architect who fills girlish visions with beauty, by erecting palaces of delight, and even in the dreamland through which the thoughts wander in mature life, with structures of almost impossible splendor, dazzling eyes whose practised vision demands brilliant colors and grand proportions to satisfy wider desires, seldom finds a rival in real life; for the imagination is more

boundless in *its* realm than is the capacity of the
actual.

The Cathedral, after St. Peter's, is the largest in
Italy, exceeding all others in the rare beauty of its
fret-work and intricate and delicate tracery in carving.
Built of white marble, its exterior is absolutely dazzling. It is adorned by one hundred and six pinnacles and four thousand five hundred statues; the
dome surmounted by a tower, on whose apex is a
gigantic statue of the Virgin in bronze. We·realize
now the full significance of the poet's meaning when
she pronounces architecture to be "frozen music."
Such harmony, such darting of beauty from every
point seem to penetrate the soul with that delicious
content that springs often from the inception into our
thought and sense of some prolonged strains of
melody, whose every note reverberates through the
innermost recesses of our being.

The length of the Cathedral is four hundred and
ninety feet, its breadth two hundred and ninety-eight;
and while its foundations appear stable, broad, and
enduring, the upper portion is the embodiment of
grace, pinnacles, like exhalations, rising from every
point. We enter; shall we be disappointed? Amazed
by the beauty and grace of the exterior, we almost fear
to find a nearer view less gratifying. We stand within
one of the finest temples "made with hands" in the

world; but *hands* that were endowed with a skill
seldom equalled. Supported by fifty-two pillars of
seventy feet in height and eight in diameter, its form
is that of a Latin cross. The interior abounds in
statuary, paintings, and the most gorgeous stained glass,
the three large windows behind the choir depicting three
hundred scriptural scenes; their colors of ruby and
blue of such remarkable· beauty that our eyes constantly seek them as sources, in themselves, of the
most artistic delight. We sympathize with Ruskin's
thought when he declares that " of all God's gifts to
the sight of man, color is the holiest, the most divine,
the most solemn;" to us, embodying thoughts or emotions "too deep for tears." The love of color may be
a sensuous taste, as is that of odor, but that it awakens
dormant sentiment who can doubt? While gazing
upon brilliant tints in the sky or upon those that dye
the flowers of the field, it may be thoughts of the Infinite who planned and originated their beauty that
moves our spiritual sense; but when looking upon a
simple dash of gorgeous color on a more prosaic object,
or as seen in many of the stained windows in the grand
cathedrals of Europe, who shall say that under its spell
a harsh mood has not been softened, irritation soothed,
and apathy won into the active, warm exercise of the
heart's best emotions? And we believe that it is
through this and the kindred tastes of music and odor

—as in the incense—that the sentiment of worship in these Romish churches is developed and stimulated.

There is something magnificent in loftiness, and as we walk beneath a dome two hundred and eight feet in height, enclosed within columns colossal in size, we experience sensations approaching awe, with a realization of physical littleness that would effectually obliterate any exaggerated sense of self-importance.

Near one of the altars is a bronze candelabrum representing a tree inlaid with precious stones. It is a relic of the thirteenth century.

Under the choir is the vault of St. Carlo Borromeo. He was a count of an ancient Milanese family, and nephew of Pius IV. From his earliest youth he was rigidly pious and severe in self-discipline. Having a large share in the civil government, he also accomplished much for the papal authority, effecting by his great influence the results of the Council of Trent. As archbishop of Milan he established many noble institutions and was unwearied in good works. Dying at the age of forty-six, he was canonized some years after; his embalmed body dressed in pontifical robes, which are richly and profusely studded with precious gems, was placed in a crystal sarcophagus. The display of rare workmanship and of immense jewels is surprising. The crosiers and mitre are of great value and beauty, while the sarcophagus, which is supported by ornaments of wrought silver, bears the cross in heavy gold of Philip IV. of Spain, who presented it. Indeed, the body of the saint is covered with gifts from crowned heads and of the nobility. The ceiling of the vault is inlaid with tablets of silver, representing the prominent events in the life of the celebrated prelate, particularly of his self-sacrificing efforts to assuage the sufferings of the sick and dying during the plague of 1576.

Not far from the choir stands a marble statue as remarkable in execution as it is striking in conception. It is that of St. Bartholomew represented as flayed,—the entire skin, retaining the form of the still living body, hangs over his shoulder. The sculptor has proved his skill by making the representation so curiously real as to be almost shocking to, at least, feminine sensibilities. It is comforting to know, however, that it is a work of the imagination, as history assures us his death was effected by crucifixion.

To obtain a more accurate idea of this wonderful Cathedral and to enjoy an experience very novel in its character, we accede to the proposition of the guide to ascend to the roof, and there wander through its labyrinthine foot-paths amid statues innumerable; pinnacles of Gothic form covered with fret-work; spires jutting everywhere; and towers and ornaments in great variety. The whole roof, "a multiform unit," is com-

posed of flat blocks of white marble, the long spaces
of devious way varied by occasional successions of
steps. A long journey before we are bidden to halt
and gaze upon a view well worth the effort made to
obtain it. There lies the city in the midst of a fertile,
pleasant plain ; the river Olona gliding by, the Alps
hovering near, and the Apennines looming up in the far
horizon. It is a strange situation, roaming on the lofty
top of a building so broad and so intricate in its wind-
ings as to excite the fear of being lost amidst its forest
of marble spires.

One of the most ancient churches we have visited is
that of Sant' Ambrogio. The marble pulpit, which is
itself deserving of studious attention, is said to be the
same as that from which St. Ambrose preached A.D.
387. Among many curious and antiquated relics of
ages gone by are the missals, held in sacred keeping
and shown only by a priest, who himself turns their
precious pages. Dating from the twelfth century, they
are written on parchment, very legibly, and even
beautifully. At the beginning of each chapter are
many sketches brilliantly illuminated in rich colors.
The young priest who displays these treasures to us invites scrutiny. Drooping shoulders and an ungainly
figure deprives him of much physical advantage, but a
keen, intelligent eye, and smile so bright and sunny
that it can even lighten priestly gloom, helps to re-

deem other deficiencies. Discovering our ignorance of
his native tongue, he meets us on common ground in
the French, through whose airy medium his lively
sense of the ludicrous, his ready wit and rich fund of
information make sparkling and piquant his comments
upon the pictured ornamentations of the missals and
other odd features of the ancient church. On a pillar
of porphyry, near the centre of the church, a brazen
serpent is twined, rearing its frightful head aloft. It
is affirmed that the common people consider this the
identical serpent which Moses held up in the desert,
inviting the gaze of the Israelites that they might be
healed. It is also believed among them that at the end
of the world this serpent will hiss. Pointing to this
brazen representation, our priestly guide explains that
many think this is the veritable serpent of the wilder-
ness, but, with a contemptuous shake of the head, he
declares the belief to be the outgrowth of "*superstition,
superstition.*" Associating priestly reticence and rigidity
of manner with the sect he represents, we are surprised
by his great affability and communicativeness, and
much amused by his evident ignoring of the masculine
element of our party and his devotion to the fairest of
the other sex, giving earnest invitation to repeat the
visit, when he with pleasure will again act as our
cicerone. So gentlemanly is his mien that we feel
some awkwardness in proffering the usual gratuity,

and he, too, feels some embarrassment, as on receiving it he volunteers the unusual explanation that it shall be devoted to the poor.

In the former refectory of the Dominican convent belonging to the church Santa Maria, is Leonardo da Vinci's most famous painting, "The Last Supper." Under the blighting effects of time this justly celebrated picture had become much faded and marred. But its ruin was almost consummated when Napoleon I. taking possession of Milan, the convent was transformed into barracks; its refectory, containing one of the art-gems of the world, being used as a stable for horses. We cannot believe that Napoleon, such a lover of the arts as to be thievingly covetous of their treasures, transporting them from every city he conquered to Paris, and there proudly displaying them as trophies of war, could have known "to what vile use had come at last" this apartment, made sacred by the marvellous representation of one of the most pathetic, solemn, and sublime scenes in our Saviour's human experience.

The fresco covers one entire end of the large room, rewarding even in its partial obliteration and impaired beauty, repeated visits. Leonardo, it is said, concentrated his thought for two entire years upon the manner in which best to depict on the face of Judas the abject meanness, the consummate depravity, the devilish perfidy of his heart. Perhaps the world is indebted to the fact—in moral view to be deplored—of his entertaining vindictive hatred to the prior of the convent. which sought gratification by giving to his features the satanic expression of our Lord's betrayer. If this be a fact, it would seem that the existence of malignity in the heart, may endow with inspiration the hand that strives to give it outward expression.

LAKE COMO.

Perhaps we draw too heavily upon our imagination, and should, if challenged, be unable to substantiate our belief, when we think that there are localities as adapted to the various mental conditions as others are to the physical. Nature, with a tact and power inimitable, has brought together certain elements, not always tangible,—but perceptible to the senses,—to bear upon the changing moods which characterize our imperfect humanity. These are more noticeable, perhaps, in our sex than in that more rugged one, whose blunter sensibilities make it more invulnerable to the many influences that vibrate upon the chords of the feminine heart. Should this thought be resolved into a fact, would not the lofty, rugged mountain ranges of Switzerland be most congenial to the strong, undaunted courage of the brave-hearted; its heights struggling heavenward, in sympathy with the aspirations of the

ambitious soul; its frosty air and rough winds adapted
to the temperament of those to whom softness or gen-
tleness of spirit is a stranger, and who find in them
a semblance to the stormy passions that sweep through
their own hearts? But to those whose nature is the
nestling place of tender emotions, dreamy thoughts,
and brooding fancies, how much that favors its growth
and grants it sweet indulgence is there in the very
atmosphere, seeming filled with poetry, of the balmy
land of Italy, in its soft, fleecy clouds, and in the
manifold influences which nature holds in her keeping!

We first look upon Lake Como in June, the loveliest of months, and on one of its loveliest days,
through whose bright hours the sun has shone un-
weariedly, but with a fervor tempered by the breezes,
which have caught freshness from the waters as they
skim over them. The very name of the lake implies
beauty, or is it that we have always so associated
beauty with Lake Como that its name has grown to
be synonymous with it? However that may be, when
the word Como falls upon our ear or meets our eye on
printed page, there is a scene of beauty and charm
floating before us that seems could only be borne on the
wings of dreamy fancy.

The lake is at the foot of the Alps, the mountains
extending around and above it to the height often of
eight or nine hundred feet. Most of them are clothed

in a mantle of green, with growth of tree and shrub, while others are wearing proudly their robes of purest snow. In the boat that is taking us to Bellagio, situated at a point which is midway of the lake and where its beauty seems to culminate, we are reminded that there is something in the scenery singularly adapted to the languid mood which has settled upon us. A languor that is not the lassitude which is the offspring of an enfeebled condition, or the accompaniment of disease,—one of its most trying features,—but that state of being when all disturbing causes having been banished, the mind is in perfect repose, a soft dreaminess flooding the soul, allowing the gentle thought to flow without let or hindrance. Drifting along in luxurious content, one's individuality fades out into a state of utter negation, which is ofttimes one of placid enjoyment. Nature, here, is in sympathy with the mood. Inertia seems to have been the principle on which these exquisite scenes have been planned. All about us is suggestive of rest. The line of ponderous peaks which forms the background hints to us of a more rugged experience beyond, but the present is hedged in by influences relaxing, softening, and soothing. The hills incline in gentle undulations toward the lake, greeting it with sunny slopes studded with bright-eyed flowers; the face of the sweet waters on which we glide breaking into dimples; beautiful villas on its borders, their

gardens proving the prolificness of the clime by masses
of bloom, blossom, and clustering vines; the skies
above assuming a softness and tenderness that suggest
the fancy that they are but the fleecy veil that half
conceals the angel faces beaming upon this lower world.
The zephyrs, so deliciously sweet, may be their breath
wafting blessings to us. The "glorious piles" of
mountain peaks, whose snowy heads are often painted
by the rays of the sun with a creamy golden hue, or
with colors beautifully suggestive of rose and crimson.
Some so concealed by ambient mist that we can scarce
tell where their outline ceases and the sky begins, the
lofty summits of those in the distance seeming to repose upon the billowy bosom of the clouds; these
giants in nature, like the strong in human life, seeking,
Samson-like, to recline upon a lesser strength!

A marked peculiarity of this famed and beautiful
lake is its graceful irregularity. Often we imagine
ourselves at its terminus, apparently shut in by towering hills and bordering meadows, until suddenly a
silvery flowing pathway opens to us new views of such
beauty as in Lake Como reaches the acme of natural
charm. The trip is a succession of sweet surprises;
nor is it strange that they should remind us of their
counterpart in life's experiences. How often does the
soul seem environed by apprehensions and by perplex-
ing cares; fate shutting it in to a gloom from which

light seems effectually secluded; no opportunity possible for escape from what appears inevitable! But unexpectedly the clouds of adversity disperse, the glorious beams of the sun flood the darkened soul, showers of divine mercy refresh the weary spirit, and joy comes in bright array!

CHAPTER VIII.

SWITZERLAND.

SWITZERLAND, with its wonderful passes and lovely valleys, is to us as yet an unexplored Canaan. We anticipate with eagerness the pleasure we know to be in store for the lover of nature. We have brought with us a rich sauce for the feast, in an enthusiasm which will give relish to all that is to be spread before our vision. It has ever been our conviction that this attribute of the soul, this sentiment of the heart, which we call enthusiasm, is a requisite to the full enjoyment of life and beauty. It is inspiring; it is the energy with which the soul recognizes and digests the richest meaning of the powers of nature; whereby the mountains excite deep veneration, the flowers of the field convey "mysterious truths," and the heavenly bodies speak to us in illuminated texts. Life—who can deny it?—is so full of the chilling prose of reserve; so formal in its manifestations; so commonplace, shallow, and artificial in many of its phases, that we find an earnest sentiment, true feeling, or, in other words,

a well-disciplined enthusiasm, gives a warm impulse
to the currents of life; and while it enriches the
nature from which it emanates, sheds a reflected glow
upon other and colder natures.

Endowed, then, with this joy-giving sentiment, we
are prepared to read upon the inspired pages of nature
the grand truths which she would reveal to her own
children. No interpreter is needed, as her language is
a universal one. On the Alpine heights we read the
title of her works, " Excelsior"; and in her valleys, the
sweet humility which adds grace and beauty to the soul
of God's creating. We discover nature's treasures to
be more satisfying than are the gems of art; the former
revealed to us in Switzerland, the latter in Italy.

Riding in the " diligences" over the passes of Switzerland is one of the principal and most delightful
features of travel in that country. The element of
danger, always prominent,—although creating less fear
in some than in others, according to the individual
temperament,—adds much to the exciting interest of
the experience. Indeed, all the circumstances are
refreshingly novel. The position, perhaps never before assumed, on the top of the lumbering coach is
in itself amusing. The peculiar gurgling sound that
the driver makes in urging his trusty animals to
greater speed is as characteristic as the warning-cry of
the Venetian gondolier. The prolonged crack of the

whip as it whizzes around the ears of the horses, who know by long experience that its sound is more threatening than its touch is painful, is almost as stimulating to the passenger's spirits as it is to the horse's pace. Then the wonderful panorama that flits by our delighted eyes as we dash on our course, keeping every sense on the *qui vive* lest some choice bit of nature, some *chef-d'œuvre* of her master-hand, shall escape our eager attention.

The little town of Coire is situated very prettily in the fertile valley of the Signe Caddie. Here we take the diligence for St. Moritz by the Albula Pass.

On ascending the mountain-side we are afforded distinct views of the pleasant little village we have left. So comfortably secure does it seem in its quiet, secluded nook; so free from the noisy bustle of distant cities, naught but the soothing ripple of its gentle river; so peaceful and content in its natural shelter of high hills, that we wonder if we shall not regret the indulgence of our ambition to scale the dizzy heights beyond, and find that the first estate was more desirable than the elevation toward which we are aiming. But the village is soon lost to view, as early joys are to memory, by subsequent experiences, and our thought and attention are absorbed by the varied scene before us. Prodigious mountains, by their side hills which seem like lambs lying down by the lion; modest streams flowing beneath the heavy shadows, leaving, feminine-like, their influence of beauty, although so quietly exerted; châlets on the mountain peaks,—do their occupants think to ·make their transit from this earthly to their heavenly home less difficult and long?—cascades leaping from immeasurable heights to our feet; terrific gorges gaping beside us; the bells on the horses jingling merrily while they prance gayly on, as if indifferent to the fact that one false step would plunge us into the fathomless abyss on whose very edge we are driving. Even when several thousand feet above the level of the sea we pass small Alpine villages, and sometimes a single châlet. The smoke from its roof curling gracefully in and out among the dark foliage, indicating the presence of a house, is always associated in our minds with domestic comfort and content, affording a text for a dream of the home-life warmed by its fires. The clouds of this glorious day are resplendent; 'tis "the bridal of the earth and sky," a harmonious union. The heavens shed a bright beauty and light upon field, tree, and hill-top; and the earth, grateful for these happy gifts, responds by reflecting the charms of its own inherent beauty. Banks of fleecy clouds sink low on the mountain's side, just as beauty droops its graceful form or head upon the ample breast which loves to shelter it. The snow-tipped mountains lift their pure crowns on high, as if to offer them to heaven's acceptance. Little graveyards full of touching memorials of the dead occupy sunny slopes, for even in this pure air death comes to all. Frowning rocks, black and threatening; mountains densely covered with the darkest green foliage; others lying in their shroud of snow, on a line—although higher—with those that are decked with the culminating richness of midsummer's verdure.

At times we wend our way through narrow defiles, and on emerging a scene dawns upon our view such as would develop enthusiasm in a soul which had never before thrilled with the glorious emotion. Again the scenery changes; a pall seems to have fallen upon the face of nature. All is weird, dreary, and barren. The air burdened with a weight intangible, penetrates our souls, and we sigh in sympathetic heaviness of spirit; soon again, however, we dash into a new experience, full of gladness and beauty. Ah! there is in life, too, but a step, often, between the sombre and the bright, the dull and the gay. We pass through many picturesque villages, whose surrounding meadows are deep in bloom. Often do we wade through masses of variegated blossoms, treading upon flowers as we had never dreamed of doing, *literally*.

We discover that many hamlets cluster around a large, majestic-looking town-pump. It is the medium through which the simple-hearted villagers offer hospitality to thirsty Alpine tourists. At its ample trough, too, the beasts of burden slake their thirst; but its most picturesque use is when, as the public wash-tub, it is surrounded by housewives who bend together over their tasks. Their native costumes now show off to advantage, as with bared arms they rub and rub, seasoning their efforts with much spice of tongue. What opportunity for gossip! Surely the same nature animates these Alpine folk, living midway between the sea-level and the clouds, as inspires their sisters in our own land over the sea!

While crossing over the Simplon we meet with an unusual experience. The severity of the preceding winter has manifested itself in vast accumulations of snow, which, falling from the lofty heights above, obstructed the roads so seriously as to render them impassable. Under the magic touch of the frost-king this has become at one point a glacier of ice. As the material prosperity of this country, in a considerable degree, is dependent upon the influx of strangers who yearly travel over its great mountain passes, it was thought expedient to tunnel a passage through the ice, and this having been successfully accomplished, we attempt, a week later, to penetrate its frosty length. Before entering we instinctively halt, as if to summon fortitude for an encounter with the ice-king. A moment later and we are encircled by walls and vault of crystal, for it shines and glitters with a dazzling purity. The air is cold and chilling, and as we gather our mantles closer about us a reserve creeps over the party, not a word being spoken during the ten minutes occupied in making the transit, *although the majority are ladies!* Who can tell, but at any moment we may be crushed and buried by falling masses of ice? Emerging from our ice-bound passage, we ride many miles farther between lofty walls of snow, a road having been dug out at great trouble and expense. On reaching the summit of the pass, we rest a while at the " New Hospice," so called, which was founded by Napoleon I. More than fifteen thousand travellers are entertained here every year, and are expected to leave a gratuity. It is a spot of peculiar dreariness, subject all the year round to falls of snow; its altitude being six thousand five hundred and ninety-four feet above the sea-level. The building is very large, plain, and substantial. Built of stone, it resists successfully the assaults of the elements, to which, from its elevated position, it is greatly exposed. Deep gorges yawn before it, while on every side, either near or remote, " Alps rise on Alps." For many consecutive months the " Hospice" is inaccessible, and here, " cribbed, cabined, and confined," is a forlorn company of monks. We enter the building from curiosity, but find its cold, cheerless walls and stone floors more repelling than the outside desolation, for there the blue sky looks friendly, and somewhat redeems the barren gloom and frigid isolation of the scene. A monk with smiling face dispenses the wine, which, in this country, is so simple in its nature that it merely "cheers and not inebriates." With great compassion we contemplate his circumstances and those of his fellows. His face is irradiated with smiles, it is true, but are they not due to the pleasure, a temporary one, of renewing his intercourse with a world from which the rigorous severity of his religion has shut him out? He is evidently enjoying the warm, reviving influences brought from the busy scenes far down below the clouds, in which he shivers out his youth and early manhood. We wonder why any creed should assume that asceticism which banishes from the heart the glow that Heaven meant should illumine it! Why not take for its model the religion which inculcates "mercy and not sacrifice;" which does not encourage the ignoring of those domestic ties which humanize men's natures, and kindle in their souls emotions that have something of angel-light in them? Paul, the great expounder of our faith, declared, it is true, that *he preferred* a life of celibacy, and hinted at the disadvantages of the married state; but would not he have been happier if a Mrs. Paul had lightened his sorrows by sharing them; brightening the gloom which inevitably shadows, at times, such grand souls

7

as his, by a love full of feminine tenderness and tact? Perhaps she might have plucked from his "flesh" that mysterious "thorn" to which he pathetically alludes, or at least have, through fond sympathy, mitigated its smart!

We think, then, while looking over the cheerless apartments and empty corridors of this monastic abode, that were domestic influences allowed here, an inviting, home-like air would make attractive what is now really repelling; and that the Alpine wanderer would then turn with grateful word and more eager step to bide the morning sunrise by an ingle, made the cheerier for a woman's kindly greeting and children's bright smiles. Believing with Victor Hugo, that "the double life is the happy one," we wish that every self-denying laborer in God's vineyard was a happy Benedict and a pater-familias.

Studying nature during these wonderful drives, we enjoy drawing the parallel between it and the *human* nature, whose prototype it is; finding in its mighty heart much that is in unison with the throbbing pulses of humanity, and so close a similarity to the workings and manifestations of the female nature, that we claim the justness of its title to the feminine gender. To be sure, in its strongest types, when it rises to majestic forms, which masterfully overshadow the smiling landscape; when with overwhelming force it pours in thundering cataract or impetuous torrent down the mountain-side, conquering the sweet valleys by its floods; or when, in mighty tempest, it sweeps through the land, claiming in its victorious march the more delicate forms of tree, shrub, and flower as its trophies; or when, in the sublime power of the ocean, it bears heavy fleets in its strong embrace, and cements continents indissolubly, it seems to lose its feminine character; yet we remember that in the feminine sex there are exceptional cases, in which masculine elements of character are conspicuous, the gentler, lovelier, and milder types, however, predominating.

Nature has, in its bright, fair aspects, many that are analogous to the phases of womanly character and feeling, and others that correspond to the general experience of life.

When during our Alpine journeys we reach a higher plane, we are surprised by the quick transit of a passing cloud, followed by the falling of a momentary shower, and then a dazzling sunlight that, making prisms of the drops, fills the sky with added beauty; so, often have we seen in the highest types of female organization a soft shade of sadness steal into the eye, succeeded by the shedding of gentle tears, which, even as they flow, are brightened by sunny smiles. Tearful eyes are often the outlook of a soul of deepest sensibility and tenderness, as the fervid sky of a summer day often, burdened with warmth, relieves itself by a gentle shower. Then, too, while looking upon nature from a level stand-point, we have compared it to a *casual* view of woman's nature. How little does a superficial observer realize the depth and capacity of her soul; its self-sacrificing devotion; the wealth of its emotions! But as we approach nearer and penetrate its recesses, we are reminded of the fertile valleys whose depths reveal so much of charm. Their pure crystal lakes,—which reflect the skies, God's throne,—whose borders are fringed with forget-me-nots, symbols of fidelity; lilies of the valley, types of innocence and purity; and with starlike flowers, suggestive of heavenly aspirations. The soil of these deep valleys is like, in richness, a true woman's soul, abundantly rewarding him who would probe to its depth and test its resources.

In tracing the analogy we do not forget the occasional wayward moods of nature; when squalls arise, sometimes sudden and always disagreeable; deranging the sweet order of meadows and gardens, the home of flowers. Spiteful rain-drops falling from angry clouds, obscuring the smile of the sun; cold breezes chilling the atmosphere. Can *many* lives boast an *entire* exemption from similar experiences? Do not dismal rains of sorrow and pain sometimes beat against the home of our emotions,—the heart,—sighing winds echoing through its darkened chambers? Sometimes shrieking blasts bursting its doors, uprooting the sweet growth of blooming affections, destroying every bud of promise; its secret recesses resounding with groanings and wailings of human misery.

CHAPTER IX.

CHAMOUNI—GENEVA—CHILLON.

CHAMOUNI.

" Mont Blanc is the monarch of mountains.
    They crowned him long ago
On a throne of rocks, in a robe of clouds,
    With a diadem of snow."

THE Valley of Chamouni is celebrated not only for its inherent beauty, but for its juxtaposition to its majestic neighbor, Mont Blanc. We are introduced to his majesty, and, looking up to the hoary head, are filled with reverence for what bears upon its noble brow the stamp of sovereignty, its presence indicating vast superiority to the august members of his suite who cluster around him. The glacier, formed by the snow which falls from the summit of Mont Blanc, lies on its side, revealing to unaccustomed eyes some of the curious and interesting features of this freak of nature. Its undulated and crystallized surface is like a palette on which the sun, the greatest of colorists, mixes at morn and eve his richest dyes.

134

Establishing ourselves at the Hôtel d'Angleterre, at Chamouni, we take donkeys and guides and start one morning on an excursion to the Mer de Glace. Crossing the little bridge in front of the hotel, we jolt on in a devious path some distance before beginning the ascent. Soon after a very fine view of the valley, with the imposing line of opposite mountains, opens to us, and as we ride higher and higher on our zigzag course the panorama extends and widens, discovering to us a long stretch of the valley, with its fertilizing stream dividing the double range of mountains. At length, after a toilsome pull for the poor donkeys, whose backs have often been weighed down by American burdens, we stop abruptly on the edge of a steep declivity and look upon dazzling masses of snow and ice. Their dense accumulations suggest the rigors of a Polar scene. A sea is indeed before us, but it is as if its life's flow had been suspended, its currents congealed; as if the o'erlapping waves had been arrested in the midst of tumultuous activity. As though the Divine mandate, "Peace, be still," had been uttered during a "great storm of wind;" when the waves, lashed into fury, hearing suddenly *the only voice which could still them*, had instantly calmed, before smoothing the deep furrows ploughed into their angry surface. The ice is of a greenish hue, the color adding to its effectiveness. The extreme end of the Mer de Glace, at the bottom of the valley, is called the Glacier des Bois. At the upper extremity it forms two branches, bearing different names; these are prominent adjuncts to a really hyperborean scene, affording to the scientist varied phenomena for study and solution.

The members of another party, a company of pedestrians, cross the Mer de Glace and pursue a circuitous route. Constantly ascending, they soon come to the famous "Mauvais Pas," which consists in the rounding of a jutting rock, on a pathway made on its face, as it were. All would instinctively ejaculate a prayer and consign themselves to a higher power, for, while hemmed in by a gigantic rock on one side, a very Charybdis yawns on the other, ready to engulf them should their feet slip. *We* are almost enclosed within bulwarks of massive, towering rocks, at whose base a sea once flowed, but which now, with dumb eloquence, invokes the wondering attention of all beholders. So we sit in happy security, following through powerful glasses the progress of the bolder party as they wend their ghostly way over the crystal-like sea.

How dwarfed they appear in the distance below us! but as they gradually ascend a height parallel and equal to our own, with bated breath we watch their passage over the perilous spot with name of ominous sound,— "Mauvais Pas." They have reached it! a guide preceding, extends his hand, which is grasped by a Mr. Faintheart or a Miss Timorous, who are won, through much coaxing, round the curve. We shout our congratulations and breathe freer, as we rise and prepare to mount our donkeys, to return to the little village of Chamouni, which nature seems to have taken under its strong protection, by building about it ramparts of rocks and mountains.

As we descend the declivities which we have so recently climbed, we find ourselves often in danger of doing so in a manner at once indecorous and dangerous, —head first. The clouds have gathered and broken in a drenching shower, but when we are midway on our journey the sun bursts forth and gives us a glad welcome to our village resting-place, and so continues to bless us until we bid farewell to the peaceful, picturesque vale of Chamouni.

In reviewing the experience we are reminded of its analogous bearing upon many situations in life. There are often crises in men's histories when, through combinations of circumstances, they find their temporal prosperity—and perhaps their spiritual welfare is involved—dependent upon escape from a threatened disaster. Should they bridge the gulf, their lives will " lead on to fortune," and it may be their eternal interest, also, be insured; but should they fail to reach the visible goal by a fatal false step, they are compromised and engulfed in irredeemable ruin. Heaven is watching the conflict, and, perchance, one of its ministering angels in human guise, with encouraging voice and helping hand, guides the almost despairing man past the point, beyond which is the security and happiness he seeks.

GENEVA.

Geneva has few objects of art to amuse the traveller, and yet it wooes many to a protracted stay amid such natural beauty as appeals eloquently to the universal heart and bids it rejoice in nature's works. The city is associated with historic events which linger in the memory of the intelligent mind. It is dear to the Protestant, whose faith was here cherished, fostered, and ripened under the warm sympathy of its Calvinistic friends and supporters. Here Calvin and Knox found refuge and hospitable protection from enemies and persecutors. Indeed, Geneva was the Swiss cradle in which the tumult of opposition was soothed and the Reformation nursed into a more robust growth. The pulpit chair which Calvin occupied still retains its honored place in the Cathedral, and is reverenced as a souvenir of a man who, although a harsh controversialist, a bitter opponent, an intolerant upholder of the new dogma, yet commands our respect, because of the intense sincerity which was the undercurrent of his life. Although the Christian world cannot endorse certain of his acts, imputing them to a fanatical zeal, yet we must not forget that such men and times are not to be judged from the stand-point of the present age. As one of the fathers of the Reformation, which was struggling in the weakness of its infancy with nations and potentates for its mighty enemies; the powers of hell arrayed against it; the superhuman effort of papal strength sworn to strangle its young life; he must *needs* exercise a combative spirit, and in the dire emergency of the case put forth all the resistive power of his strong nature and astute intellect to succor and support the spiritual bantling, as the disciples of the Romish creed considered it. And so with fiery breath, injudicious ardor, and, we grieve to confess, in some instances, relentless cruelty, he fought with desperate intensity for the new faith, the adopted child of his religious nature.

The city is built upon the southern extremity of Lake Geneva, whose waters, always blue, and its borders, which nature has beautified and art has further embellished, are attractions that delight the traveller. Skimming the blue surface are little vessels, whose unique sails form a striking feature in the pretty scene. They are formed like the quills once used as pens and crossed, so that their appearance at a short distance is very peculiar and picturesque. Many splendid hotels are built on the very borders of the lake; stately palaces proudly overlook it,—one a magnificent home of the Rothschilds; villages cluster under the shadow of the sweeping range of mountains, above which Mont Blanc shines pre-eminent, " with its diadem of snow;" fine bridges span the river at its confluence with the lake, a short suspension bridge connecting one of them with the little isle, in whose shady bowers Rousseau is said to have delighted to sit and ruminate.

The Public Gardens are situated on the borders of the lake, to whose surface swans lend a graceful beauty. Strangers win them to a near approach by feeding them, and they are considered public pets. Music adds its animating influence, while rich verdure, bowers of green, and skies of unusual brilliancy and of blue most ethereal, make the scene one of great loveliness. The river Rhone, which flows through Lake Geneva, makes its noisy exit not far below, dashing with impetuous rapidity from the waters with which it has mingled, as if impatient to resume its original personality. At a still lower point a most curious sight is presented to the traveller. Standing on the bridge, one looks down upon long floating sheds, in which many women are assembled washing clothing; inclined planks answer the purpose of wash-boards, and the river is the universal tub. Energetic action, corresponding with the activity of many tongues, makes the scene a lively one, and although a prosaic it is not an uninteresting feature to the spectator.

Lying like a green nest upon the blue waters is Rousseau's little island. We look upon his statue erected here many years since by his fellow-citizens, and wonder that, as he gazed upon the everlasting hills which encompassed him, his moral thought was not elevated by their contemplation; that the sweet calm of the scene, with the soothing flowing of the tide, did not speak peace to his perturbed spirit; that his morbid misanthropy was not dissipated by the sunny beauty that met his eye; that his philosophy did not become more cheerful, and his views assume a more rational character; for the lesson nature would teach is one that gives a healthier tone to the diseased mental and moral system; and strange it seems that any one of its devotees could prove a dull pupil under such tuition !

Geneva was the adopted home of many who were famed in the world of letters, all its influences being favorable to mental growth and labor. Among these were Voltaire and Madame de Staël. The former spent the last twenty-two years of his life at Ferney, four miles from the city, and many now visit the spot so closely associated with the literary life of the remarkable man, for here he wrote some of his best works. While through his versatile talents literature was enriched in many departments, his character, vain, cynical, and impious, failed to reflect credit upon humanity. The great lack in his intellectual efforts, as in his life, was the grand soul which is needed to illuminate both; its animated glow giving living fire to thought; and color, richness, and warmth to sentiment. When intellectual force is unwedded to soul-power, the grand source of inspiration, its results fail to awaken warm enthusiasm, even while they receive the critical commendation of scholarly minds.

We turn with pleasure to the great female celebrity, whose name belongs, probably, to the greatest of all female writers. We admire this wonderful woman the more as her intellect, although so profound as to entrench in its power upon the masculine, was united to a quickness of perception and richness of imagination purely feminine; for we believe this combination to be a rare one. Generally, it is the prosaic workman who lays the ponderous foundations of a structure, and other and delicately-skilled hands that form the ornate embellishment. And so the profound thinker and philosophical essayist is seldom one with the graceful novelist, whose pretty play of fancy belongs to an intellect of lighter calibre. We recognize, too, in Madame de Staël the beautiful union of mind and heart; the remarkable power of the one not absorbing that of the other. We give tender pity to the richly-endowed woman who, with the greenest of laurel thick upon her

brow; the great of the earth doing her honor; her aid
and friendship solicited, although too late, by one of the
most brilliant of temporary monarchs; the world com-
posing her admirers; yet exclaimed, in referring to one
who was eminently winning in person and manner, "I
would give every brilliant thought I ever conceived
myself, or developed in another, for such power to win
affection." Here the feminine nature asserted itself,
and, we think, nobly, for the thirst for affection is a
holy one. Her intellectual appetite was abundantly
appeased, yet her great womanly heart cried out with
a yearning that culture, honor, wealth, or any other
material good could not satisfy. We have read that
she was plain and unattractive in person; and we believe that nature, although we would speak reverently
and even lovingly of her, takes a grim pleasure in enclosing her richest gems of soul and intellect within
settings singularly incongruous. But we also believe
that a woman with a fine soul cannot be ugly; the
torch of genius or rich emotion lit in the soul must
shed sparkling light through its windows,—the eyes,—
irradiating the whole face with glow almost divine.

While wondering at her taste, we rejoice to read of
her marriage with the young French officer, De Rocca,
who, after distinguishing himself by his bravery in
Spain, enfeebled by his wounds, came to live in
Geneva.. Madame de Staël's sympathy, happily ex-

pressed, won his heart. Deeply enamored, he declared, "I love her so passionately that she will marry me at last." And so she did; and, notwithstanding the disparity in their ages, they lived happily together until death divorced them, six years after, her marriage being kept secret until after her death.

CHILLON.

It is at the close of an afternoon in midsummer that the Castle of Chillon, in all its sombre majesty, greets our sight. Built upon a solitary rock, which projects twenty yards into the lake, it is connected with the shore by a bridge. Very irregular in its construction, of massive walls and large central tower, it looms up in the landscape in a gloom, symbolical of the middle ages, when it was built for a fortress, serving now as an arsenal.

The hour chosen to visit it is an appropriate one; the day has been brilliant, sparkling, and bright with joyous sunshine. Nature now has suspended her activities; a becoming languor has stolen over her; the sun is descending from his throne on high; shadows begin to lengthen on the hill-sides; the birds have ceased their heyday song and are twittering "good-night" in leafy bowers; and the bees are satiated with their prolonged feast amid the clover-bloom. The breezes, after gayly frolicking with the enticing flowers,

softly brushing their velvety cheeks, have died away,
perhaps in "aromatic pain," and Flora, unlike her
human sisters, betrays weariness in flaunting her gay
colors in the summer air.

A sweet hush has fallen upon nature, and in sympathy with her prevailing mood we quietly saunter
along the pleasant country road to the castle, a half-
mile distant from our hotel. Obtaining entrance, we
first explore the depths of the famed fortress. In a
large dungeon stands a pillar with chain affixed to its
side by a heavy staple. To this the prisoner Bonni-
vard had been attached, and here, like a chained beast,
he had walked around as far as his chain would permit,
until deep ruts had been worn into the hard clay floor.
For six years had this patriotic soul borne this cruel
martyrdom. How must its fine fibre have chafed
against its iron fate! and when restored to the city of
his love, Geneva, for whose liberation from tyrannic
rule he had fought before being conquered and thus
imprisoned, one can imagine that no after-dream of
happiness could efface the memory of this nightmare,
of a night extending through long, weary years. The
iron ring to which his chain was fastened remains in
its original position, and the traces on the pillar caused
by the grating of the chain are deeply marked. It is
appalling to contemplate the goading, wearing friction
on the heart and brain of this refined nature and noble

spirit, and we wonder that he survived his frightful ordeal thirty-five years, during which he was the object of the special regard of his grateful and admiring fellow-citizens. Other dungeons, deeper, smaller, and darker still, are shown us, where criminals were consigned to a living death. An aperture is pointed out lined with sharp knives, down which a victim would be thrust, his mutilated body finding its final rest in the waters of the lake at its base. Their beautiful blue has often been reddened thus with human blood, *in*humanly sacrificed; and although all earthly traces of such crime have long been washed away, yet not even its broad, deep currents can erase their *eternal* record.

We see many apartments in the upper portion of the castle curious in their antiquity. The wooden ceilings, and the walls of the banqueting-room, covered with the painted emblems of the different Swiss Cantons. Here feasted and lived at times the dukes of Savoy, all unmindful of the groans of their wretched victims, which mingled with the sighing of the wind and the plashing of the waves around the castled rock.

On leaving the grand old castle, which gives character to all the landscape, we meet the peasantry returning to their homes after the day's toil in the hay-fields. They add much, as they ever do, to the view; their homely attire, always brightened by a dash

of color, is so piquant and quaint that we have learned
to believe no picture of a country scene complete without its introduction.

As we look toward the sky we see that the sweetness
of the hour is there culminating. The sun is nearing
the western horizon; its effulgence spreading over the
heavens as we stand spell-bound before charms which
light up our vision with dazzling splendor. The orb
of day is like a great ball of fire, whose flames, catching the clouds, spread the conflagration, until the sky
is like a vast molten sea of glory. Flashes of radiant
light spring from the grand centre, piercing with their
golden shafts the billowy blue, darting through banks
of roseate clouds, dissolving them into masses of shim-
mering light and color. As we gaze, our souls filled
with joy by the celestial beauty, clouds of pale azure,
lined and fringed with burnished silver, melt little by
little into the great canopy of gold and crimson, which
fill the whole firmament with splendor incomparable.
From a distance come sailing on quiet, gray clouds,
beautiful, because soft and fleecy, but as they glide
into the gorgeous arena they are glorified by color,
quickly girdled with silver, crowned with gold, and
tinted with crimson.

Upon a cerulean background suddenly there blossoms a silvery star, or is it a jewel fallen from the diadem of the Invisible King? Its tiny rays shine from

afar, as it modestly beams in the wake of the departed sun.

Ah, if the outer walls of the Celestial City be so brilliant and radiant, so glowing with beauty, what must be the *Heavenly Jerusalem itself?* As we gaze we recall the words of the Great King : "Eye hath not seen, nor ear heard, neither have entered into the heart of man, the things which God hath prepared for them that love him."

We recognize the exquisite sentiment of the Persian instinct which, in ignorance of "The True God," leads to the worship of so divine a symbol as the sun, typical in its power, in its marvellous light, and in its indescribable glory, of the Supreme Power, the Divine Illuminator, and the omnipotence of the Creator of the World.

CHAPTER X.

LAUSANNE.

LAUSANNE, on the north side of Lake Geneva, occupying a very elevated position, enjoys views remarkable for their extent and beauty. Ouchy, whose grand hotel attracts many visitors, lies below it on the very borders of the lake, and affords, in its nestling security, a pretty view to the town above. "Montbenon," the public promenade of Lausanne, is bordered with many trees of an age that the oldest inhabitant fails to compute, and of a size really prodigious. So carefully are they preserved by the town authorities that wide iron bands are made to encircle their gnarled trunks; the decay producing large fissures, arrested by a filling of plaster, which, as it becomes hard and smooth, resembles a tablet inserted in a wall, awaiting its inscription.

From the terrace of Montbenon one enjoys a fine view of the lake sluggishly basking in the bright sunlight; the slopes on the opposite shores beautiful with

151

spired villages, antique towers, spreading vineyards, and turreted villas. Sweeping along the horizon are the Piedmontese Alps, greeting their opposite neighbor, the Jura range, their lofty heights rising above the clouds, which often in foamy masses repose below them; sometimes enveloping themselves in a fleecy robe of blue mist, which, like the delicate drapery over a beautiful bust, only enhances the charms it affects to conceal. Many of the snowy peaks turn at night their whitened faces toward the moon, blushing red under the morning smiles of the rising sun as he goes forth to run his race. And when the sunlight crowns the mountain-tops and lights up the hill-sides, who can stand unmoved by the effects of its illuminating splendor!

In the heart of the town stands the Hôtel Gibbon, formerly the residence of the famous historian of that name. Attached to it is the garden where he sat on a moonlight night in June, 1787, writing the final words of his history; and he describes in his memoirs the thrilling emotions with which he contemplated the completed work which was to immortalize his name.

Our hotel is situated in the midst of a garden filled with fragrance and beauty. Within its enclosure is a cottage, occupied by the owner of the hotel and his aged wife. One evening she sat upon one of the rustic seats, amid the flowers she loved to cultivate, in pleasant converse with some of the hotel guests. As the nine o'clock bell struck upon the evening air with its mellow sound, she arose, and, bidding her companions "*bon soir,*" entered her little châlet.

What consternation fell upon the household the next morning when the death of the dear old lady was announced! She had just been found lying peacefully in the arms of death; having passed away without the knowledge of her husband, who lay beside her. Her "good-night" had been uttered amid the flowers of earthly growth, while the shadows of evening were deepening about her, but angels had whispered their "good-morning" in a brighter clime, amid perpetual bloom, where her feeble age was already transformed into immortal youth.

Judge of the astonishment created by seeing through the open windows, two hours later, the freshly-made widower pruning the plants! The ladies very naturally resented the cruel indignity laid upon one of their sex, until some kindly disposed person suggested that he was probably paying respect to his late wife's memory by bestowing upon the flowers she loved the tender care which had been her daily pleasure.

FREYBURG.

Freyburg occupies an elevated and very picturesque situation, containing besides its organ several other attractions. From a balcony in the rear of our hotel we look upon a deep ravine spanned by a suspension bridge which is considered a triumph of mechanical skill; the wire chains which support it are fastened to rocks on each side instead of pillars. Another very fine suspension bridge crosses the river Saarine; it is supported by four chains, which form a single arch. A drive over the two bridges to the suburbs of the town richly rewards us, by pretty views obtained of the winding river and of the town from higher points.

The tourist is always expected to visit the famous lime-tree in front of Council Hall. Tradition tells us that after the battle at Morat in 1476, a young man, native of Freyburg, rushed breathless and exhausted into the town announcing the victory. The word " victory" was all he could command strength to utter, expiring soon after. In his hand he had borne a twig, which was planted, and having grown into a tree of mammoth size, fourteen feet in circumference, is an object of the special regard and watchful care of the citizens and of curiosity to strangers. Its branches are supported by pillars, a wooden fence being built around it, with seats for garrulous old age, and as a trysting-place for village lovers.

In the Cathedral of St. Nicholas is the organ to which the town is indebted for its influx of visitors. It is considered one of the finest in Europe, and with its sixty-seven stops and seven thousand eight hundred pipes, some of them thirty-three feet long, requires a masterly hand to perform upon it.

Wending our way to the Cathedral at eight o'clock, we find it enshrouded in partial darkness, being but feebly illuminated by one light "dimly burning." This is most agreeable, the effect of the music being much more impressive than if the glare of daylight shone about us. It is a weird scene. By the obscure light we can faintly discern a few human figures scattered through the pews; occasionally a solitary person will steal noiselessly in, and, gliding through the shadows, drop into a distant seat. Gloom lurks in all the corners of the great church, the pictures and altar decorations looking ghastly in the feeble glimmer; while we sit as if in preparation for some inquisitorial business, a funereal silence settling upon the meagre assembly composed of about fifteen persons. We begin to be "scared with visions," and instinctively nestle a little nearer our companions, when suddenly the air, it seems the universe, is filled with sound, overwhelming, grand, magnificent! We are borne along on its deep, rapid current, breathless with a delight mingled with awe, when gradually, almost insensibly, we are guided into gentler ways, on the bosom of calmer seas, the lulling sound of the rippling waters exquisitely attuned to the tenderest feeling.

Now comes the imitation of storm, chaos,—perhaps an intimation of the final destruction. The muttering of distant thunder swells into a great clamor, rushing nearer, with the rattling of heaven's artillery, the crashing of the elements, until we almost cower under the power of sound. And yet this same instrument, obedient to the conquering hand of the gifted performer, can breathe in tones so mild as would not disturb an infant's sleep, and so sweet as would lap it into deeper slumber by the most ethereal notes. The vast organ which belches torrents of wrath and power, and breathes gentlest whisperings of joy and love with equal ease, seems possessed with a grand soul; at times torn with the force of its human passions, and again imbued with a divine tenderness and peace. The most wonderful of its achievements is its imitation of the human voice. With one hand the accompaniment is played, while the simulation of vocal strains is produced with the other. The effect is most remarkable. The magic voice seems to be wafted to our entranced ears through misty space, ascending the scale to highest notes, filling the air and soul with delicious melody, as descending it melts into the sweetest whisper.

LUCERNE.

The ride by rail from Freyburg to Lucerne is made enjoyable by the beauty of the panoramic views of the landscapes, which, shifting rapidly, seem as fleeting as pleasing dreams. The day is in the dew of its youth. We delight in the hour,—'tis early morn,—for Dame Nature as seen in her maturity at mid-day is less charming than in the freshness of her youth in the morning. The birds in their elevated choirs are holding their morning service of song; it seems to be nature's bridal hour, for she is timidly waiting in fresh and sweet array to receive the kiss of the bridegroom as he comes forth like a strong man from his chamber of the clouds. On her face are the beautiful dew-drops, which glitter as his radiant glances beam upon her. Sweet shadows, at first, hang about her, but are dispelled by the nearer approach of his warm, bright presence. Now, indeed, all is sunlight and joy, and we who witness this tender meeting think that men might well imitate the wooing of this stately sun of the morning!

The sweet burden of new-mown meadows exhales its perfume, rising like incense to the sun; fields of ripening corn give pleasing signs of plenty; in pretty pastures of rich green the clumsy kine feed lazily. Brightening the view are acres of wheat, whose golden surface is exquisitely relieved by the scarlet poppy,

which is here so abundantly scattered through it.   The
faint breeze of a summer's day gently breathes upon
the rippling treasure, blending the colors into one.
The hum of many insects gives a soporific influence
to the air.   The sunlight is now spread broadcast over
the landscape, sparkling streams saucily flashing back
its glances.   Women in their quaint costume, as seen
in the distance, deftly wielding the hoe or turning the
odorous hay to the warm rays of the sun, add to the
picturesqueness of the view.   Many of the· billowy
mountains along the horizon are robed in snowy white,
emblematic of the purity above them; modest valleys,
where nestle many vine-clad cottages, their attractive
loveliness resurrecting memories of the girlish dreams
of long ago, when the sentiment,

> " Give me a cot
>   In the valley I love,"

filled the imagination.

Ah, that charm which brings tears to the eyes must
be of sacred beauty; and we feel that the influences
of such revelations as nature has made to us this day
must stimulate, even develop, the finest emotions of our
natures.

The great attraction of Lucerne consists in the peculiar advantages of its position.   It is situated on the
river Reuss, as it emerges from Lake Lucerne, which is

spread out before it, with Mont Pilatus on the right
and the Rigi in front. Lake Lucerne is considered the
most beautiful of all the Swiss lakes, and is the more
attractive from its irregularity. Taking the steamer,
we traverse the entire length of the lake, finding great
enjoyment in its diversity of scenery. Clustering
around the base of the Rigi are sunny gardens abounding in fruit-trees, pretty cottages interspersed among
them, with shady woods and green pastures on the
higher slopes. On the opposite side of the lake is
Mont Pilatus, which forms in its dark, frowning presence a strong contrast to the brighter aspects of the
Rigi; but to these antipodal effects much grandeur and
beauty are attributable. Indeed, the mind of man demands variety of objects and character to gratify its
every phase of taste and feeling; and to antagonistic
influences, and to the varied forms of scenery, do we
owe that pleasure which arises from the exercise of our
reasoning faculties, and from the contrast of the simple
with the grand; the pretty, bright, and picturesque
with the magnificent, the imposing, and the sublime.

Our patriotism having taken on new fervor during
absence from our native land, we feel, as we near Tell's-
platte, a sympathetic interest in the associations of the
spot which the Swiss people hold sacred, as connected
with memories of their ancient hero and liberator.
Whether mythical or not, the reminiscences are a nucleus

for the patriotic thought and feeling, which burn with such vivid flame in the public heart of the staunch little Republic; and his name is a talisman against any treasonable sentiment or act. The spot upon which we gaze with such lively attention is one where the Chapel of Tell stands. This was erected by the Canton of Uri, it is said, in 1388 to commemorate the escape of the patriot from Gesler's boat, but it is evidently of more modern date. On the Sabbath following Ascension-day, mass is performed here, great numbers attending in boats, gayly decorated, to hear the patriotic sermon which is always preached on that occasion. The sentiment inculcated is so noble a one, that we would have it fostered by these yearly ceremonies, believing this man, whose patriotic memory they half "ignorantly worship," to be the embodiment of one of the grandest passions of the soul, and so, worthy of their enthusiastic devotion.

As we approach the terminus of the lake the mountains assume most imposing grandeur, as if to leave upon all minds an impression of august dignity. On returning to our hotel at Lucerne, we renew our former pleasures amid scenes less impressive, but sunnier. Perhaps with the thought of nearing the skies, the better to enjoy the Sabbath observances, we cross the lake and, taking a carriage, reach by a good road the large hotel built on the Burgenstock, some two thousand six hundred feet above the sea-level. The view of the lake, and of the mountain kings enthroned above it, is superb. In very pretty woods adjoining the hotel, by paths easily climbed, we attain to greater heights, and, through vistas skilfully arranged, obtain glimpses of several lakes, vast mountain peaks and distant ranges, with the gem of all the adjacent waters, Lake Lucerne, gracefully curling in and out below and beyond us.

The air is deliciously fresh, suggestive of health, strength, and buoyant life. The views are something ever to remember, for it is our faith that impressions of beauty and grandeur imprinted upon the eye are caught by the spirit, and ere lost or faded are engraved upon the tablets of memory, and often incorporated into the moral character, elevating it above the paltry objects of the lower world by introducing it to the higher influences of nature in her exalted phases.

Seated on a balcony overhanging the lake, we can look upon the waters of Lakes Zug and Sempach. Mont Pilatus, its face generally clouded, scowls down upon the sweet landscape, unmindful that the lake below reflects its frown; while the Rigi, with more feminine proportions,—and disposition too, shall we say?—casts brighter glances around, and lit up with smiles, reflected from peak to peak, vainly strives to propitiate its neighbor, who is enshrouded in almost perpetual gloom. The lights of the distant town throw their quivering rays athwart the waters, the moon vying with them in illuminating the scene; lighting up rugged mountain crags; throwing a veil of silvery sheen over the broad face of the lake; bringing out in bold relief the little boats idly floating on its surface; and concealing by its modest light defects which the sun wantonly reveals. By its hallowed beams it clothes all visible objects with sacred beauty, investing even the most prosaic with a spiritual or poetic beauty.

What wonder, amid such enchantment, if a gossiping breeze bears to our ears the tones of love? Glancing at the foreign faces on every side, we bethink us what an accomplished little urchin is Cupid, who whispers in every known and unknown tongue! And how wonderfully preserved is his youth, remembering that he was a contemporary even of Adam and Eve! playing as mischievous a rôle in the lives of the antediluvians as now, when in wanton glee he toys with his pretty weapon, piercing with magic arrow maidens' hearts; sharpening it anew to penetrate the more obdurate organ of the sterner sex!

The following morning, summoning the courage upon which heavy drafts have already been made, we enter the car to ascend the Rigi. As the passengers sit with their backs toward the front of the car, the sensation might be unpleasant to some, but we think the opportunity for enjoying the view better in that position than in the ordinary one. As usual, our ambition soars to the highest point. We are ticketed for the Rigi-Kulm, the highest peak, five thousand nine hundred feet above the sea-level. Losing all sense of fear, we surrender ourselves to enjoyment, each moment unfolding to our view some new feature of delight and wonder. Arrived at the hotel, we lose no time in exploring the locality. It is remarkable for its breadth of vision, and for the confusing number and variety of objects comprehended in the view. The sunset is a disappointment, foreboding a foggy morrow, and so, although scarcely daring to *pray* for a clear sunrise, we *wish* for it, as to see the great king of day as he emerges from his couch of clouds and enters the sky—the vast audience-chamber of the world—is the prime object of the trip.

We retire early, doubtful of the morrow's prospects. Humming the familiar lines,

> " Watchman, tell us of the night,
> What its signs of promise are,"

the thought and wish blend with our dreams, and we sleep until the Alpine horn sounds the noisy reveille at three o'clock in the morning.

Dressed as we are, for we had not ventured to go literally " to bed," we throw shawls and cloaks about us and join the sleepy, murmuring crowd which, issuing

from every corridor, is flocking to the grand rendezvous, a hill in rear of the hotel. Alas! alas! we are
quickly enveloped in fog and cloud, typical of the condition of the sun, who, although so many are awaiting
his coming, fails to indicate even his whereabouts.

Disconsolate, tired, sleepy, and bedraggled with dew,
we return to the hotel, and a few hours later, amid a
violent rain-storm, descend the mount.

The grand artistic treasure of Lucerne is "The Lion,"
executed in 1821, in memory of the massacred Swiss
Guard of twenty-six officers and seven hundred and
sixty soldiers who fell in defence of the Tuileries, August
10, 1792. A vociferous mob surrounded the palace,
and, refusing to disperse, was fired upon by the Guard.
The people, believing that the firing had been ordered
by the king, maddened by fury, forced an entrance into
the palace and murdered all found within it.

The dying lion is represented as endeavoring still to
protect the shield of France, one huge paw covering it.
The figure is colossal,—twenty-eight feet by eighteen.
Transfixed by a broken spear, it half reclines in the
agonies of death, reminding us of its representative
human counterpart,—the dying gladiator at Rome.
The Lion, modelled by the Danish sculptor, Thorwald-
sen, is grand in conception and masterly in execution.
It is hewn out of the face of an immense sandstone
rock; at the base of which are the ·dark waters of a

small pond fed from a spring which flows down by the side of the rock. Dense shrubbery adds to the gloom of the death-scene. It is a striking spectacle, and in every particular testifies to the rare cunning of the artistic brain and hand. The face expresses, with almost human fidelity, physical anguish and piteous distress. Looking upon the monster in his quiet agony, one is deeply impressed by its representation of what is rarely seen,—the *sublimity of suffering.*

LAKE THUN.

Lake Thun, while it boasts of no remarkable feature, is certainly a little gem among the more stately waters of a country that abounds in natural attractions of lakes, mountains, and glaciers.

We wonder not that the Swiss are possessed, as a people, of those virtues which distinguish the highest moral character. Universally industrious and honest, proverbially patriotic, domestic, simple, and chaste in their lives, we discover the origin of this innate excellence in their peculiar surroundings. Surely the climate and the formation of a country, particularly if its landscapes abound in striking features, must exert a marked influence upon the tastes, the nature, and the character of its people. Could a man environed by lofty mountains, dazzling heights, and glittering glaciers be the same as one living upon unbroken plains, feed-

ing his breath from the still, sluggish air that steals
over them? Must not his whole organism differ from
one whose first breath, even, is drawn from the clear,
bracing winds that come sweeping down from the
lofty peaks; whose eyes ever rest upon the sublime
in nature? Nor would it be strange if his soul
should assume the purity of which the perpetual
snow and ice are symbolical: "Chaste as ice and
pure as snow."

The banks of Lake Thun are for some distance
thickly studded with ornamental villas, many of them
very elegant, surrounded by dense and very beautiful
growths of shrubs and flowers; their gardens sloping
down to the water's edge, add beauty to a view to
which the surrounding mountains impart the elements
of grandeur. Many pretty villages dot the banks,
their vineyards covering the hill-sides; and occasionally
an ancient and picturesque château and little churches,
whose modest spires point the thought to heaven. Indeed, this lake with its pretty bordering banks seems to
us like a little poem set to music, so smooth and rhyth-
mical in its flow; so harmonious in its parts; so suggestive of beautiful thought; so full of delicate pictures of life in its sweetest form, without its rude,
rough prose. Lambs gambolling in green pastures;
little churches where the manly youth and gentle
maiden plight their troth; and beautiful hills whose

tops are Pisgahs where they may read their happy future, as typified in the graceful, sunny landscape that lies before them.

A slight shower compels a temporary withdrawing to the salon below, but on emerging again, the attention of all is attracted toward a rainbow which half spans the lake. It is unusually defined in form and vivid in color. At this moment we are nearing the narrow portion of the lake, and are apparently about to pass under the bow of promise in the clouds. "Oh," we exclaim, "if it would only extend and completely span the lake, it would be like a triumphal arch to pass under!" The words are scarcely uttered ere the heavenly artist has traced with divine touch the other half, so that the bow literally stretches from one side of the lake to the other, the extreme points seeming to touch the earth on either side. A universal exclamation of rapturous delight bursts from the lips of all the passengers, who have flocked to the bow of the boat to witness the renewal of the covenant made with Noah: "I do set my bow in the cloud, and it shall be for a token of a covenant between me and the earth."

INTERLACHEN.

Arrived at Interlachen, we find our "lines have been cast" in one of the most delightful spots in Switzerland. The village is situated in a valley formed

between the two lakes of Thun and Brienz, which are
on the east and west of it, the valley of the Lauterbrunnen lying toward the south. The principal street,
or avenue, is the Hoheweg, bordered on both sides by
large walnut-trees. The many hotels which line one
side of this fine avenue vie with each other in floral
display. One walks through a miniature Eden before
entering their doors, and all within is made very inviting. The windows of our rooms look upon the
"Jungfrau," which in dazzling robe of snow is a
fascinating object for all eyes. As its name signifies
"virgin," we must try to realize its femininity. Although arrayed in trailing robe of white, spangled by
the sun's rays, and often wearing a bridal-like veil of
fleecy clouds, yet despite this glamour and the silence
she maintains as to her age,—like many *human* spinsters,
—we recognize her to be a very ancient maiden. She is
of Amazonian proportions, the fourth among the Swiss
and the eighth among European mountains, thirteen
thousand seven hundred feet above the level of the sea.

A drive to Grindelwald is full of delight; here,
after dining, we mount mules and proceed to the glaciers. In one a grotto has been hewn. We enter it
to enjoy the better its exquisite transparency and color
of emerald, but meet with such a cold reception as
compels us to retire hastily.

Another interesting excursion is by carriage through

the Lauterbrunnen Valley, or it might properly be styled a ravine, bordered on both sides by immense precipitous rocks from one thousand to fifteen hundred feet high. Numerous springs suggest its name. The fertile valley is sheltered by the gigantic rocks, shaded by many trees, and made fresh and sparkling by its many cascades falling from the heights above. The principal one is called the Staubbach,—dust-brook. Its source is comparatively insignificant, being simply a brook; but its fall of nine hundred and eighty feet gives it an exaggerated appearance of volume, gaining dignity from height and distance. It descends at first impetuously, but when the wind catches the water, scatters, spreads, divides, and subdivides it, carrying it whither it will, flinging it into fantastic shapes, weaving it into a waving, transparent, silvery veil, we look upon it with intense pleasure. It is a pretty plaything for the breezes, and through their wand is tossed into its many forms of beauty. Often when the sunshine sports with it and glimmers through its radiant drops it is further beautified by rainbows.

CHAPTER XI.

MUNICH—CARLSBAD.

MUNICH.

MUNICH, the capital of Bavaria, lies in a plain, and is built upon both sides of the Iser. It is considered one of the handsomest cities in Germany, ranking as the fourth in population. We are delighted with not only its fine, broad, open streets; its squares, monuments, and its bright, inviting appearance; but with the galleries abounding in artistic wealth; its Palace, which, although of unpretending exterior, is truly magnificent within; and in the numberless facilities offered for pleasure, to secure which, is the tourist's avowed purpose. Indeed, it is difficult to find a "convenient season" to leave it; and beginning after a few days to suspect that it is the country of the Lotus-plant, which is said to have the effect of obliterating from the mind all longings for native land, and of rendering departure very difficult, we follow the example of Ulysses in a similar emergency, and drag ourselves

away to other cities, who, siren-like, are wooing us on
to an enjoyment of *their* pleasures. Meanwhile, what
throngs of migrating travellers arrive! Excitement
and bustle are constantly agitating the air and scene
until our hotel, crowded to its utmost capacity, is
obliged to close its doors against new-comers. Our
hotel is admirably situated upon one of the finest
streets, whose gay, moving crowds afford material for
pleasant contemplation. At eventide, particularly, the
panorama is an animated and brilliant one. The German husband and wife, with their children, dressed in
gala costume, sally forth to spend an enjoyable hour or
so at the beer-gardens, which are popular institutions in this country. Travellers contribute another
element to the throng and to the babel of tongues.
The military, of whom there are about twenty-five
thousand in the city, by their jaunty manner, the gay
colors of their uniforms, and the inspiriting ring of
their rattling swords, form a conspicuous feature of the
scene. We have always found that a mingling of the
military in a crowd is very effective and exhilarating.
The flashing in and out of their gaudy colors amid the
more sombre hues of the civilians' dress; the imposing
epaulets and other showy decorations, glittering even
in the dusk of evening, and, above all, the perpetual
ringing of swords, give a spirited tone to an occasion
otherwise tame and ordinary. There are evidently

many epauletted Lotharios circulating in the crowd, waiting to be caught by some feminine *hook*, needing no other bait than pretty, inviting *eyes*.

In visiting the Palace, we are lost in a perfect maze of splendor. Full of art-treasures, our eyes are yet diverted to other objects, such as the bed in one of the royal chambers, whose draperies cost the almost incredible sum of eighty thousand pounds! They are of brocade, entirely covered with hand-wrought embroidery in pure gold thread. The needle-work is wonderfully done, and the gold employed in its manufacture of fabulous amount, as it almost conceals the groundwork of the material. Other rooms abound in costly ornaments and chandeliers, rare pictures, porcelain, paintings, and in frescoes, which form an illustrated history of the past, introducing characters and depicting the prominent events in the history of the Bavarian Kingdom. We know of no palace that excels this in richness of treasure and in the showiness of its appointments. The Throne Hall, the last of the seemingly endless suite of royal apartments, is one hundred and six feet long, and seventy-three wide. On each side are ten pillars of white marble in the Corinthian style, which, surmounted by gilded capitals, support the galleries. Between the columns are twelve statues representing princes of the houses of Wittelbach in gilded bronze. Each statue weighs about one and a half tons.

Wishing to witness the effect of the whole range of salons, we mount the steps leading to the throne, which stands opposite the open doors, commanding a view extending six hundred and fifty-six feet beyond! The custodian, probably recognizing our nationality, and seeing that we do not aspire to the throne itself, as some royal neighbors have done in times past, offers no resistance. Each apartment being grand in itself, the effect of all, as seen instantaneously, can be but faintly imagined.

In the suburbs of the city, on a hill, stands a colossal bronze statue, representing the Protectress of Bavaria, with a lion at her side. It is elevated upon a platform, on which rests the pedestal; the two equal the height of the statue, which is sixty-one and a half feet high. Entering the figure, we see a flight of iron steps, sixty-six in number, which leads through the pedestal to the knees. Now appears a narrow spiral staircase which terminates at the head, within which are seats for any eight persons who have the courage to ascend thus far. Becoming almost stifled with the heat, a little frightened by the contracted space, and dizzy with the height, we turn on reaching the chest, and contrive to regain terra firma intact. Others of the party, however, venture to the apex, enjoying the extended view through the mammoth eyes of the statue. Does not Shakspeare exclaim, " How bitter a thing it is to look into happiness through another man's eyes"? This is a woman; a fact which may, however, *add* to the beauty, because seen through the *feminine* medium.

The "English Garden" is one of the most pleasing of parks, and indeed we find in almost every city a common breathing-place for the people, such as inflates the public lungs with the purest air, scented with the freshest fragrance from living flowers; emerald lawns; fountains whose crystal sprays, when entangled in the sunbeams, rain illuminated drops, like opals, far and wide; temples, pavilions, and towers, all pretty conceits of architecture in its light and playful mood; and trees that, inanimate as they are, suggest to human minds native dignity, nobility, and firm endurance.

This Bavarian city owes much of its improvements and embellishments to King Ludwig I., who was a special patron of art in its varied forms of architecture, sculpture, and painting. He helped materially to make Munich the inviting city it is in beauty and in manifold fascinations.

How strange it is that one whose soul is animated with quick perceptions of the elevated and beautiful; whose ideas assume æsthetic forms; whose thoughts wander in the realm of harmony, art, and lovely ideals; whose longings go out toward the graceful, the grand, and the artistic;—how strange, we think, that such a soul should fail to possess in its *moral* instincts a corresponding delicacy of thought and sentiment; that he who was so keenly awake to the beauty of art, to its purity of conception, and to its faultless symmetrical expression should foster in the same soul the germ of impurity, permitting it to ripen through gross indulgence!

We remember, then, with mingled surprise and regret, that Ludwig I., to whom the Bavarian capital, and through it, the travelled world, are indebted for an abundant ministry to their cultured, æsthetic tastes by grand architecture, superb paintings, and sculptured monuments, was, through his vices and follies, which disgraced even his old age, compelled by a disgusted people to abdicate in favor of his son.

CARLSBAD.

There are many places at which the traveller touches that seem, like certain human characters, to be so exuberant with life, so bright, cheery, and sunny, that one gladly seeks them and lingers in their proximity, hoping to absorb a portion of their surplus joyousness. These are great light-centres which we approach with eagerness and hover near through an irresistible attraction; and so susceptible is our spiritual nature that we are deeply impressed by these influences, and so absorbent, too, that we can scarcely fail to bear away with us a supply of acquired stimulation, which only disappears gradually from the receptive store-house of our mind.

Such a spot is Carlsbad, one of the most famous water-ing-places in Germany; its springs among the most celebrated in the world. The town is situated very prettily in a deep valley of the river Tepl, and is very enticing in its suburbs, affording beautiful drives and embracing very fine views. The really providential discovery of these springs was made, according to the tradition of the country, in a very singular manner. Although known in the seventh century, they were forgotten, or not utilized, until the year 1358, when Charles IV., while hunting one day, hearing the piteous cries of one of his hounds, discovered him in a hot spring, where he had fallen while pursuing game. The king's physician suggested his trying the waters with the hope of obtaining relief for a disorder in his foot. The malady disappearing upon repeated applications, the fame of the springs was established, their waters from that time being devoted "to the healing of the nations." They were called after their royal discoverer, the name Carlsbad signifying "Charles's bath." Their tempera-ture varying from one hundred and seventeen to one hundred and sixty-five degrees Fahrenheit, they are the hottest springs in Europe. The Sprudel, the hot-test of the nine, rises with great volume three feet high, and makes the atmosphere around it uncomfortable by its steam and heat.

Leaving our hotel at one end of the valley, we saunter

down the street and mingle in a scene full of brilliancy
and animation. Although the natural surroundings
and the situation of the sequestered village are very
romantic,—its buildings clustering in a deep ravine or
valley, penetrated by a river with one small bridge of
one pretty arch; hills overshadowing it and most umbrageous trees embowering its streets,—yet we think the
fascination is vested in its extreme phase of social life.
The broad street lined with hotels is swarming with
life as gay, as happy as we have ever seen, the very
air is murmurous with voices, all in their lightest tones.
No duty harassing, no haste visible on the faces or in
the manner of the brilliant dames, sparkling youths, and
fashionable men who throng the street. Life here,
apparently, has no duties. Elegant leisure rules the
hour. Hundreds of chairs outside the cafés all filled
with bright chatterers; music drowning in deeper
melody the minor notes of the human voice; verdure
abounding, and flowers, as if jealous of the tinted cheeks
and rosy lips on every side, wave their bright banners
yet more gayly in the sunny breeze. Open bazaars display gorgeous ornaments and gems; all is gay bustle and
pleasant confusion. It would be difficult for any sober
stay-at-home American who, if he drinks, does it pri-
vately, and when he eats sits within-doors, to imagine
polished men and refined, but fashionable, women
sitting out on the public thoroughfare flirting, laughing,

and talking over brimming, sparkling glasses of foaming beer, drinking even deeper draughts of worldly
pleasure.

The scene is dazzling and full of effervescing spirit.
No hint is there of sickness, poverty, or death. If such
thoughts intrude they seem vagaries of the brain, and
flit by, untenacious, amid such a whirl of idle, although
innocent, dissipation.

The sweetest pleasure often awaits one when, after
taking a carriage and lolling back luxuriously, an utter
surrender is made of every faculty to the ephemeral
influences of the hour.   And yet no, not ephemeral,
for when the soul revels in a joy fed by the purest
fountains of nature, catching the brightness of the sunbeams; fancy borrowing the celestial blue of the sky in
which to paint her thought; the breezes perhaps stimulating into fresher exercise those servants of the brain,
unfettered imagination, dreamy revery, and idle phan-
tasy, memory, jealous of its prerogative, hastens to assert
it, and records with diamond point, upon her imperish-
able tablets, moments thus spent in richest pleasure.
We are sure that with ineffaceable touch she will record
the sweet experiences of this summer afternoon, when
the "gods" so fill the hour, that when it closes we shall
not exclaim, " Behold, an hour of our life is gone," but
rather, " We have *lived* an hour !"

We approach a wood and penetrate its beautiful

vistas, meeting many of the gay denizens of the little village we have left, who, with their sparkling gems, are lighting up, as with stars, the shady bowers of the grove; appearing, with their bright dresses, like variegated flowers amid the waving grass. Great cafés embowered in green are tempting the saunterers, and music arises from all parts of the extensive grove. On we drive through miles of beauty, catching glimpses occasionally of "hills peeping o'er hills," and of the faraway glory of the radiant sky above and around them, until we reach a large manufactory, where our eyes are delighted, and the purses of many are depleted, by the tempting display of exquisite porcelain.

9

CHAPTER XII.

BERLIN—POTSDAM—NUREMBERG.

BERLIN.

BERLIN is one of the most brilliant of European cities. Its finest street, Unter den Linden, is really magnificent in width, foliage, imposing palaces, fine hotels, and showy stores. It is fifty-three feet wide, with a double row of lime-trees, to which it owes its name. Several years since, the trees which bordered this grand boulevard were the pride of the city; but the comparatively recent introduction of the gas-pipes injured them to such a degree that gradually one after another died, being immediately replaced by younger and smaller ones. We hear many regrets expressed that the grand old trees have yielded to the blighting effects of modern improvements, and that so long a time must elapse before their successors can win an equal reputation for size and beauty. The Unter den Linden extends to the Brandenburg Gate, which is surmounted by a chariot drawn by four horses, in which a figure symbolizing "Victory" is seated. The chariot

178

was taken to Paris by the French in 1807, but was recovered after the battle of Waterloo in 1814.

The streets of Berlin, grand in their width, regularity, and architectural buildings, are further embellished with numberless monuments and statues of military heroes and the great in science and art. The equestrian statue of Frederick the Great at the east end of the Linden is universally conceded to be the finest monument of its kind in Europe. While the main purpose has been to commemorate the greatness of the "great" king, and to testify to a nation's enduring remembrance, yet he is made the nucleus of much subordinate distinction, many of the celebrated characters of his reign having a niche for a sculptured tribute in the sections of the pedestal. The foundation-stone of this magnificent memorial was laid on May 31, 1840, the one hundredth anniversary of Frederick's accession to the Prussian throne; its inauguration taking place in 1851. That kingdoms are not always forgetful and ungrateful, is proven by this superb tribute to the unselfish patriotism of a man who sought in every way to secure the aggrandizement of his native land, making his remarkable genius tributary to its advancement and power.

The vanity and pride of the people are perpetually fed by a conspicuous reminder of their military prowess in the dazzling and splendid monument of "Victory"

in the centre of König's-Platz. It stands one hundred
and ninety-eight feet high; the square pedestal is covered with reliefs in bronze, celebrating early victories
and those of 1870–71: on the north, the battle of
Königgrätz; on the east side, the Danish war of 1864;
on the west, the battle of Sedan, 1870; and on the
south, the return of the troops, 1871. A few steps
higher is the "Hall of Victory," encircled by Doric
columns. From this hall ascends a pillar of sandstone,
in the flutings of which are placed three rows of Danish,
Austrian, and French cannon. The summit consists of
a figure gorgeously gilt, forty-two feet high.

The palace occupied by the present Emperor is remarkably unostentatious in its dimensions and appearance externally; but the Royal Palace or Schloss, time-
honored, having been founded as a fortress in 1443,
was completed, after various intervening changes, in
1716, and is now principally used on festive occasions
and in entertaining royal guests. The palace contains
six hundred apartments, only a few representative ones
being shown. In the Throne-Room is an immense buffet
covered with gold plate. Near this is a large ornamental beer-barrel with silver faucet and trimmings,
provided for the king Frederick William I., father of
Frederick the Great, whose royal thirst was so excessive that it must be thus liberally provided for. We
think if he could only have imbibed more freely of the

" milk of human kindness," the life of his illustrious
son would have been a happier one. A magnificent
chandelier of rock-crystal, suspended in the same apartment, is the one under which Martin Luther is said to
have stood when he made his famous defence at Worms.
It was subsequently purchased and transferred to the
Berlin Palace. We look upon the silent, unconscious
witness of the heroic man's trial with intense interest;
recalling his words when urged to fly the danger
thought to be waiting him at Worms: " Though there
are as many devils in Worms as tiles upon the house-
tops, I will enter it." Intrepid soul! and so he did;
and before a tribunal of three hundred inimical judges
—the Emperor and his nobility—he argued, as did Paul
before Felix, "reasoning of righteousness;" vindicating,
through the Scriptures, the justness of his opinions and
the glory of his faith; and, guarded by ministering
angels, like Paul, he was allowed to go his " way for
this time."

On we wander, through salons glittering in gold and
silver decorations and in satin brocades a hundred years
old; our eyes gratified by pictures, portraits of celebrated men, statues of Carrara marble, and frescoes of
great beauty. Our delight culminates in the wonderful
dimensions and chaste ornamentation of the " White
Hall,"—the largest room in the palace, one hundred
and eight feet long and fifty-one wide,—hung with

sparkling crystal chandeliers, and adorned with marble statues, among which is an exquisite figure of "Victory," by Rauch.

The Royal Chapel contains a crucifix of silver, seven feet in height, set with precious stones and valued at eighty thousand pounds. The altar also invites inspection, being of alabaster, a present from Mehemet Ali, Viceroy of Egypt.

Driving through the streets to the depot, on leaving Berlin, we pass by a plain, substantial mansion, standing back from the street, with a pleasant yard in front, filled with massive groups of green shrubbery. It wears an air of eminent respectability, of solid satisfaction, as it were, with itself; as if its inmates were at peace with themselves and with the world at large; life and they shaking hands in good-fellowship. We turn inquiringly to the guide, who answers our unspoken inquiry in the simple words, " 'Tis Bismark's house." We are glad to see the home of the giant-brained man who has made his country the leading monarchical power of Europe, and who has left his impress strongly marked upon the political history of the nineteenth century. We trust that he will be allowed to retire while his honors lie thick upon him, and before the coming king, who is said to be inimical to him, has opportunity of doing him any disrespect.

POTSDAM.

Potsdam, very naturally styled the "Versailles of Prussia," is half an hour distant by rail from Berlin. We first visit the Royal Palace, and wander with pleasure through the apartments once occupied by Frederick the Great, which, remaining unchanged, contain many souvenirs, such as his hat, scarf, and writing-table spotted with ink, his music-stand, and the furniture, whose covering is defaced by the dogs who were his petted and favorite companions.

His bedroom opens into a small dining-room having a trap-door set in the floor, through which the table rose laden, with perhaps eel-pie, as that was his favorite dish, disappearing at the conclusion of his meal in the same magical manner, thus doing away with the presence of curious servants during political or private discussions.

But the most agreeable visit is made to Sans Souci, in the suburbs of Potsdam, whose palace park is an Elim, with its beautiful waters and trees. The great fountain, which throws a jet nearly one hundred and twenty feet high, its basin surrounded by marble groups of mythological characters, is at the foot of the hill on which stands the charming little palace, reached by terraces covered with flowering trees and conservatories. This was Frederick's favorite resort, and where he entertained his ungrateful and cynical friend Voltaire. The king's apartments are as he left them. His choice collection of books, some of which retain the critical remarks pencilled on their margin by Voltaire; the couch and chair, both of which contradictorily share the honor of having supported the dying king in his last moments; and the clock which he had been in the habit of winding, its hands pointing to the hour of his death, twenty minutes past two; its ticking said to have ceased at the moment of the spirit's departure. There it has stood untouched for nearly a hundred years, a silent memento of a solemn and sacred scene. How sad to think that the great spirit, so full of worldly wisdom, left the earthly throne, which it had adorned, to appear before the heavenly one, doubting, skeptical, or utterly indifferent to the realities of an eternal future! That he who boasted of having set his earthly kingdom in perfect order, even to the smallest details, should have spent no thought or made no known preparation for the endless life of his own immortal soul! Not far from Frederick's apartments are those which were occupied by Voltaire when the familiar and honored guest of the Prussian king. These also remain as when left by this man, great in brain-power, but too little and mean in heart-qualities to retain the friendship won by the fascination which a brilliant intellect exercises over other cultured minds. His innate vanity and inherent selfishness always blighted the bud of affection felt for him, or if perchance it blossomed prematurely in the light of his brilliant talents, it was inevitably blasted through his cynicism and inordinate self-conceit. In examining the furniture we found its tapestry covered with illustrations from La Fontaine's Fables, a fact which affords a little incident characteristic of the pleasant intercourse existing between the host, royal in rank, and the guest, royal in intellect. Voltaire, always disparaging La Fontaine, whose powers, although not profound, were surely possessed of some elements of excellence, instigated perhaps by literary jealousy, refused to concede to the Fables the merit which the world awards them. Frederick, espousing the cause of La Fontaine, took advantage of a temporary absence of Voltaire and ordered his furniture to be covered with representations of some of the principal Fables. Tradition fails to picture the chagrin of the subject of the joke, who, as a guest, could not complain of the appointments of his apartments. Another substantial proof of the king's playful humor towards his friends is seen in the corridor of the palace, where stands on a pedestal a fine statue of Venus. Below it, on the floor, rests the bust of one of his generals. This poor unfortunate, as the fact of his being a woman-hater proves him to have been, took great pleasure in giving free expression to his aversion to the sex. Frederick, who, although not a lover of his kind, yet cherished no special dislike to woman, devised the ingenious plan of punishing so unnatural and unmanly a trait by procuring a bust of the general and giving it permanent place at the *feet* of the marble statue which adorns so conspicuous a place in his palace.

Must there not have been a jarring chord in that brave soldier's nature, that at the touch of some memory gave forth discordant notes, but which, on the strange principle of compensation, might have been tuned into harmony by *some* feminine hand?

"To a man who has had a mother" should not "all women be sacred for her sake"? And may not respect and regard for the sex prove an "ægis" to a bachelor, and a sun, as well as shield, warming into active life those emotions and principles which are often dormant in the masculine nature?

Passing out of the bright little palace, whose windows look upon as fair a scene as the eye or soul could covet, we walk a few steps to the end of the terrace, and stand beside several flat tablets, whose inscriptions inform us that the favorite dogs and the charger of the king are buried here. The king's fondness for these was a marked peculiarity of his character, giving to these dumb, soulless, and yet intelligent creatures the affection he withheld from human kind. And so skeptical was he of those noblest traits—sincerity and

fidelity—in his fellow-men, that he preferred to bestow upon the brute creation the affection he refused
to his wife and to others. It is said that in a certain
battle one of his dogs was lost, remaining absent for
some time, and that upon its return it manifested such
excessive delight on seeing its master that the king
burst into tears. It is also a well-known fact that
he directed that his body after death should share the
grave with his already buried horse. This request,
however, was not complied with.

A short distance from the palace stands the historic
windmill, occupying ground *now* belonging to the
crown, but which once so strongly excited the covetous
desire of Frederick. Well was it, for the modern Na-
both, that he was not resisting an Ahab, whose wife
could resort to sanguinary means to secure the treasure.
As it is, the quaint old mill stands as a memorial of
justice and a vindicator of the majesty of law.

And now that we have, through familiar souvenirs,
seen the home-life of Frederick, we follow him to his
final resting-place in the "Garrison Church," in the
village of Potsdam. It is an exceeding plain, old structure, erected by Frederick's father, Frederick William
I. On the walls hang flags, taken in various battles, and
in rear of the pulpit are mahogany receptacles, where
are preserved the uniforms worn by the three sovereigns
who formed the "Holy Alliance." Not in a subter-

ranean vault, although beneath the pulpit, is the plain metallic coffin which contains the remains of a "mighty man of valor," one who in the face of tremendous disadvantages compelled the great nations of Europe to acknowledge his military genius and to succumb to his superior military tactics. We remember that the lowest order of man may have brute or physical force, and successfully exercise it; but pre-eminent above physical courage, and even that genius that boldly organizes mighty campaigns, leading vast armies on to battle and to conquest, is the moral strength that supports a grand spirit amid, it would seem, overwhelming discouragements; and that irresistible pluck which carries him through difficulties before which even many stout hearts would quail. The world now, in the unimpassioned view by which time permits past actions and long-buried lives to be judged,—and 'tis a certain test,—pronounces this man to be worthy of the grand and rarely deserved title of "Great." We turn our eyes to the marble sarcophagus of the only other silent incumbent of this sepulchral chamber. We gaze almost ironically, at least bitterly, upon it. The massive casket encloses the heartless form of Frederick William I., the father of the "Great" King, and his immediate predecessor.

We believe that there is almost a divine element in parental sentiment and relations; that parentage is the coronation of married life; that heaven in the bestowal of a child is endowing wedlock with a sublime trust; that its immortal soul is like a precious, although crude, gem, to be shaped and polished with the tenderest care, that it may one day be worthy to shine in the Redeemer's crown; that to insure the happiness—as well as to minister to the moral and mental training— of the child is a solemn obligation; that a child may claim as its *birthright* a happy childhood; that smiles should play around its youthful steps, as heaven has taught the sunbeams to brighten the world's pathway. That no shadows should be voluntarily allowed to throw their lengthening gloom over a long life; that while the child should be restrained by uniform and gentle firmness, it be made glad by the fond affection of the parents' hearts.

We can see, without aid of imagination, the pernicious effects upon King Frederick's whole after-life of a gloomy childhood, in his case of a frightfully dark one. His father, a man of brutal instincts, tortured the childhood and tyrannized over the youth and manhood of his noble son; using personal violence, and even meditating the condemning him to death. Few temperaments could prove invulnerable to these influences. Failing to receive affection from the source where he had a *right* to expect it, he became skeptical of the existence of all lesser emotions. Disgusted with a religion whose most rigorous forms had been imposed upon him; seeing none of its gentle benignity in the life of the father who compelled its strictest observance, he eschewed it forever, when freed from the father's tyranny, and died without hope in the immortal life. Forced to marry a woman for whom he had no regard, he ignored the duties compulsorily thrust upon him, declining to accept the wife of another's choosing; testifying, however, before his death to the unblemished character and virtue of his virgin wife.

"Pitying him," as did Desdemona Othello, "for the distressful strokes that his youth suffered," who would not heave a sigh as they stand by the tomb of this "great" man, who found so little of cheer in this world's social and friendly relations, as to prefer to lie in death beside his horse, who was wont in life to neigh at his approach and to return, according to his capacity, the affection bestowed by his fond master?

As we look down upon the simple coffin, we hope that the *heavenly* Father has been more merciful than was the *earthly* to the son, who, we believe, had he been reared in an atmosphere of love and kindness; who if his life had not been robbed of heaven's richest boon,—a happy childhood,—would have been free from many of those faults and foibles which marred his otherwise noble character. That if a wife voluntarily won, and children the fruit of that love, had cheered his private life, a portraiture of his social and domestic habits might have brightened the pages of history, blending with the dazzling glory of his storied achievements as a military leader and as a king.

NUREMBERG.

Nuremberg is a curious, quaint old city. We are glad to find that progress—the modern usurper—has failed to obliterate many traces of the mediæval ages; so that one may readily forget his identity and become lost in this great past, whose relics abound on every side. We delight in these unique phases of ancient life, and fear that we shall never again have respect for what is not musty with age. Indeed, we have found ourselves gazing upon embrowned crumbling mummies with a reverential awe that a modern subject would not inspire; and upon grimmed old buildings with an inquisitive enthusiasm which no recent structure could excite. So fresh are American eyes, so unaccustomed to rest upon objects of antiquity, that it is with keen relish we allow our attention to be diverted into these channels of interest and thought. With no venerable "past at our back," the *future* is the god of the American's worship. We live in advance of our time; opening up new territory; establishing new settlements, founding new institutions, and constantly building up for future generations; pressing always forward, and never loitering on the way to confer with that wisest of teachers,—the world's past, —with which " 'tis greatly wise to talk," gathering knowledge and suggestion from its lessons.

Like many other cities we have seen, Nuremberg is divided by a river, which, with its bridges, adds to its beauty and picturesqueness. As we ride over one of them, we are pleased with the immediate view of ancient buildings, including a tower now used as a prison. Perhaps the chief feature is the castle, one thousand years old, a part of which is fitted up for the royal family. It is built high upon a rock, from which the view is grand. In an adjacent tower we contemplate many repulsive objects with that fascination which the horrible affords. It was in olden time the prison where criminals were tortured and executed. Within its massive walls are collected a great variety of instruments of torture, which look as if they had been frequently employed upon suffering humanity. It seems a pity that the names of their inventors should not always have been associated with these proofs of their satanic ingenuity, so that the execrations of each succeeding generation might be heaped upon their memories! Following Haman's precedent, they should have been made to demonstrate the utility of the instruments upon their own shrinking bodies. The thumb-screw;

the pillory; the wheel on which criminals were broken; the chair on which the condemned sat while being beheaded; a separate bench, with two seats, to accommodate the doctor and the executioner, the doctor's having a back attached to it; a chair whose seat was formed of sharp points, on which the prisoner was pressed; the horrors perhaps culminating in the "iron virgin." This is a massive figure seven feet high, its interior bristling with spikes which penetrated the prisoner when thrust into it. His death accomplished, the body was released and allowed to fall through a trap-door leading to subterranean vaults. We see the wooden pen, dark and frightful, in which a condemned criminal passed the night preceding his execution. But among these barbarous relics is one which suggests so fitting a punishment for those who "put an enemy in their mouths to steal away their brains" that we would be glad to see it adopted in our own country. It is a common barrel, in which the drunkard, after being placed within it, his head projecting over the top, was driven through the public streets. A deep moat lying below this curious old tower, and originally filled with water, is now a bed of luxuriant grass, shrubs, and trees.

The Church of "St. Lawrence," built in the thirteenth century, is of beautiful Gothic architecture, with many ornamental towers and spires. Its interior is

full of interest. A Gothic pix of white granite, most
elaborately carved, rises to a height of sixty-four feet,
and is a marvel of grace and beauty. Its apex is in
the form of a shepherd's crook, and bends over as if to
protect the sculptured beauty below it. Longfellow
thus describes it:—

"In the church of sainted Lawrence stands a pix of sculpture
    rare,
  Like the foamy sheaf of fountains rising through the painted
    air."

The windows of the church are unusually fine, and
it is through them that the air is "painted" in rich
glowing color. This church, now belonging to the
Lutherans, was originally dedicated to the Roman
Catholic faith, and still retains several of its souvenirs.
In one corner of the church we see an ancient altar of
unpainted iron, and our curiosity is excited by discovering several human bones visible through a grating.
Their presence is explained in this wise. A family of
high rank missed a valuable silver tankard; diligent
search having been made in vain, suspicion fell upon
the steward, who, although protesting his innocence,
was condemned to torture, confession being extorted
under its power. Not restoring, however, the missing
article, he was executed. Some time after, his innocence being proved by the accidental discovery of the

tankard in a remote cupboard, the family, burdened with remorse, built this curious old shrine, and in expiation of their unjust censure, and to atone for its fatal consequences, exhumed the poor fellow's bones, placing them over the altar consecrated to his vindicated memory.

In an opposite nave the site of a former confessional is pointed out as associated with a tragic event of days long gone by. A young priest, in accordance with God-given instincts, the indulgence of which heaven encourages, but contrary to the unnatural law of his church,—fell in love! The object of his affection loved another, and revealed the fact to the enamored priest in the confessional. Upon leaving it, he hanged himself upon a heavy bronze candelabrum suspended near by, and, being discovered soon after, by his indignant fellow-priests, was cut down and summarily ejected from the neighboring window.

There are two bronze fountains in the town very noticeable because of their unique design. One is called the "Fountain of the Virtues," the water flowing from the breasts of several large female figures. The quaintness of the design, as well as the merit of its execution, attracts the eye. Near the market is another fountain, representing a man of small proportions, in the quaint garb of a farmer, holding under his arm a goose, from whose bill issues a jet of water. This is to commemorate the welcome appearance of the first poultry-vender who had the courage to enter the plague-stricken city after the disease had spent itself. So one is never allowed in these ancient cities to forget the striking events of past ages. All revel in the remembrance of a rich past; its heroes, never buried in forgetfulness, live in sculptured forms before the world. The intelligent traveller finds ample illustration of the events of former times, with which he is familiar through reading, and feels somewhat fossil-like himself, being surrounded by the stone, bronze, and marble effigies of ancient worthies. We begin to feel that there is great prestige in age and in having a voluminous history, and when speaking of our own country fall back upon the fact that it existed—inhabited, to be sure, by mere aborigines—centuries before its discovery by Columbus.

CHAPTER XIII.

HEIDELBERG—FRANKFORT.

HEIDELBERG.

How often in some bright sunny day of summertime have we watched the busy bee as it would flit from flower to flower in the enamelled field, spending a fleeting moment in absorbing the sweetness of the humble clover; and then, although agreeably catered to, yet, with almost human fickleness, flying to another blossom, perhaps to the simple sweet-brier, whose beauty suggests a feast even more luscious; and so, in turn, each gay, flaunting flower of the meadow tempts the giddy bee to sip its nectar. Does not the insect find its counterpart in the tourist, whose aim is to taste, although not exhaust, the inherent charm of each city, as he speeds on his "flying trip"? And each one possesses that individuality which we associate with the human character; some peculiar attraction, strictly personal; each enjoyable, but *all together* presenting that variety which forms the pleasure of continuous travel.

Starting anew, we soon find ourselves in the famous

University town of Heidelberg, which is beautifully
situated on the Neckar, at the base of the hill Königs-
tuhl. Leaving the train, we saunter up to the hotel,
but a few steps distant, and there find, in its pretty
gardens glowing with gay flowers, its broad, pleasant
verandas, and cheerful aspect, a bright welcome. We
have arrived most opportunely. The yearly com-
mencement has just completed its exercises, and the
culminating act of the drama, a brilliant illumination
of the celebrated castle, is to be accomplished this very
evening. This unusual demonstration, only occurring
at long intervals, is considered so gorgeously grand that
many have come from far and near to witness the display. The streets are thronged; vehicles in great demand; the hotels crowded; and expectation beaming in
every face. We secure a carriage and start out for an
evening's entertainment. Toiling up the hill-side over
a good spiral road, we enjoy a fine prospect of the
adjacent country. The town lies below us, with its
crowded streets; the Neckar flowing by its side, and
the magnificent old castle on an elevated position, "the
observed of all observers." But the evening shades
are gathering; a signal for the coming event. We
descend the hill, cross the river, and remain in the
carriage, taking a favorable position to witness the
promised display. The crowd fills the highway; music
strives to drown the discord; the river presents an ani-

mated scene, covered with gayly-decorated boats filled with lively, dashing young students in their varied and jaunty little caps, their colors indicating the classes to which the wearers belong. That the moon refuses her light none regret, as the illumination will be the more effective in her absence. But the *stars* also, in petulant mood, suspecting, perhaps, that their mild sweet light is to be eclipsed,—like many of their vocal and dramatic sisters,—decline at the last moment to appear. The air becomes murky, the human temper impatient, when suddenly, just as expectation has ripened, the heavens open, and a heavy thunder-shower threatens to engulf us. The people disappear—who knows where? Their retreat is always accomplished, under such circumstances, in a mysterious way. Nature soon exhausting her reservoirs, peace is again restored to the elements; the crowds regather, and all eyes are riveted upon the castle, which is, in its old age, to be rejuvenated with youthful fire and to shine and dazzle as with supernatural glow. It looms up in solitary grandeur on the hill-side before us; gloom pervades its grand spaces; darkness looks grimly out at its portals; its rich, full robes of ivied green protecting its sides from the dampness of night. It is reposing upon its strength of centuries, defying Time with that majestic dignity that commands respect for even an inanimate object.

From a boat on the river a signal is given, not seen

by the waiting crowds, but recognized by watching eyes at the castle; and now such a sight as we have never before witnessed bursts upon our vision. Instantaneously the whole structure, magnificent in its proportions, superb in its carved ornamentation, statued façades, and in its stately tower, glows with a light indescribable in glory and color; at first absolutely bathed in a ruby-like, flameless fire, instantly changing into one of green that rivals the emerald in hue. The brilliancy gradually fades out, except from the tower, which is irradiated with a light almost unearthly in its splendor, and, this dying away, the colossal fabric is again enshrouded in the gloom of night.

The expenses of this illumination are defrayed by the students, and although it is but of few moments' duration is very costly. As the departure of the students takes place on the day following the exhibition, they, like other blessings, may be said to

"Brighten as they take their flight."

The next morning, during a drive to and from the castle, we meet many of the students, of whose duelling practices we, in common with the world, have often heard. In the bustle of departure they are circulating everywhere; the streets are thronged with them, and we are astonished at the large numbers whose scarred visages bear the marks of disgraceful encounters.

Fair youthful foreheads seamed with deep sabre-cuts; cheeks gashed; ears split; and eyes distorted,—barely escaping utter loss. With what shamefacedness should they hereafter present their countenances, marred as with the brand of Cain, in polite society! Were their gaping wounds received on the battle-field in honorable conflict, they would win them sympathy and renown. Were the horrid red lines that are deeply graven across their seared faces received in defence of their country, they would be like badges of honor, reminding the world that those who wore them were of such stuff as heroes are made of, and their disfigured faces would be passports to the favor of the gentle sex, who admire bravery, patriotism, and all heroic qualities. We are informed by resident parties that the evil is assuming formidable proportions, and that the government is waking up to the consciousness of its enormity. The police either cower under the united strength of some hundreds of gay, reckless youths, and so wink at their infringement of the laws; or they are corrupted by the full purses of the rich, and often titled, young scapegraces. The code originated by these impetuous spirits allows no affront to pass without being effaced by human blood; they seem to thirst, as does the tiger of the jungle, for its taste. A German Whittier should sing to them this blessed sentiment:

" O, brother man ! fold to thy heart thy brother ;
　　Where pity dwells, the peace of God is there ;
　　To worship rightly, is to love each other,
　　Each smile a hymn, each kindly deed a prayer."

In the cellar of the Castle we see a renowned
curiosity in the mammoth tun, thirty-six feet long and
twenty-four feet high. Its capacity is eight hundred
hogsheads. There are steps leading to the top of it,
on which is a platform where the students in former
times were wont, on certain gala occasions, to have a
dance. Had the flooring given way, they might have
been drowned in the spirituous liquor, a manner of
death that the Duke of Clarence preferred to any
other. Near by stands the grotesquely painted wooden
image of the court jester, who was made notorious by
his apparently infinite capacity for imbibing. A clock
of rude construction hangs near him, with a string
appended to it which the unwary visitor is invited to
pull. Should he comply, a large bushy tail is suddenly
projected into his face, to his personal chagrin and to
the malicious amusement of the spectators.

FRANKFORT.

Frankfort-on-the-Main is a city that impresses one
with its respectability and solid merit; but, unlike many
of the cities to which this description might apply, it
has much sweet poetry of light attraction to mingle with

the prose of its substantial and more matter-of-fact advantages. The city is not as popular among tourists as many others, and although we find a sojourn of several days pleasantly employed, a *few hours* would make us acquainted with its leading features. It is eminently a business city; the headquarters of money and banking interests; the birthplace of the first of the Rothschilds, and also of the famous banker Bethmann. We are much gratified by a drive through the old part of the city, our attention being often directed to the venerable buildings, with their quaint gables overshadowing the lower stories, and in the Jewish quarter of the city to the exceedingly high dwellings, among which is one pointed out as the house in which Rothschild, the head of that famous family, was born. The house, like others of its class, is swarming with life, occupied by many families. Grim, dirty, and blackened with age, it bears little resemblance to the many stately palaces now occupied by the descendants of the great financier who built up not only a personal reputation, but a family name, honorably represented in many European countries.

There is another house so associated with greatness —a different phase, however—that we gladly turn our steps towards it. Goethe was born in Frankfort, and not only is the house in which he passed his precocious childhood to be seen, but the room is pointed out where the mother bore the child who, almost lifeless, was with difficulty reanimated. How much more earnest would have been the efforts of the midwife and attendants had they suspected that the life of the inaugurator of a new intellectual experience for Germany —one whose birth was to prove an epoch in the nation's history—hung in the balance! How little, too, the mother dreamed that the feeble physical life enshrined a mental organization of such power and genius as had never before dawned upon Germany; who was to be an object of not only an empire's enthusiastic appreciation, but of the world's admiring regard, and that at the death of the philosopher poet two worlds would mourn him! How much to be regretted that the soul of a man upon whose utterances the world waited, and who wielded an incalculable influence upon the general mind, should have been so befogged in mysticism, failing to recognize in his life The Hand that guides the world, and in the problem of life and in the enigma of death the germ of Christian truth and faith!

The room in which the eyes of the wonderful babe first opened is small, and utterly devoid of all decoration. The study and desk are shown to the interested traveller, and in one of the chambers familiar to his childhood the picture, with several other souvenirs, of the woman whom his love may have idealized, but who stands out brightly in the light of her home. There she presided, taking tender care of young brothers and sisters who had sustained, with her, the loss of a mother. This Charlotte of sweet memory was necessarily shut out from the after-life of her gifted lover, because of an engagement to another; but her appreciative friendship was enjoyed by him, and he, in turn, by making his love for her one of the inspiring subjects of his famed novel, "The Sorrows of Werther," has immortalized her name. In one room hangs the picture of his mother, who was evidently fair, comely, and sweetly womanly. We stand and gaze upon her benignant smile and shapely features with deep interest, as we ever do upon the living form or pictured face of one who has borne a genius or mothered a hero. Who can estimate the glorious dignity of motherhood, and the exquisite pleasure of claiming, in the lovely maidenhood of the daughters and in the vigorous manhood of the sons, a personal right so close that none but a heavenly-ordained power could bestow it! The wonderful link between the mother and child is of symbolic gold, so beautiful and pure that it could be of no other than Heaven's forging.

The house once occupied by Martin Luther is also to be seen, the fact memorialized by his bust placed upon its front. Thus is the memory of this German apostle, the prodigious champion of our Christian faith, honored in all the places that once resounded to his tread. Alas that in his own native land the echoes of those victorious footsteps should now be so faintly heard, and that a gospel which he so fearlessly promulgated, with the enthusiastic zeal of a soul but recently rescued from the bonds of slavish error, should be so feebly supported, and, indeed, in its sublime purity and simplicity almost ignored!

The banker, Bethmann, having in the statue Ariadne, by Dannecker, a superb treasure, has erected for it a small building within his garden. For a trifling gratuity strangers may feast upon the rare graces of the sculptured beauty. A curtain is withdrawn, and there we see the life-sized form sitting on a leopard. It seems to us the personification of female loveliness and a triumph of the sculptor's skill. It might well suggest to the modern bachelor a feminine ideal of not only those personal charms to which all are susceptible, but of the mental graces which seem to irradiate even these marble features; and which, united with the former, "show how divine a thing a woman may be made."

Through the red skylight a tempered color is thrown upon the statue. A glow tinges the pale cheek, seems to illumine the eyes, and to give a flush of feeling to the figure, apparently instinct with the shy, modest, sweet sentiment of a living soul. We gaze and wonder how Theseus, the possessor of such rare beauty as is here represented, could ever have turned his back upon it, and sailed away to encounter all the desolating gloom of widowerhood.

CHAPTER XIV.

BADEN-BADEN—COLOGNE.

BADEN-BADEN.

BADEN-BADEN, before the consolidation of the German Empire, was the rendezvous of all gay pleasure-seekers in Europe, and not only of that class of reckless adventurers who live by their wits, but of those who found the novel scene it exhibited so fascinating that they sought it for amusement, even while they refused to succumb to its pernicious allurements. The gaming-tables, which were the "cynosure of all eyes," drew multitudes, who, when deprived of their facilities or of their spectacular attraction, failing to find in the natural advantages of the watering-place and in its milder forms of diversion sufficient enticement, forsook the once favorite haunt. Germany, although over its national character there floats a scum of infidelity, observes great decorum in its legalized amusements, and when Baden Baden came under its control it was divested and purified of its moral cancer, gambling. It is a penetrating disease, absorbing a man's whole thought, depriving him of will-power, and so corrupting his judgment and reason that his entire being is infected with the moral poison. We honor that government which will reject the financial advantages accruing from the establishment of these great gambling centres, encouraging in lieu of them those amusements which are not prejudicial to the growth of a healthy moral sentiment in the community. This should be the policy of all governments, and, even if selfishness lurks at its roots, it will still bear good fruit.

Baden-Baden is cosily situated in the valley of the Vos, which in its petty trickling scarce deserves the title of river. The town encroaches somewhat upon the slopes of the bordering hills, pretty gardens smiling in the sunshine. The "Neue Trinkhalle" is the focus of attraction at the usual drinking-hour, while the somewhat unsavory waters are made tolerable by the delightful strains of a good band, the ear being ministered to at the expense of the palate. This hall is a colonnade, richly frescoed; contiguous to it are the Promenade and "Conversationshaus." The latter is a commodious building, with a portico in Corinthian style. It contains a splendid hall-room, concert-rooms, restaurant, and reading-room. The saloons, too, whose gaming-tables once drew the presence of the world, are still dazzling and gorgeous in glittering show, but vacant and silent, as befits the burial-place of so many hopes, fortunes, and reputations. Still, there are many seductive charms to delight the visitors who throng the promenade at evening. We take chairs, and, in payment, order ices, and there sit, with Heaven's blue canopy studded with stars glittering above us; flowers nodding drowsily, the evening breeze stirring their slumbers with its soft breath, the atmosphere dropping its diamond dew-drops upon their drooping petals; the music of choice selection and delicious in melody, touching all hearts; while the giddy crowds pass and repass, seeming happy in light, frivolous talk. A Chinese pagoda costing ten thousand dollars, near the Hall, accommodates the band, which is worthy of so costly a pavilion. We leave many stray francs at the shops, which are replete with elegant ornaments and knick-knacks, forming, as they do at all such resorts, a conspicuous feature and an irresistible temptation.

A ride follows, of some miles, in itself affording keen pleasure, through "lanes and valleys green, dingles and bushy dells," and fine old woods. We are at length compelled to alight and climb a hill to reach the grand ruins of an ancient Schloss, or castle, built by the Romans many centuries ago,—how many no one can tell. It is an enormous, rambling structure, its towers rising higher than we dare to ascend, lower positions affording a view sufficiently extensive, rich, and varied. Far away, the hills of the Black Forest are discernible;

then the spreading plain, threaded by the faintly-traced Rhine; while nearer lies the sweet valley of the hospitable little town of Baden-Baden, with its pretty clustering homes and modest little river. The grandeur of the ruins is in no way diminished, but made perfect by the union of pretty, clinging vines, which in their dense, wild luxuriance seem to revel in their freedom, clambering with riotous growth over lofty towers, sending down graceful festoons, which shade the walls and toy with every passing breeze.

But we must leave this venerable monument of past ages, with its clinging, bride-like vines, to visit the scene of the singular private drama of a life whose shameless record is perpetuated in many visible objects.

We catch a glimpse through a broad fine vista of an elegant château. It is very prettily situated, half encircled by woods, with pleasant lawns stretching before it; but its interior is unusually inviting and opens up to us new forms of gay, brilliant, and unique ornamentation. The palace was built and furnished by the Margravine Sybilla, a woman of luxurious and perhaps somewhat gaudy taste, and of life most unchristian; a voluptuary of wide-spread fame, and of such beauty as delighted to repeat itself. In an apartment called the mirror room we find the walls and ceiling formed of small mirrors so ingeniously arranged that there is but one place in which one fails to see his reflection.

In another room are seventy pictures of herself in every possible guise and attitude. In still another apartment the walls are literally covered with portraits of men of her time,—perhaps the art-gallery picturing her dissolute life. The grand bedchamber is hung in richest tapestry wrought by herself and her ladies. The walls of one room are lined with pictured porcelain, a singular and very costly finish. It would be impossible to enumerate the vast number of ornaments scattered with regal profusion through the beautiful suite of apartments. The life, gay, frivolous, unwomanly, and impure, that once animated these places has long since fled; although it seems, in penetrating the private apartments full of the familiar objects of domestic life, that we might encounter at any moment the unfortunate spirit that once brightened these rooms, so invested do they seem with the immediate presence of their notorious mistress. As we emerge from the pleasant mansion, we hear the wind as it sweeps through the leafy branches of the lofty trees that surround it, sounding to our imagination, which has become captive to the spell that by this time is woven around us, like a dirge moaning over a sad and wasted life. Within the grounds is a small round chapel, called the " Hermitage," where the rich, beautiful, and sinful woman was in the habit of spending in strict seclusion, and in a superficially penitential mood, the forty days of Lent.

Each year at that season would she lay aside her gorgeous apparel and the unhallowed practices of her life, and, assuming a dress of coarsest serge, would enter the little chapel to remain alone with her offended Maker. The days and nights were devoted to expiatory penances, such as self-scourging, wearing an iron shirt, and in seeking repose only upon a rope mat, eschewing every luxury and the attendance that belonged to her rank; condescending to the performance of the most menial offices; returning at the expiration of the season to the sinful follies of her previous life.

We enter the tiny building with eager curiosity. It is divided into several very small apartments,—one, an oratory, where is a life-sized waxen figure of our Lord stretched out beneath the rude shrine at which she performed her devotions. On the wall hangs a scourge, and a shirt of rough, prickly iron which she wore next her person. In the next room is a small wooden table where she ate, *waxen figures representing the Virgin Mary and the Saviour seated at the opposite side.* In the adjoining room is the coarse woven mat on which she slept; a repulsive human skull is suspended near, which it was her duty to contemplate. Next to her dormitory was the kitchen where she prepared her scanty meals. The floors of the "Hermitage" are of rough pine, and all the appointments such as we associate with abject poverty.

The little building in which we stand is full of suggestion, and fires a new train of thought. As we contemplate this Magdalen's character, we think of the stigma which justly falls upon an unhallowed life, and of the unequal view which the world takes of lax morality in the sexes. Why is it, we ask ourselves, that man should be allowed to sow his "*wild oats,*" while woman is expected to sow *wheat?* Why should a man demand of the woman he marries an unspotted maidenhood and an unblemished life, while his past has been tarnished by sin? Why require that her vestal fires should have burned purely, while in his heart are the ashes of unholy passions? Why the difference? Will *Heaven* require of the weaker sex a higher degree of moral excellence than of the stronger? Should condemnation fall more heavily upon the tempted than upon the tempter? One of Solon's laws decreed that that man should be declared infamous who condoned his wife's infidelity. Right so far; but why not frame a twin law that the wife should be declared infamous who tolerated her husband's unfaithfulness, or the maiden who ignored her lover's derelictions? But so it has ever been; public opinion heaping maledictions upon the *female* culprit, while winking at the unsanctified habits of man. So has the world wagged since the days of Abraham, when poor Sarah compelled the dismissal of Hagar.

Woman is essentially superior in her moral nature to man; her religious tendencies are more marked; her instincts nobler, purer; her moral perceptions more delicate and acute. While we cannot affirm that her feelings and affections are more profound, yet we do believe them to be more delicate and chaste. When we realize that her power underlies the whole social economy, that through it the passions of men are swayed, their emotions moved, their tastes biassed, and often their prejudices excited, we recognize the providential aspects of the case. What man can deny the overwhelming influence of woman in the social as well as domestic sphere? What *one man is there* whose life has not been more or less affected, often even directed, through a woman's influence?—a subtilely working power, but the more pervading for that. Indeed, we believe that every woman is more or less responsible not only for the earthly career, but for the eternal destiny, of some one man at least!

Woman should be man's guiding star, pointing to heaven and leading the way. Through the influence of her refined, cultivated society are developed the latent virtues, and perchance nobility, slumbering in his nature, just as the sun's rays woo the budded flower to unfold its hidden beauty. The influence and love of a good woman—alas that there are any other!—may be the means, like Jacob's ladder, through which man may be won into communion with heaven, whose purity and truth should be typified in the female character.

We would not magnify our sex to the disparagement of the other, for we honor man. Our Saviour, in assuming man's form, dignified manhood and crowned it with majesty. What in the moral world is more grand than a rich, heroic manhood, around which cluster all those noble attributes which go to make up the ideal masculine character! Like a rock he stands, immovable, strong, grand; and yet the clear, purling stream, which flows often at its side, by its gentle influence, woman-like, gradually wears into smoothness its rough points. Firm in principle, true to instincts, and faithful to all trusts, the highest type of man stands,

> " A combination and a form indeed,
> Where every god does seem to set his seal
> To give the world assurance of a man !"

COLOGNE.

Aside from the cathedral there is comparatively little of note in the old city of Cologne to entertain the traveller. Its streets are simply noticeable because they are those of a foreign city; a city once famed for its great commercial importance. Besides the cathedral there are several churches which secure at least passing attention.

Entering the church of "St. Ursula," a dreary and singular sight greets one, the walls being lined with shelves, on which are deposited a vast collection of bones, their presence explained through the following legend. St. Ursula, the daughter of a British king, accompanied by eleven thousand virgins, made a successful pilgrimage to Rome in the year 453, but on their way back they were attacked and massacred at Cologne by the Huns, while in defence of their maiden vows. Their bones were subsequently collected, and have been for many hundred years exposed to view in different portions of the church which is dedicated to the memory of their heroic death. The sight of these dried human relics is repulsive and disagreeably suggestive; and yet we would not rob the sweet innocents of the reward which is thought to be bestowed upon their virtuous memory, for

"Dear to heaven is saintly chastity."

In another church may be seen, by payment of a gratuity, Rubens's "Crucifixion of St. Peter," painted a short time before the artist's death. It is a marvellous conception of human suffering, and its perfection of form, we think, evinces a thorough knowledge of anatomy. We are aware that, by some, incorrectness in this particular is attributed to Rubens; yet the defect was perhaps manifest only in his female figures. The brilliancy of coloring which characterizes all his efforts is, in this picture, observable, although distributed with so much judgment and taste as to be effective and not obtrusive. We think we never looked upon a more powerful representation of human agony than this, and we wonder if the myth-like story told of Guido Reni's painting of the "Crucifixion" might not apply to this almost inspired effort. To paint a face with ordinary expression—in repose—requires a hand of cunning skill. But to portray in every lineament anguish unspeakable, such anguish as distorts every line of the face; the smooth curves ruffled into deep furrows; the veins swollen and knotted; the eyes protruding and glassy; the mouth drawn and tense; every vein swelling with rushing blood-currents; the limbs of the body, too, corresponding to the face in signs of mortal agony;—to accomplish all this; to make every feature, muscle, and limb eloquent with the suffering of martyrdom in its culmination of torture, must, in the absence of a model, require a genius of whose vast, almost supernatural power those who are destitute of artistic talent can have no idea. The artist's imagination must have been of abnormal development; the mental conception of almost inspired birth.

Tradition, seldom reliable, has it, that Guido Reni became so frenzied with zeal, so completely imbued with the spirit of his subject, that, catching up a stiletto, he plunged it into the body of his living model, that he might more faithfully depict the expression of dying agony upon his picture of the Saviour's face.

But to return to Rubens's picture of "St. Peter's Crucifixion." The martyr, by request, is undergoing the frightful suffering with head downward, refusing to be honored with the position in which his beloved Master had been crucified. Noble, magnanimous, loving soul, how thoroughly did he expiate the criminal weakness of the denial of his Lord! With what deep, untiring, uninterrupted devotion did he seek ever after to atone for his temporary disloyalty! How generous his atonement, how warm his love, and how sincere his sacrificing worship of Him who had forgiven and who ever loved the impetuous disciple, was proven by his subsequent experience, and by the final surrender of life itself, under circumstances of voluntary aggravation of martyrdom. The picture—whose figures are life-size—is so striking, so impressive in its delineating power, that we think a quiet contemplation of it would stimulate to warmer zeal all lukewarm followers of the blessed Saviour, who forgives like a God, and who bestows a victor's crown upon him who, conquering finally, through much tribulation, enters the Heavenly City at last!

While driving through Cologne, we are amazed to see in an upper window of a large, fine house the heads of two white wooden horses. What can it mean? We must inquire, we say, and, on doing so, are entertained, by way of explanation, with the following legend. During the year 1440, when a terrible pestilence swept over Germany, the wife of Sir Aducht fell sick of the distemper, and, dying, was hastily entombed. The cupidity of the sexton was fully aroused on seeing the costly jewels which ornamented the hands of the deceased, and he determined to divest her of such superfluous decoration. Upon visiting her tomb that night and breaking open her coffin, he was terrified to see her turn and hear her faintly sigh. Superstitious fear taking possession of him, he fled without accomplishing his purpose.

The lady, slowly recovering full consciousness, and realizing the horrors of her situation, called for help; but, no one hearing her, she stepped from her coffin, and with faltering steps sought her home.

It was at a late hour when she reached the house of her sorrowing husband, who, disturbed by the persistent knocking at the door, opened the window and demanded the business of the intruder.

" It is your wife, Richmondis, whom you buried as

dead. Oh, come quickly, dear husband, for I am overcome with fear and cold."

"You are a villain to attempt such a joke with an afflicted widower."

"No, no; I am your own living wife."

"That is as impossible as for my horses to ascend the stairs."

At that moment the heavy tread of horses' feet was heard on the stairs, and looking down he saw their two white heads projecting from one of the windows, as they gazed into the street.

Trembling with fear, he descended, and, opening the door, received into his arms the exhausted form of his beloved wife.

Both survived this wonderful event many happy years, and, to commemorate it, Sir Aducht ordered two wooden horses to be placed at the window, where they remain to this day.

The cathedral at Cologne is one of the architectural wonders of the world, and, as we stand and gaze at the elaborate intricacies of its Gothic ornamentation, we are thrilled with a renewed appreciation of the human genius that was capable of such a stupendous achievement. When we realize that to the mind of the architect must have been revealed a vision of just such a magnificent creation as this, before it could have been reduced to a definite plan; that every tower, buttress,

and pinnacle had been erected in the mind's eye; that
the whole temple, with its numberless appointments
and decorations, was reared in the vast realm of man's
imagination, before it assumed its present tangible form;
we are dumb with amazement at the palpable proof
given of the marvellous capacity of man, who surely
"*is* but a little lower than the angels." We rejoice
that this vast and mighty effort of human genius
should be so appropriately made a tribute to Him who
is the *architect of worlds!*

Within, the choir first arrests the eye. How high,
how majestic! How artistic the disposition of columns,
statues, and chapels! How exquisite the painted windows! always a bright medium through which our
thoughts are turned heavenward. For not only are
their subjects of Scriptural meaning elevating in
theme, but we, who find something sublime in color,
love to look through it up to the Divine Artist, who
has given expression to his love for his earthly creatures by painting for their delight the sky in sweet
color, the grass in reviving green, and the flowers of
the field in every hue and tint to please the eye of
man.

As we enter the cathedral one day, our ear catching
the sweet notes of music, the words of Goethe flash
upon our memory,—" Architecture is petrified music.
The tone of the mind produced by architecture ap-

proaches the effect of music." We look around us.
Have the numberless graceful pillars, the fine old
carved stalls, and all the delicate fretwork warmed into
life? and are they *singing* the beauty which has hith-
erto *mutely* appealed to us? and when rich organ-
sounds suddenly swell the melody, filling the grand
old temple, we lift our eyes to the wonderful dome,
to see if *it*, too, has become endowed with musical
expression.

While wandering through the "fretted aisles" and
splendid naves of these old churches and majestic cathedrals, we feel a thrill of gratitude for the wise pro-
vision made for devotees and for tourists, who so gladly
seek these sacred places,—the one for a whispered
prayer, beaded paternoster, or for solemn meditation,
the other for delicious revery amid the wondrous
beauty of pictured walls, frescoed ceilings, painted windows, and the lofty, statuesque, and grand in architecture.   Is not beauty an accessory to worship? is it not
a true and beautiful medium, by which our thought is
borne heavenward to that Divine Essence of all beauty
which fills the eternal spheres?   What more appropriate place to seek the Divine benison; to meditate
upon holy things; to renew covenant vows; to seek a
blessing on some new plan; to offer our children anew
upon the altar of God's love and mercy; and to recon-
secrate our future lives to His service, than a church?

Why should *our* churches be closed during the week? Would we not tread the solitary aisles and seek the vacant pew with different emotions on the weekday, from those we feel on the Sabbath when surrounded by a bustling throng of worshippers?

Silence conduces to devotional feeling; a solemn gloom enshrouds the holy place; we feel alone with our conscience and our Maker. Who can tell what sanctifying influences, won through such peaceful communion within the hallowed walls, may go with us as we return to the outside world refreshed and strengthened in the inner man?

Then let us *never close the doors of our churches*, thus inviting to a silent altar, within walls dedicated to the Hearer of prayer, the worn and wearied soul, him who, weak in faith, would rally his spiritual forces, and those who, suffering in mind, seek relief at the foot of the cross, amid the hallowed quiet of the sanctuary. No, never close the churches, when even to the careless visitor their sacred associations suggest holy themes, and that worship which should fill the soul,—the truest Temple of God.

> " Are there no sinners in the churchless week
> Who wish to sanctify a vowed repentance?
> Are there no hearts bereft, which fain would seek
> The only balm for death's unpitying sentence?
> Why are they shut?

" Are there no poor, no wronged, no heirs of grief,
 No sick who, when their strength or courage falters,
Long for a moment's respite or relief,
 By kneeling at the God of mercy's altars?
   Why are they shut?

" If there be one—one only—who might share
 This sanctifying weekday adoration,
Were but our churches open to his prayer,
 Why,—I demand with earnest iteration,—
   Why are they shut?"

CHAPTER XV.

LONDON—SPURGEON—HAMPTON COURT.

LONDON.

THE compartment of the first-class car in which we
travel to London, capable of accommodating eight persons, is delightfully spacious and comfortable, and if
by chance no stranger is introduced to it, a company of
friends may enjoy themselves in unrestrained converse,
or a husband and wife be treated to a domestic *tête-à-
tête*. At intervals in the winter season the guard places
a long tin, filled with hot water, under the feet, this
being the only means of conveying heat, proving sufficient for the climate.

Arrived at London and established at our hotel, we
hasten to look about us, and are not disappointed
to find our eyes resting upon the building which is
of absorbing interest to all lovers of the ancient, the
historic, and the sacred,—Westminster Abbey. Here
history finds illustration in the presence of those who
made it; here art seeks its noblest representation in
those works of genius which, as monuments to the

great dead, line the walls and fill the niches; here science, philosophy, prose, and poetry receive admiring recognition through the marvellous tributes of the sculptor to their interpreters and exponents; here the renowned military hero is made through defiant mien and uplifted sword, to "fight his battles o'er again." The "sacred preacher" is presented to us in his clerical robes; Shakspeare, the king of the drama, is "winding the clock of his wit," as he stands before us in thoughtful attitude. Milton, who by his inspired imagination has opened Paradise to our delighted vision, is, through his blind eyes, seeming to pierce heavenly mysteries. Chaucer, the ancient "father" of the art we love, lies in effigy before us. Addison, whose liquid prose will ever continue to fascinate the cultivated mind; Macaulay, whose rich and massive style amply rewards the reader; and Scott, through whose weird, ingenious, and unequalled fancy we tread baronial halls, consort with kings and queens, are made to join in the revelries and mingle in the battles of bygone ages, are all, with many others, introduced to us in sculptured forms.

"A dim religious light," appropriate to such a hallowed sanctuary, pervades the gloomy aisles and chapels, and one feels almost oppressed, as if with the burdened memories of the great past, whose mighty ghosts seem stalking by our side; and with the richness of the present age, whose heroes of political and military renown and its giants in intellect slumber by the side of the illustrious of early times.

In one of the chapels, called The Confessor's, are the chairs used for the coronation of English sovereigns, in one of which is enclosed the famous stone of Scone, the coronation-seat of the kings of Scotland, brought to England by Edward I. in the year 1296.

Westminster Abbey is built in the form of a cross, and is the more interesting as it cannot be said to be of any one style of architecture, presenting specimens of many forms, from the Anglo-Saxon to Early Renaissance. "A Gothic church," Victor Hugo declares to be "a sublime book"; but what could be more worthy of the comparison than this venerable shrine?—a volume to be read, studied, pondered, and re-read again and again. One feels, in wandering through the aisles whose vault is so lofty and of such marvellous execution, and between columns that cluster like massive trees in a forest, that the architectural art has here attained its triumph, and that 'tis fitting that pilgrims should come from distant lands to marvel at its intricacies and to acknowledge its successes.

London, the largest city in the world, presents a singular conglomeration, in its architecture, of the antiquated and modern. The English, unlike the French, take great pleasure in retaining their old buildings;

doing little to remodel them. Immensely tall, ungraceful edifices, covered with the must of ages, frown down upon us everywhere. Time and the atmosphere—so damp and foggy—seem to vie with each other in producing a dark, blackened appearance upon brick and mortar, which gives the city a sombre aspect; indeed, London requires the most unmitigated sunlight to brighten it, and would absorb much more than nature often affords it. Brick is seldom painted here, because the prevailing humidity soon obliterates all colors—but black.

Let the Englishman sit down in his pride and enjoy the appearance of antiquity which the crumbling tiled houses, with their moss-covered and grimmed surfaces, give his famous city; we of America will have the nobler satisfaction of seeing in freshly-hewn marble, in granite, and in iron, the hand of progress traced in all our cities. But while we give America the preference in this respect, we would that we might imitate the example which the English set us in the profound reverence and homage they pay to their buried heroes. Not a park, square,—in which London abounds,—or public edifice, but contains the carved or mounted effigy of their great dead. Why should not we, triumphant America, pay such honor to *our* great generals, intellectual giants, and political leaders? why should not Washington, Jefferson, Adams, Clay, Webster, and

others, who reflected by the light of their great intellects and by their patriotic services glory upon our
country, be thus remembered in all our larger cities?
And on enduring brass, or in marble pure and unspotted as his fame, let the grand record of the country's
latest idol and martyred President be written in letters
of gold, that the youth of future generations may pause
to read and admire the story of a man great in his good-
ness, wise in his simplicity, honest in his convictions,
and resolute in his will. All hail to the memory of
our martyred dead!

One is often tempted to criticise the physical Englishman as seen on the promenade, and wonder that he
is so heavy and ungraceful in his build, so unlike in
appearance his more attractive neighbor, the Frenchman, who is lithe, easy, and elegant in person and
movement. The English in their human structure
exhibit the solidity and compactness which are characteristic also of the style of their architecture, and to
view them generally, one would imagine all ideality to
be buried in a hallowed corner—the poets'—in that
revered old pile, Westminster Abbey.

We have always thought of Spurgeon and Beecher
as being the representative preachers of the orthodox
faith in England and America, and were naturally
desirous of seeing and hearing the English clerical
orator, having often been the amused, if not benefited,

listener of the American apostle. We say amused, for
ofttimes we have seen the serenity of a vast congregation disturbed by a ripple of mirth which threatened to
culminate in a wave of laughter, under the influence of
the grotesque contortions of Beecher's singularly mobile
features, and of a humor so genuine as to prove irresistible.

One beautiful Sabbath morning we attempt to find
" The Tabernacle," as Spurgeon's church is called.
It is situated in Surrey District, quite removed from
the heart of London. Arrived at our destination, we
find ourselves at the doors of a very plain, but immense, building, which, large as it is, accommodates
with difficulty the crowds who flock to hear the great
preacher.

Entering, we see that the interior is as conspicuously
plain as the exterior, with capacity for seating four
thousand four hundred persons. The pulpit is simply
a very elevated platform, on which are placed a table
and a chair. With almost incredible rapidity the
church becomes packed, taxing to the utmost the efforts
of the courteous ushers. Turning to one of them, we
ask if the crowd is always as large. "Oh, yes," is the
answer; "although I have rented a pew here for many
years, I never find a place in it to sit, unless our pastor
is absent." "You experience the inconvenience," we
say, "of having one of the most popular preachers of

the day, a man whose reputation is as well established
in our country, over the sea, as here." He seems
pleased with the assurance, and makes many inquiries
about Beecher, as if associating the two men, as the
world seems involuntarily to do.

Seated in a front pew of the gallery, we can command a fine view of the entire congregation. It presents an interesting study ; a large number are strangers
from our own land, brought together by a common
desire to see and hear the man who "sits high in the
opinion" of the Christian world, whose talents and
powers, whatever they may be, are never supplemented
by any oratorical trickery or flourish, no trace of the
clap-trap sensationalism, of which we believe Beecher
also to be innocent, but through which a pulpit, near
his own, is so shamelessly notorious.

What a sea of faces! Could any man stand before
such an immense audience and not feel intellectual fire
kindle within him, its sparks lighting up a sympathetic
enthusiasm in the *hearers* as well? Must not an orator
be stimulated to a species of inspiration as he looks
down upon a waiting multitude? And if "the root
of the matter" is in him, does not the glow of spiritual
life within take on new warmth, as he feeds the hungry
souls before him with a feast of delectable things?
bearing them on the tide of his eloquence to that great
ocean of thought,—the plan of redemption,—finally

bringing them to the haven of rest, the foot of the cross.

A lull,—eager expectation expressed in attitudes and faces, and the preacher enters! A short, thick-set man, of unwieldy proportions and ungainly figure, with a face heavy, but not dull; a brown eye, not naturally bright, but lighting up on occasion; a countenance altogether expressive of genial benevolence, but, we think, not of mental power. After reading the Scripture, expounding its meaning at great length, he offers prayer. And here is his power manifest. It seems to us that, through its earnest reverence of tone, its persuasive appeal, its imploring importunity, its sincere but not abject humility with its prevailing spirit of worshipful devotion, it *must* win a heavenly benediction; nor are ours the only moist eyes at its conclusion. Such a prayer, one of the most remarkable we have ever heard, would plough deep into any heart, however hard and sterile, preparing it for the sowing of the seed so abundantly scattered by the sermon which follows.

Ah, what a sermon! It is based upon the text, "Who forgiveth all thine iniquities." Clear, logical, and conclusive is his reasoning, not beyond the comprehension of the most ordinary mind or of an intelligent child, but containing the germ of rich thought, and showing much originality in its treatment. His argument is lucid and systematic, his rhetoric remark-

able for its simplicity, and his oratory evidently the
result only of impulse, the truest guide, and not of pre-
meditated study. We venture to say that "every head
with a heart to it, and every heart with a head to it,
answers to the appeal" which closes the never-to-be-
forgotten sermon.

Many must be enamored of the grace and beauty of
a good and noble life as he pictures it, and many, too,
conceive a greater aversion to sin as they listen to his
vivid portrayal of its penalties and horrors. Like
Dryden's "Good Parson," "he preaches the joys of
heaven and pains of hell" with a graphic power that
wins us to the hope of the one and fills us with increased
dread of the other.

And yet it is difficult to analyze his power and discover wherein lies the secret of his unwaning popu-
larity. No appeal is ever intentionally made to the
humorous element of our nature during his discourses,
and while wit does not tickle, neither is fancy made to
allure our senses through *its* charm. His efforts are
characterized by an intense earnestness, united with a
full purpose of heart and an unswerving adherence to
the simple tenets of the most orthodox creed. A keen
insight into the heart of man, a knowledge of its workings, gives him the power to attack successfully its
weakest points, and to "discover to ourselves that of
ourselves which we knew not of."

His is a thoroughly well balanced mind and character, a remarkably-developed common sense restraining him from the commission of those petty follies which impair a minister's usefulness, as flaws in the precious diamond depreciate its value in the estimation of the world.

His private life—if such a man may be said to have one—defies the investigation of even an enemy, and is as unblemished and beautiful in its consistency as the most carping critic could demand.

How rarely discovered is such a human jewel, a well-rounded character! An intellect and power deep enough to sustain and feed a great reputation year after year; thoughts constantly bubbling forth from the unfailing fountain of his heart and mind, which, by their clearness, force, and beauty, command the admiration of the learned as well as the unlettered; a will so strong and a principle so well grounded as to remain unshaken through the vicissitudes of a comparatively long life, resisting all the temptation which assails even the purest soul; a faith so firmly established on the "Rock of Ages" as never to be blown into those heresies which, to say the least, are innovations upon the rigorous simplicity and purity of our grand creed.

With a morbidly sensitive nervous system, over-wrought by the exorbitant demands made upon it, and a body much of the time tortured by pain, he performs herculean labors, seeming to act upon the conviction that the harvest-time in which to garner *his* sheaves will be short, seeing probably a cloud in the sky which, now no larger than a man's hand, may ere long burst in storm upon his devoted head.

During a personal interview with Mr. Spurgeon we discover his social powers and manner to be as charming as his pulpit efforts are edifying.

HAMPTON COURT.

One of those sunny, exquisite views that memory loves often to reproduce, and which defy time's obliterating power, is that of the Thames from Richmond Terrace. But the vista, so beautiful, opens to us *many* features that help to adorn a landscape. Were the soul tempest-tossed, it would learn a lesson of repose and peacefulness that would allay its unrest and lull it into a tranquillity such as the eye there dwells upon, for we believe that the spirit of every lover of Nature catches its tone and is in harmony with it. When shadows fill the sky, dimming its brightness, and the air is murky and heavy with gloom, is not the spirit burdened and oppressed? Or when the sun lights up the face of Nature with its cheerful beams, the atmosphere bright and electric, does not the soul catch its glow and reflect its warmth?

And should the birds, through whose joyous notes Nature expresses her jubilance, fill the air with their thrilling melody, the very soul, in sympathetic accord, bursts into glad song, the human heart beating in unison with the great pulse of Nature.

The carriage stops as we reach the favored spot, and we alight, the better to enjoy a scene which is considered by some to offer one of the finest views of the Thames in England. But as the sky is not satisfied with its grand luminary, the moon, but calls to its aid the auxiliary light of the stars, so Nature to the beauties of the Thames has added those of meadow, brook, hill, and copse, which are not unworthy of bordering the train of her graceful sweep. The queenly river is seen in the distance meandering through the landscape, while between it and us is a pastoral view of such beauty as fully vindicates its fame. We look upon the rich bordering meadows, where cattle lazily browse under the shadow of spreading trees; gentle undulations displaying to advantage their beautiful green; trees of every shade and many varieties; the hawthorn and other shrubs vying with them in luxuriance; and gliding streams embroidering, as with silver threads, the velvety green of the pastures. The sun, as if jealous of other beautifying influences, seems determined to embellish with superb skill a scene so fair, and we stand admiring the pencilled lines of light and shade, observing that the beauty before us is much enhanced by the coquettish play of shadow and sunbeam.

Driving a mile and a half through the broad avenue of Bushey Park, we enjoy the remarkable sight of a double row, on each side, of immense horse-chestnut-trees. We believe it would be impossible to find another such display of trees.

Hampton Court Palace, at which this avenue ends, was built by Cardinal Wolsey, who presented it to Henry VIII. It was afterwards a favorite residence of Oliver Cromwell, and was enlarged by William III. The splendor of the furniture and of the apartments has faded out, but the paintings, chiefly by Benjamin West, are very fine. The grandest apartment of the palace, we think, is Wolsey's Great Hall. This, of Gothic architecture, is noble in size. The carving of the ceiling is remarkably intricate and beautiful, and the stained glass of the windows is in keeping. The Hall is hung with very ancient tapestry, representing scenes from the life of Abraham.

The signs of dilapidation, decay, and forlornness pervading this once magnificent apartment, and, indeed, every portion of the interior of the palace, are symbolical of the complete ruin and disaster which overtook its founder. History hardly affords another such example of vaulting ambition, daring assumption of royal state and prerogative, and the extreme arrogance which is their natural outgrowth, as the life of this unspiritual prelate exhibits; presenting a drama whose gorgeous acts were in such singular contrast to the pitiable drop-scene which closed all to human vision. What school-boy is not familiar with the pathetic words which Shakspeare borrowed from the dying utterances of the once haughty cardinal, when his "fallen greatness" had succeeded his unparalleled prosperity?

The gardens are delightful, offering the variety of lawn, shaded walks, and flowers, with terraces which overlook the river. In a conservatory is to be seen the largest grape-vine, it is thought, in the world. It measures one hundred and ten feet in the extent of its branches from the stem; the principal stem having a circumference of nearly thirty inches. It often bears three thousand bunches a year, and these are sent to the Queen.

There the fruit hangs in rich, purple clusters. Tantalus-like, we see it swaying before our eyes but beyond our grasp. Was Eve tempted thus? Alas! if so, she has been too harshly condemned.

"Will you not sell us at least a leaf of this wonderful vine as a souvenir?" we plead with the keeper. "Oh, no, not for any amount of money," he replies. "I might make my fortune quickly if I accepted all the bribes offered me; but, you see, it belongs to the Queen."

Turning from the coveted fruit, we cannot withhold our commendation of his incorruptible honesty, which, whether it originates from innate principle or from policy, we feel should be encouraged.

CHAPTER XVI.

WINDSOR CASTLE—STOKE-POGIS—THE DAIRYMAN'S DAUGHTER.

WINDSOR CASTLE.

TAKING the train at London, we arrive at Windsor after an hour's pleasant ride. The castle, as one approaches it, presents a grandly imposing appearance, being one of the most magnificent royal palaces in the world. It is difficult for one unaccustomed to monarchical institutions to associate a *home* with such a mammoth pile.

As we thread its grand corridors and walk through its vast apartments,—almost lost in immensity,—realizing its capacity to accommodate the inhabitants of an ordinary-sized village, we think that the possessor of a cosy home, whose sacred privacy is its chief charm; whose walls are so near that one may realize their encircling protection; whose fireside is a snug retreat from the weary exactions of social life; where one may foster those sweet domestic tastes which seek the shade of retirement and avoid the glare of public

240

life, would scarce covet such a home as this and other
kingly palaces afford; shrinking from their dreary
vastness and stately grandeur, for the joys of home-life
are essentially simple in their nature.

The dining-rooms are grand banqueting-halls; the
sleeping-apartments in their loftiness and spaciousness
suggesting to modesty a desire for the privacy which
they do not seem to afford. But we remember that
the occupants were bred amid such scenes, and that
their tastes may require just such pompous surroundings for their fullest gratification.

The castle, the embodiment of solidity and vast
proportions, with its thirteen turrets and round tower
or keep in the centre; its elevation, overlooking the
Thames for many miles; its beautiful terraces, park,
and gardens, helps to realize our early imaginings of a
castle palace.

The chapel in which the royal nuptials are celebrated, and which, from all its associations, must be
very interesting, is closed for extensive repairs. We
enjoy, however, the privilege of a visit to the private
chapel which has been erected by the Queen as a memorial to the Prince Consort. It is ostentatious and
costly. The floor and walls are formed of a mosaic of
the richest marbles of many colors, with texts of Scripture inserted in each panel. White marble statuary
and exceedingly beautiful stained glass add to its

effective beauty. On a marble bier in the centre of the chapel lies the effigy of the noble man, who was in every way worthy of the affectionate honor paid his memory.

Every patriotic American may well drop a tear at the sepulchre of him, who was to our country a staunch friend in her hour of need, anticipating, through his clear-sighted and far-seeing judgment, in the grand result of our conflict, the glorious vindication of divine justice and human right.

Taking a carriage, we ride to Eton Hall and view its venerable, classic walls. This famous school has nurtured much youthful genius which has ripened later into splendid maturity, as many distinguished men, in the varied professions, have been its pupils. The hall, being situated on the opposite side of the Thames, forms, with its "distant spires and antique towers," a pleasing prospect from the castle.

Driving farther on, we come to the village of Stoke-Pogis, where the poet Gray lived for many years, and where he is buried.

STOKE-POGIS.

At the close of a busy day, as the sun is filling the western sky with its departing glory; the air full of dim shadows; the sweet notes of the birds dying away; all nature sinking into an early repose, we stand by the little gate which opens into the graveyard where Gray wrote his immortal "Elegy." It is a quiet and impressive scene, all the influences of the hour harmonizing with it, and so in accordance with the spirit of the poem, that we involuntarily listen for "the curfew" to toll "the knell of parting day." There is the little church, with its pretty tower, peeping forth from amid its ivy mantle; the vine of luxuriant growth, enfolding the whole church with its tendrils, imparts to the simple architecture a picturesque beauty which lacks no charm.

Opposite, and overshadowing the rustic porch, is the yew-tree under whose drooping branches we stand, recalling to mind the exquisite poem which had delighted our childhood, and which, unlike most youthful tastes, has not lost in maturer life its sweet flavor. Surrounding us are the " narrow cells" of the " rude forefathers." Conspicuous among them is the tomb of the poet who made this rural little graveyard an object of tender regard to the world. It is of plain brick, covered with a slab of slate, on which is the following inscription, written by Gray, in memory of his mother and aunt, whose death preceded his:

" In the vault beneath are deposited, in hope of a joyful resurrection, the remains of Mary Antrobus. She died unmarried, Nov. 5th, 1749, aged sixty-six. In the same pious confidence, beside her friend and sister, here sleep the remains of Dorothy

Gray, widow; the tender, careful mother of many children, one of whom alone had the misfortune to survive her. She died March 11th, 1758, aged sixty-seven."

A tablet inserted in the wall of the church, opposite the tomb, records the fact that the poet also is buried here. Near the churchyard stands a monument erected to his memory. It is of freestone, consisting of a sarcophagus supported upon a square pedestal. On each side are inscriptions taken from his poems.

With lingering step we walk down the narrow path lined on each side by lowly mounds; and, leaning over the little gate, strive to photograph on heart and memory the sweet and lovely picture. The simple beauty of the scene is heightened by its quiet seclusion. No noisy hum of human voices disturbs the "solemn stillness" of the dead, whose very dust is so sacred; no busy haunts of men crowd upon the view; only the natural beauty of the green-spreading "lea," the venerable trees, the circling hedges, and an occasional pretty cottage, meeting the eye.

THE DAIRYMAN'S DAUGHTER.

Taking a carriage at Ventnor, on the Isle of Wight, we drive to Newport, making a détour to visit the cottage of the "Dairyman's Daughter" at Arreton, and the graveyard beyond, where she lies buried.

We fall into a pleasing revery as we ride through

the quiet country roads, bordered on both sides by arable fields enclosed by green hawthorn hedges. And here let us testify to this pretty feature in the English landscape, as being infinitely preferable to our own unpicturesque rail fences.

We think of the strangeness of our mission: for weeks and months we have journeyed, turning here and there aside to visit some renowned spot memorable in the history of the country and of the world; many grand cathedrals, superb in architecture, and wondrous in age; many storied ruins which have withstood the havoc of time, and are standing in mute eloquence to tell of the grandeur and opulence of former ages; and many palaces of royalty, glittering in gold and ornament, yet cheerless in their vastness. Many times, too, have we stood by the ostentatious monuments of the dead, whose living celebrity finds commemoration in death through the display of richest marble shaped by rare skill. But now we, in common with others, are seeking a grave so humble that one must look sharply to find it; no marble sarcophagus, or imposing pillar of granite, distinguishing it above the simple slabs marking the surrounding mounds; the grave, too, of a lowly uneducated girl, whose humble home, a few miles distant, is also a shrine for the pilgrim.

What a triumph is this for truth and piety! As we bow reverently over the slumbering dead, we are paying our humble tribute to the grandeur of that Christian faith which found such powerful exemplification in the character of the humble " Dairyman's Daughter." The name of the dead, and the respective dates of her birth and death, are preceded by the following lines written by her honored biographer, Legh Richmond:

" Stranger! if e'er, by chance or feeling led,
Upon this hallowed turf thy footsteps tread,
Turn, think on her whose spirit rests with God.
Lowly her lot on earth, but He who bore
Tidings of grace and blessings to the poor
Gave her this truth and faithfulness, to prove
The choicest treasures of His boundless love—
Faith, that dispelled affliction's darkest gloom;
Hope, that could cheer the passage to the tomb;
Peace, that not Hell's dark regions could destroy;
And love, that filled the soul with heavenly joy;
Death, of its sting disarmed, she knew no fear,
But tasted Heaven e'en while she lingered here.
O happy saint! may we, like thee, be blest,
In life be faithful, and in death find rest!"

Filled with solemn thought, we turn away and enter the plain old church, which is enclosed within the small graveyard; here the pew is pointed out where the youthful saint sat beneath the eye of that earnest exponent of gospel truth, her pastor at one time, and subsequently her biographer.

The cottage where her simple life was passed is of

very humble construction; low, with a thatched roof, and covered still with clambering vines, which festoon the small windows, darkening the little family room, into which the front door opens. A shed attached to one end of the cottage, where the dairyman sheltered the few cows which afforded him his meagre support, still offers protection to "lowly kine." We open the little wicket-gate and ascend the walk which leads to the cottage. Homely domestic plants line the simple flagging and fill the narrow flower-beds beside the door at which we knock. We wait long, trembling lest our pilgrimage should prove unsuccessful, and then, repeating our rap, hear unwilling steps approach from within. An old woman opens narrowly the door and scans us ungraciously. We tell her we have come from far to see the home of the " Dairyman's Daughter," and hope she will gratify us, expressing our willingness to compensate her for the trouble. "No," she says; "hundreds come here to see the house, and I am not well, and have decided that I will refuse everybody." Seeing the disappointment her words produce, she relents so far as to say, "You can look in this room if you like," stepping aside that we may see, without giving us the opportunity of entering.

It is a small, square apartment, with very low ceiling, and having the ordinary appearance of a cottager's family room. Gladly would we mount the narrow

stairs to the chamber where the almost sainted spirit
"exhaled its flight to heaven," believing that the chamber where the pious soul meets its fate

> "Is privileged beyond the common walks
> Of virtuous life, quite in the verge of heaven."

And although the pure presence of her who made
this place sacred by association has long since fled, yet
the aroma of a good life lingers like the perfume of a
rare rose long after its leaves have withered and died.
Sanctity seems to pervade the place, and it is almost
prayerfully that we turn from the humble shrine,
plucking a leaf from the vine which shelters the little
window.

CHAPTER XVII.

XFORD—KENILWORTH—HADDON HALL—CHATS-
WORTH.

OXFORD.

OXFORD owes its celebrity chiefly to the University,
hich is one of the most famed institutions for learning,
ot only in England, but of the world. To be a grad-
ate of Oxford, or of Cambridge as well, is a literary
istinction of which England's greatest men are proud,
ieir honors ennobling any name.

The city is situated at the confluence of the two rivers
sis and Cherwell, and near the Thames; their waters
ffording facilities for the indulgence of boating exer-
se, so dear to collegiate youths in these days; some,
is to be feared, engaging more eagerly in those
quatic sports than in slaking thirst at the fountain
f knowledge. The large extent of beautiful rich
ieadow-land which lies between the rivers and the
ty affords pretty rural views for the book-wearied
res of the students to rest upon; for how grateful to
re and brain is it, when both are "worn and hard

12   249

beset," to gaze upon the sweet repose and fresh bright face of Nature! How oft, when the mind is wearied, the memory burdened, the thought perplexed, and the mental vision dimmed with the arduous study which also brings "weariness to the flesh," is rest obtained, and even inspiration won, in walking abroad in the woods, "whose very air is holy"! in looking upon the dewy freshness of leaf and grass and upon broad flowering meadows, Nature's easel, where the colors, richly combined, bring brightness to the spirit and delight to the eye!

As the University comprises nineteen colleges and five halls, we think it best to visit two of the most prominent; selecting, by advice, Magdalen and Christ Colleges as representative ones. Each college and hall forms a separate establishment of itself, having its own students and teachers, and yet all are subject to the government of the University. Its origin is lost in obscurity, many supposing that it was founded by that good and wise king and patron of letters, Alfred the Great. Some fix its date considerably later; but, however this may be, that its extreme age entitles it to our reverence none can doubt.

We find the classic halls deserted, as the summer's vacation is yet in progress, and therefore, being apparently "monarchs of all we survey," we linger long amid scenes to which time itself has given distinction, and with which we can associate much of the talent which for centuries has adorned the literature, parliament, and pulpit of England.

The college buildings form a quadrangle, the students' apartments being around it. As we enter the court of Magdalen College, we are surprised into general exclamation: the air is literally burdened with the perfume of the sweet-brier; never were we conscious of odor more heavy and pervading. Stepping forward, a pretty, picturesque little view presents itself. We penetrate into the inner court, and there, entwining each pillar and interlacing the spaces, is the sweet-brier whose delicious fragrance ministered to our delight ere we had discovered its source. The luxuriant vine gives grace to the quaint old architecture of the ornamented walls, which throw their shadow upon a plat of pretty green grass.

The dining-hall shown us is really very elegant, the wainscoting of richly-polished walnut; fine portraits embellishing its surface. The professor's table, occupying one end of the dining-room, is placed on a raised platform, the students' tables occupying the main floor.

The grounds pertaining to this college, including a deer-park, are more beautiful and extensive than those belonging to any other. We hasten to see the shaded avenue which is said to have been the favorite walk of Addison while a student here. We notice particularly

the luxuriant growth of the hawthorn, equalling that
of a full-sized tree, and many other rich varieties of
foliage. We can imagine that the contemplative mind
of the graceful essayist would find congenial influences
amid such natural beauties as here feasted his eyes and
soul, his gentle spirit, refined thought, and cultivated
mind seeking nutriment from Nature's inexhaustible
sources. Who, indeed, has ever drained them, or, hun-
gering and thirsting for divine knowledge, spiritual
strength, or mental suggestion, has left her grand cathedral, with its spired trees, towering hills, and dome of
blue, that did not feel elevated by the worship, armed
for life's moral conflicts, and equipped for intellectual
victories?

As the Magdalen is the most beautiful and picturesque, so Christ College is the largest and grandest.
Its chapel, dating from 1154, is very curious in its
ancient tombs, and elegant in its more modern features.
Its architecture is chiefly Norman-Gothic, although
many later styles have been introduced.

Riding through the old city, our driver halts, and,
pointing to a stone in the middle of a street, declares it
to be the identical spot where the aged martyrs Latimer
and Ridley were burned at the stake. The flat stone
inserted there to identify the spot is in the shape of a
cross. Farther on, in St. Giles Street, is the "Martyrs'
Memorial." Unfortunately, the narrowness of the street

in which they so heroically met their cruel fate would not admit of the erection of the grand monument. Its inscription includes the name of Cranmer, who was subjected to a similar martyrdom six months later.

A remarkable fact in connection with the death of Latimer and Ridley is related in history of Bishop Gardiner, whose animosity towards these saintly men was such that he declared on the day of their death that he would not dine, until he received information that fire was set to the fagots with which they were to be burned.

The information not reaching him as soon as expected, the Duke of Norfolk, who was his guest that day, was compelled to wait for his dinner from eleven o'clock, the usual dinner-hour, until three o'clock. But the wicked, bigoted bishop was destined not to partake of the dinner, for when it was served, on the arrival of the longed-for intelligence, he was taken suddenly ill, and, being put to bed, soon died.

KENILWORTH.

So successful was Walter Scott in investing Kenilworth Castle, through his delightful novel, with romantic charm, that while preparing to visit its famous ruins we find scenes from the sad history of Amy Robsart are floating on our minds and becoming entangled in our thoughts.

In tracing the origin of the castle we learn that it was founded by Geoffrey de Clinton, chamberlain and treasurer to Henry I. Most of the buildings now extant were erected by John of Gaunt, father of Henry IV. Continuing in possession of the crown, Elizabeth bestowed it upon Robert Dudley, Earl of Leicester, who is said to have expended sixty thousand pounds upon its enlargement and decoration, and with fabulous munificence to have entertained here his enamored sovereign and her court for seventeen days.

What must this princely abode and ancient stronghold have been in the days of its prime, when now in its decay it commands our wondering admiration, astonishing us with its mammoth proportions and remains of architectural beauty!

So formidable is the entrance that, as we apply for admittance, we almost expect to be challenged by an armed sentry; instead of which a meek-eyed woman opens the portals to us. Passing through, we soon confront the grand mass of ruins. What a tale they tell of ancient prowess and grandeur! Built on a knoll, they are the more imposing. Cæsar's tower, or the keep, stands on one side, and, being compact, solid, and intact, looks grand in its strength. There it has stood for ages, frowning down upon the peaceful village and smiling landscape. Its walls are of almost incredible thickness, and are completely covered with a vine whose

root is of a size we never saw equalled in the ivy.
The central ruin consists mainly of the banqueting-hall,
whose architectural ornamentation is the greatest attraction of the ruins. The lofty casements, curtained by
drooping vines, are exquisite in symmetry and grace.
As we gaze upon these relics of bygone splendor, involuntarily we repeople the deserted banquet-hall with the
old-time chivalry and with the grace and beauty of the
court. A glittering pageant flashes upon our view,—
the haughty earl, host to the virgin queen, leading with
her the courtly train ; a brilliant company in dazzling
array, representing the highest nobility of the land;
gay courtiers and high-born dames with stately tread
brush past; and penetrating the royal scene our fancy
has conjured, comes the thought of the unhappy Amy
left in the neighboring town by her faithful escort,
Hamilton.

But we are rudely restored to our identity by the
summons to clamber up a flight of stairs that one of
our party has discovered, resuming as hastily as may
be our rôle of modern tourist. The interior of the
remainder of the castle fails to reward prolonged inspection, for, having been built originally as a stronghold, it seems truly more like a fortress than a palace-
home.

How strange indeed it is that Elizabeth, who displayed so much masculine strength and decision of

character in the administration of public affairs, who proved her penetrating sagacity in the choice of her prime ministers and other officers of government, adopting so sound a policy in her monarchical relations, exercising so wise and beneficent a judgment as to win the admiring approval of the world then, and the more dispassionate verdict of all time since, should have proved herself to be the *weakest of women* in matters of the heart! The history of her emotional experience evinces a positive craving for love and its joys, and had it not been for the equally marked love of power, —and between these rival desires there was a constant struggle and conflict,—she would have probably married one of the three noblemen upon whom she lavished her regard. And, after all, did not the feminine element of her nature prevail in the end, when, ambition forgotten, affairs of state neglected, womanly dignity laid aside, self-respect, even, forfeited, she literally died of a remorse born of love?

Is not woman always happier as *queen in the home*-life,—her kingdom, the family circle; her sceptre, the wand of love; her loving subjects, the children whose early will she is to control, character to mould, mind to cultivate, and heart to sow with seed that shall spring up, blossom, and bear rich fruit for time and for eternity?

HADDON HALL AND CHATSWORTH.

"Look on this picture, then on that."

Haddon Hall and Chatsworth are representative illustrations of the homes of the powerful and rich of olden and of modern times. The former is a remarkably preserved baronial castle, built in the reign of Edward III. Soon after the Conquest it came into possession of the Vernon family, whose last male descendant died in the seventh year of Queen Elizabeth's reign. Haddon then fell into the hands of the family of Manners, whom the Duke of Rutland now represents. It occupies a bold, elevated position, and is an absorbing object in the landscape.

At the foot of the hill on which it is built is the humble but pretty cottage in which the custodian of the castle lives. While waiting for the attendant to don her fashionably-made panniered dress, we examine the exterior of the colossal structure. It seems in its strength able to resist the most belligerent assailants, and we contrast the domestic experiences of its original occupants, who were compelled to live within entrenched walls of such massive thickness as would repel armed hosts, and to challenge each comer as though he were a foe, with the peaceful serenity of present home-life, when the English nobleman may " live under his own vine and fig-tree," " with none to

molest or make him afraid;" no watchman necessary
to give hasty warning of the approaching enemy; and
instead of soldierly retainers, liveried servants; and
in lieu of bristling walls of impregnable strength, the
beautiful flowering hedge, offering no bar, but embellishing the fields it encloses with its simple blossom
and pretty green.

The somewhat elaborate toilet of the guide completed, she appears with keys in hand, inviting us to
an inspection of the curious old castle. First we are
shown a little room where, on a rude wooden table, are
a pair of clumsy, heavy long boots, which, tradition
affirms, once encased the legs of that rugged soldier—
and, we believe, honest patriot—Oliver Cromwell.
This small room, somewhat apart from the main building, is thought to have been occupied by the priest of
the household. Why this *sacred* appendage to the
establishment was needed it is difficult to determine,
unless the clerical wink and convivial aid in their riotous bacchanalian revelries gave spiritual sanction to
their excesses!

Farther on we enter the chapel, merely an ordinary
apartment with a plain ancient pulpit and rough
wooden benches. We visit next the large rambling
kitchen, noting particularly its crude arrangements. A
large, round block covered with deep indentations, just
such as is used now by butchers; fireplaces large enough

to roast whole oxen, which we read were necessary to supply the daily demands of the garrison-like families who occupied the castles of olden times. A *very large* receptacle for holding salt completes the contents of the kitchen. Contiguous to it is the banqueting-hall. Oh, how rough and crude its appointments!

Near the door, on the wall, is an iron ring, in which the arm of him who failed to drink his allotted share of the "good cheer" was upheld, while cold water was poured down his sleeve until he would promise to drink that portion which he had neglected to imbibe at table.

After wandering through long series of chambers above, bare, desolate, and despoiled, we turn away, glad that the ancient landmark has been spared to grace the landscape, but thankful that the march of civilization has improved domestic habits, lives, and homes, so that now we may enjoy those refining influences, such as will, in their highest development, be found in the modern residence of the Duke of Devonshire.

CHATSWORTH

is the famed country-seat of the Duke of Devonshire. We ride for a long time through a vast area of country—uncultivated, apparently lying waste—belonging to this powerful and wealthy family.

Land-monopoly is the great curse of this fair country. A relic of feudal times, it is not consistent with

the march of intelligent progress.   Now that the evils
of the law of entail are being recognized by some of
its very subjects, we feel that perhaps, even in our own
time, the many idle hands of the worthy poor will be
guiding the plough over the waste soil now in the possession of the few, winning sustenance from its resources for the general good.

As the *masses* are the substrata of social life, under-
lying the upper crust, we believe that a recognition by
them of the great national evil will, by producing an
agitation, shake the foundation and cause to crumble,
and finally overthrow, an institution so disastrous to
the welfare of the majority.   Any national error preju-
dicing the interests of the masses is like a sore on the
body politic, which, festering and gathering force, will
sooner or later burst, and exuding from its core the
corruption, will finally heal the nation of that which
impedes its progress toward a *healthful* national prosperity.   What nation oblivious of those evils which
retard the progress of *the people* towards independ-
ence and proprietorship, forcing them into conditions
depressing and impoverishing, withholding from them
means of self-elevation and ambitious enterprise, ever
attained to the *perfection* of national prosperity, greatness, and self-sustenance?

> " Ill fares the land, to hastening ills a prey,
>   Where wealth accumulates, and men decay;

Princes and lords may flourish, or may fade:
A breath can make them, as a breath has made;
But a bold peasantry, their country's pride,
When once destroyed can never be supplied."

Arrived at Chatsworth, we find entrance abundantly allowed to ourselves and many others. Several neatly-dressed and intelligent young women conduct the visitors through suites of stately apartments, embellished with works of art such as usually adorn royal palaces; paintings, valuable as portraits of historical characters, or as works of the old masters and of leading modern artists. We are also permitted to enjoy a fine gallery of sculpture.

The family chapel of this princely residence is elaborately decorated through its frescoed ceilings and in its rich panelled carvings; the beauty of stained glass and marble contributing to its perfect adornment. We marvel at the luxuriousness of these accessories to private family worship, yet heartily approve them, for we believe there should be a harmony of outward condition with the grace, concord, and beauty of the spiritual nature.

While the sincere worshipper needs no external circumstance to prompt his devotion, yet his whole nature recognizes and rejoices in those surroundings and influences that, in sympathy with his religious emotions, cannot fail to stimulate and enhance the enjoyment of their exercise. Milton, whose pious thought seems to have been almost inspired, and whose worship was instinctive and sincere, most happily expresses the effect of those æsthetic forms of beauty that, through the eye, minister to the soul, and those subtile influences which, through the ear, soften and often subdue the heart:

> "I love the high embowéd roof,
> With antic pillars massy proof,
> And storied windows richly dight,
> Casting a dim religious light.
> There let the pealing organ blow .
> To the full-voicéd choir below,
> In service high and anthems clear,
> As may with sweetness through my ear
> Dissolve me into ecstasies,
> And bring all heaven before my eyes."

The conservatory and gardens are among the most celebrated in England. The former is three hundred feet long by one hundred and forty-five feet wide, and occupies an area of about an acre. It is filled with rare and exquisite plants, and even trees have been imported from their distant native soil. Every clime seems to have contributed of its flowering wealth to fill this conservatory with bewildering charm. The eye is feasted with richest color, while Araby's gardens have helped to burden the air with their perfume. The air simulating through artificial means that of the native clime of these fair daughters of the soil, and the sun's beams, through the glass, being so bright, perhaps they are deluded into the belief that they are basking in the rays of a torrid sun. Roses blush beneath its fervid kiss, and lilies pale under its ardent gaze ; while trees, vines, and bushes drop prodigally their luscious treasures.

"The gardens next our admiration call."

They are planned and arranged scientifically, art often superseding nature; no natural

"Wildness to perplex the scene.
*　*　*　*　*　*
Grove nods at grove,
Each alley has a brother."

Perhaps some would enjoy more that simplicity of nature which is here exchanged for the rigid forms of artificial system.

A great curiosity is in the form of a willow made of iron, but so perfect an imitation of a natural tree that as we look upon it, apparently growing out of the soil, we can scarce be made to believe that it is a product of *human* skill. A sly touch of the guide's hand upon a hidden spring, and every leaf is made to send forth a delicate spray of water, the tree bursting into tears; *literally a weeping willow !*

CHAPTER XVIII.

STRATFORD-ON-AVON.

STRATFORD-ON-AVON, however suggestive of beauty its name may be, possesses no other attraction to its visitors than its association with and memorials of the most marvellous poet and dramatist that the world has ever known.

It is evening, long after the heavens have hung out their lights to guide just such travellers as we, that, alighting from the car, we wend our way to the "inn," where we propose to "take our ease" for the night. It is with almost shame that the next morning we acknowledge ourselves to have enjoyed a most commonplace sleep, unvisited by dreams, although we had thought that "the very gods would show us a vision" under such circumstances. Within a few steps from our inn is the house which the Fates chose to be the birthplace of a genius so brilliant that its light has dazzled the world; of a poetic fire whose glow has never died out, but burns still, and ever will, that it may warm the souls of all posterity. Awaking from our prosaic slumbers, we arise the next morning to realize the longings

264

of years, to visit the haunts of the boyhood and early
manhood, and—alas! the terminus of all—the grave of
Nature's most gifted son. Ah! why is it that she is
so prodigal of her bounty to some and so niggardly to
others? Would not the world be brighter and happier
were the aspirations measurably attained, of those who
feel themselves beggars in intellect? if Nature's stamp
of royalty was impressed upon their brow; their intellect broadened, expanded, elevated; their talent commanding in its sphere and regal in its power? It is,
we know, only certain souls that hunger after a higher
earthly attainment; to such, having a fellow-feeling, we
would say that, were they to reach the stand-point they
now long for, they would still be restless in their desires;
their ambition, o'ervaulting itself, refusing to be satisfied with *any earthly* development. And is not heaven
made more inviting, that *there*, and *there only*, will be
experienced, if not the absolute fruition, the *progressive*
condition, which must satisfy the intensest hunger and
thirst of our spiritual nature? Here the seed is sown,
and in some cases, as in his whose immortal reputation
we have come to honor, the tender leaf, ay, even the
fragrant blossom, is revealed in all its rich luxuriance to
an admiring world. But 'tis reserved for the garden
of Paradise, with its ripening influences and in the light
and warmth of the Creator's presence, to show forth
the *fruit* of intellectual and spiritual growth.

The house in which Shakspeare spent the latter years of his life, and in which he died, has been ruthlessly destroyed; but the humble, even mean, little wooden cottage where he was born, with its lowly roof, quaint windows, and porched door, is in itself, we think, a pleading relic of a time long gone by, and in connection with its associations is unsurpassed in, as it were, a sanctified charm. We knock, and are promptly admitted by a lady, whose refinement and education vindicate her claim to the title. She and her sister,—both elderly,—long since reduced from affluence to penury, have been wisely chosen and appointed to the delicate task of guiding visitors to the different apartments of the house, explaining very fully and lucidly the uses of what is seen, and giving information not to be found in books, but gleaned from traditionary sources familiar to the town. The street door opens into the family room, within whose wide fireplace is a crude stone seat, upon which we are invited to sit a moment, as it had been the favorite lounging-place of the boy poet. We accept the invitation, trying to imagine with what dreamy intentness he had gazed upon the glowing embers, each coal invested with some bright fancy; weird creations springing out of the flickering flames; sparkling visions of the future dancing before him, even as the sparks flew upward. We saunter into the outer rooms, and then, mounting the narrow, steep stairs, are

shown the room where the great spirit was ushered into
a world which was, ere many years, to resound with
his praises. We step softly into the chamber where the
tender infant soul had blossomed into life, and where
the wonderful "man-child" had first blessed his mother's
eyes. We stand gazing and dreaming; had the fortunate mother, while that little life was throbbing beneath
her heart, any prescience of the giant powers there in
embryo? And when the first cry gladdened her ears,
had she a thought that the voice would, by its utterances, delight and astonish all Christendom for all time?

But we are aroused from our revery by an invitation
to step into the museum, where are collected many mementos of Shakspeare's early life. Perhaps what
interests us most is a heavy, clumsy, wooden desk, disfigured by all sorts of boyish hieroglyphics, deep punc-
tures, and rude carvings; showing that the hands of
the young student had been no less busy than the brain
teeming with the wealth of thought and fancy. This
is the desk used by Shakspeare when at the grammar-
school, which is subsequently pointed out to us; a long,
low, rambling building situated on one of the principal
streets of the town. And now, after visiting the house
of his birth and home of his early years, and the school
where " the young idea was taught to shoot,"—although
it took a wider range than the village pedagogue could
follow,—and the site of the house which he built upon

his final return to the home of his youth, we saunter on to the church where his remains have been allowed to rest in peace. It is beautifully situated on the banks of the Avon, whose murmur, like " a low, perpetual hymn," seems to soothe into profounder repose the slumbering dead. Large and umbrageous trees form a short broad avenue to the church. Their branches, meeting and intermingling, exclude the glare of the sun. 'Tis fitting that Nature should cast a dim light over the place, for there is a sacred tenderness lurking in sweet shadows which comports more fully with the associations of such a scene than does the full blaze of a radiant sunlight. In *it* there is a sparkling gladness ; but we find the quiet, sequestered shade of her protecting foliage harmonious with a sad or dreamy spirit.

We enter the church, and are pleased to see that the morning service is in progress; the curate and the responding clerk kneel side by side, while two ladies form the congregation. We noiselessly steal into our seats, and, with a peculiar pleasure, join in the prayers ; not unconscious, however, that the bust of the great man, whose tomb we have come to visit, is beaming benignantly upon us. The bust is placed in a niche in the wall above the marble slab inserted in the pavement below, on which are inscribed the following curious words, said to have been written by Shakspeare himself:

" Good friend, for Jesus' sake forbeare
To dig the dust enclosed here.
Blest be he who spares these stones,
And curst be he who moves my bones."

His wife and favorite daughter lie beside him, their
names inscribed upon tablets like his own. We linger
long upon the favored spot, bearing away with us a
tiny spray of the vine which clings lovingly to the
outside wall of the church.

It is to be supposed that a man who would make of
his imaginary characters such irresistible lovers must
have employed in his own behalf the delicate skill of
which he was master. There was, then, an episode in
his life whose traces we are inclined to explore. The
home of Anne Hathaway, who became the wife of the
poet, is situated in a neighboring parish. "You must
go across the fields a long way," is the direction given
us; and undaunted we wend our way through "green
pastures and beside still waters," that we may lay a
flower on the altar of love. And perhaps—we
think—we are treading in the footsteps of the lover
who has so eloquently pictured love and charm, that
bachelors have sighed with envy, and maidens have
wished " that heaven had made them such a man."

On we wander, through pastoral scenes, climbing
over many a stile, until, on crossing a pretty stream
whose babbling waters seem to whisper something of

the old-time love, we find ourselves beside a little
rustic gate. This opens into the garden of the house
with which is associated so much of romance. The
cottage is in itself a prominent feature,—a long, low
building, whose thatched roof, its chimney from which
smoke is wreathing, its little windows, and tiny porch,
give it the pleasing aspect of a cosy, humble home.
We are admitted by an old woman who lives in the
house, and who claims to be a descendant of the Hathaway family.

On entering the cottage we are introduced into the
family room, where all associations are concentrated,
as here the once humble lover, but afterwards the
illustrious husband, was wont to be entertained. Beside the mammoth fireplace stands a plain, rude,
wooden bench, on which, in all probability, the wooing
was accomplished. Its original position had been on
the small porch, under a clambering vine, where the
moon,—the favorite luminary of lovers,—with her
pretty young sisters, the stars, could, with their tender
light, brighten love's sweet dream. But so successful
have been the attacks made upon it by the pocket-
knives of tourists, that, to secure its protection from
unscrupulous collectors of souvenirs, it has been placed
under the immediate supervision of the custodian of
the cottage, the garrulous old lady who entertained us.
The floor of the room is composed of stone flagging;

the low ceiling of large beams; the capacious cupboard occupying one side of the wall affording opportunity for the display of such ware as a humble housekeeper can boast. The wainscoting around the room is such as is rarely seen in the humbler houses of olden times, and is one index of the superiority of the circumstances and social position of the Hathaway family, whose homestead this cottage is proved to have been. They were probably farmers of the better class, as papers are still extant showing them to have been well-to-do land-owners and tillers of the soil.

The book, in which the old woman requests us to inscribe our names, contains those of several of the loved bards of our own native land, who had come to honor the memory of their brother poet. She proudly exhibits an ancient Bible in which the names of several of her remote ancestors are inscribed, but 'tis evident that their history and connection with the poet's wife are difficult to define. The mists of time have obscured much that would be of interest now, and but little light can be brought to bear upon circumstances connected with the early life and domestic experience of Shakspeare. That the woman of his choice was fair and comely, with a nature correspondingly attractive, who that is familiar with his conception of the female character can doubt? He has attributed to woman weaknesses, 'tis true; but would she be charming without them?

Failings, but how oft "they lean to virtue's side"!
We all know that some of his feminine creations have
become immortalized; shining, as they do, with all the
virtues which give lustre to womanhood; with those
gifts which crown her intellect; those attributes that
show her to be of full, rich soul, capable of unselfish
devotion; unassailable chastity; affection disinterested
and undying; fortitude unflinching; dignity serene
and lofty; yet with a humanity so sweet, a pliability
so winning, a temper so gentle, that the author must,
Pygmalion-like, have become enamored of his own
creation; delighted with his success in representing
womanhood pure, while warmly emotional; gifted, yet
unassuming; dignified, yet sweetly gracious; strong,
yet lovely in her weakness,—women to be won; creatures "not too bright or good for human nature's daily
food." We have no reason to believe, however, that
the mental gifts of Anne Hathaway were above medi-
ocrity; nor need we wonder at this, when we remember
that the majority of men of genius and vast intellectual
endowment have married women of very ordinary
calibre and attainments. Perhaps it is that they seek
a foil in the indifferent, and sometimes vapid, intellect,
dull wit, and undeveloped sentiment of their wives,
that their own superior minds and brilliant parts may
shine the more conspicuously. Or is it, that longing—
as man's heart ever does—for home, its domestic ties

and joys, and believing that a high development of
woman's intellectual nature would divert her thought
and absorb her time to the detriment of " household
good," they prefer the prosaic worker and skilful house-
wife to the sympathetic, literary companion? But man
is not driven to a choice of this alternative, since the
happy combination is often found of a woman of fine
natural powers which have been richly cultivated, with
a heart gifted with a capacity for the enjoyment of
home-life.

Is not such a woman the better fitted for the high
and holy office of motherhood? and do not intelligence and mental culture impart a greater charm to
love, helping to feed the flame aglow in the heart, adding
piquancy and stimulus to its indulgence?

A well-stored mind, a bright and sparkling wit, will
greatly aid a wife in beguiling the leisure of an erudite
husband; and while her literary culture enables her to
be a sympathetic companion in his *graver* pursuits, her
feminine fancy will, like the sunshine, play around his
pathway, brightening and amusing his *lighter* hours.

We would fain believe that the woman of Shakspeare's choice was sufficiently intelligent to appreciate
the marvellous genius of her husband, and that while
he poured into her ear his pretty conceits, almost inspired conceptions, and philosophic conclusions, she
listened with proud and sympathetic enthusiasm. We

can imagine that as he read to her his impassioned storied love, she was borne along on the overwhelming tide of his eloquent thought, feeling wooed and won again with the heroine of his play.

Before turning away from the humble cottage, we accept the invitation to drink from the well, whose cool waters had so often quenched the thirst of the poet-lover.

As we wander back to the inn, we mentally contemplate the character and ponder upon the works of the great man. A mind so comprehensive; a wit so sparkling; a philosophy so profound; a knowledge of the human heart so searching, so intuitive, that it would seem he had discovered the most secret springs of action, the subtlest sources of human feeling; divining all those mysteries of the soul which, to other minds, have been past finding out. With what vivid power has he described the anguish of the tortured soul; the frenzy of rage; the tumult of unholy passion; the sweet, tender joys of an innocent love! What exquisite portrayals of all that is lovely and feminine, and how powerful his delineations of the grand and heroic in the masculine character! With what subtile skill has he depicted the cringing meanness of a despicable nature, and masterfully described all the varied phases of human emotion in its divinest guises and in its most repulsive forms!

Reluctantly we bid adieu to the little town which so proudly guards its sacred trust,—the mouldering dust, relics, and memorials of the "sweet bard of Avon,"— assured that ever after we shall, with even keener relish, enjoy the mental feast which his works afford.

CHAPTER XIX.

CHESTER—THE LAKE REGION—A REMARKABLE DRIVE.

CHESTER.

As Chester, England, was the *first* city we visited after landing at Liverpool, we are aware that an account of it is rather misplaced *here*. And in ignoring all method in our *written* course of travel, flitting here and there, at "our own sweet will," we throw ourselves upon the courtesy of our readers, upon which we are conscious of drawing heavily. Indeed, in pleading guilty to the charge of an erratic style, we trust to receive the lenient judgment usually awarded to the *confessing* culprit!

We have during the past twelve days thoroughly enjoyed the distinctive beauty and grandeur belonging to the ocean, as none have the fullest opportunity of doing but "those who go down to the sea in great ships." Watching the sunlight flashing upon the rolling waves; making of the spray a rainbow, and of the swelling sea a kaleidoscope of color; our eye wandering to the distant horizon, where great vessels like our own appear·"like painted ships upon a painted ocean." Near and far the vast expanse reveals to the senses influences, at times, soothing and delightsome; the sky often seeming to bend lovingly over its rival beauty, the ever-changing sea; and at others, agitating, in their awful sublimity! Having, then, enjoyed the varied moods of Nature in her marine domain, whether of calm, as on an unruffled moonlight night, or in the majesty of her wrath, when the waves are turbulent and the sea-god rages, we turn, at length, with yearning desire, towards the land. There the youthful Spring, which during our voyage has burst forth from her thraldom,—so long detained by the icy grip of Winter,—is now displaying her tender charms, as if to give to the stranger a sweet welcome to the green bowers and shady lanes of Old England.

Crossing the ferry and taking the car, we soon find ourselves introduced to the quaint and delightful old cathedral town of Chester. Here we are comfortably established at a hotel, in a room whose belongings help us to realize that we are indeed in the Old World. And what wonder if to-night, when sleeping in the antiquated couch whose high posts and heavy hangings remind us of the beds associated with our grandparents' repose, we should dream of times when our ancestors slept their innocent sleep on just such elevated thrones, concealed from all vulgar gaze by just such enfolding draperies !

But the sun is setting, and we hasten to enjoy a walk upon the ramparts of the old city. It is encircled by a wall on whose top two persons can walk abreast. Being considerably elevated above the level of the town, it permits us to enjoy a view of wide extent. The trees, and the shrubbery which line the walk, are in full leaf and blossom; the landscape, "moist, bright, and green," smiles around us; the air is vocal with the glad song of birds, and perfumed with the breath of the prevailing verdure. Never has Nature seemed so rich. We have been so long secluded from her green fields and gardens, looking only upon "water, water everywhere," that now, when surrounded by her abounding treasures of bursting bud and leafy tree, and by the birds who seem wanton in their gladness, our spirits catch the universal joyousness.

What a memorable walk ! made delightful not only by the display of Nature's lavish beauty, but of ancient towers, arches, and various relics of the distant past, and buildings of architectural quaintness which greatly please the fresh eyes of the American travellers.

The Cathedral, which gives fame to this olden town, affords material for prolonged study. The exquisite wood-carving in the choir is said to be the finest in England. The windows of the "Lady Chapel," which are modern, are very beautiful, while the monuments and tablets are very curious. We wander into the chancel, where the morning service is being very impressively sung by youthful choristers. How solemn and sacred are the moments thus spent within the walls consecrated a thousand years ago! How many voices have here been raised and responses given by those who have for many hundred years past been chanting the Saviour's name in heaven!

We saunter through the cloisters, peer into dark and sepulchral recesses, and, leaving reluctantly the ancient · place, turn many a backward glance.

The ruins of St. John's Chapel, in another part of the town, are beautifully picturesque, draped and festooned by luxuriant and graceful vines. How almost supernaturally chaste seem such ruins by moonlight! and how happily has Madame de Staël declared that "the sun should shine on festivals, but the moon is the light for ruins"!

A REMARKABLE DRIVE.

Not a remarkable drive because it is of John-Gilpin-like speed, or that it has the supernatural character of Tam O'Shanter's immortal ride, but because of its being amid scenery famed for its beauty, and that within its limits are to be seen the homes of some of the most celebrated of England's great poets.

Taking outside seats on the coach at Windermere, we drive through a beautiful country, ofttimes obtaining glimpses of the large, fine lake of Windermere, on whose broad surface we long to sail. What indeed can be prettier than a sheet of smooth water on a summer-like day, when the soft breezes kiss it into ripples, which glide over the surface like the smiles which flit over the face of a sleeping babe as it dreams—ah, who knows of what? We have often wondered how any one could associate monotony with water in its varied forms of ocean, lake, and river. In the first there is a grandeur, an awful sublimity, which suggests eternity in its mystery and vastness. For who can fathom the depths of the ocean, or measure its resources, or by human vision define its limits? Is it invested with a soul, that in its overwhelming wrath it seems to summon ours to a dread tribunal? Or with a spirit, that appeals at times in gentlest murmurs to our finest sensibilities? when our æsthetic nature awakens to enthusiasm, as the heavenly artist paints on the broad canvas, in colors that rival the rainbow and vie with the sunset. Oft have we watched these colors, the more beautiful that they glide past in rapid succession, green, blue, golden, and silvery. And then the *music of the sea,* Nature's organ, whose deepest sweep of sound is soul-stirring, whose flute-like airs are clear and high, and again a grand æolian harp, whose breathings are of almost celestial melody.

A river, although unlike the majestic ocean or placid lake, is full of beauty, graceful in its flow, and varied in its meanderings; forming a silvery fringe to flowering meadows, and making their banks so fresh and moist as to coax into bloom the "wild thyme," the modest daisy, the yellow primrose, and the forget-me-nots, which love the dewy moisture of the "river's brim." How coquettish seems the gliding stream, as stealing through tangled wildwoods it flashes into the broad sunlight and before the open vision, anon stealing into the quiet shade of overhanging branches and drooping vines to peep forth below at some unexpected spot. Gradually broadening and expanding into statelier beauty, it changes its youthful proportions and maiden coyness to assume the dignity of an open, flowing, and grand river.

The "Lake District" of England is almost unsurpassed in beauty, for not only do the lakes display their bright mirrored charms, but the whole landscape is graceful with "hills and dales and leafy woods." Nature, in her sweetest mood, has lavished with an exceptional prodigality her treasures of water and meadow, hill and valley. Our horses, even, seem infected with the universal buoyancy, scarcely giving us time to throw a tender glance upon a vine-covered cottage, which is built upon an eminence above the road, bearing the apposite name of "Dove Nest," the former home of the gentle, womanly poetess, Mrs. Hemans. We can imagine her poetic muse to have been nurtured in just such a nest. Like a fledgling, it never soared to lofty heights, where it might roam amid heaven's bright sunlight, but twittered sweetly and tenderly amid the shadows. Her home, embosomed in trees, and protected by luxuriant vines from the inquisitive, and yet respectful, gaze of the passer-by, was such an asylum as her disappointed but chastened spirit would seek and love. Like a wounded "dove," she sought to hide her sorrows in a "nest" built high, amid Nature's soothing influences.

On we speed, drinking in full draughts of that pleasure which, although intoxicating in its exhilaration, is innocent, as drawn from the grand resources of Nature,—her buoyant sunshine; her flashing waters; her lofty trees and exuberant growth of bush, hedge, and flower.

After passing through Ambleside, a small, insignificant village, Harriet Martineau's cottage is pointed out. It stands near the highway, and is so enshrouded in dense foliage as to look gloomy and forbidding, a darkness so deep as to symbolize that of her spiritual belief. A mile and a half farther, a little apart from the main road, is Rydal Mount, the home of Wordsworth, one of Nature's grandest interpreters. The house, having been rebuilt since his death, has lost much of its attraction to the admirer of the pastoral poet. Near by is Rydal Lake, the smallest of the district, being only a mile long and one-third of a mile broad. The road, half encircling the lake, soon brings us to the humble home of the poet Coleridge; a low, mean cottage, affording an illustration of the fact that where Nature is most prodigal of her mental endowments, Providence is often the most parsimonious in the bestowal of her temporal gifts. We should think that the poetic muse, a fickle goddess, would have fled from such a haunt, and chosen rather to meet her votary outside of his dreary walls, in Nature's grand audience-chamber, under the blue sky, more beautiful than any frescoed ceiling, and within the walls of her noble hills, with carpet of velvety green, and mirrored lakes reflecting beauty all around.

A little farther, and we are surprised by the driver turning to us and abruptly saying, "Shut your eyes, and don't open them until I tell you." Instinctively we obey, and after whisking around a corner we are relieved by his permission, given in triumphant tone, to "look now."

Ah, it is indeed a scene to dazzle our eyes! The sun seems to have taken on new glory, lighting up the distant hill-tops, and making the trembling bosom of the beautiful lake Grasmere to shimmer and sparkle as with diamonds, giving a tenderer shade of green to vegetation and foliage, throwing soft shadows on the mountain slopes, and affording bright glimpses of sweet valleys. A thrill penetrates our being as the glorious view bursts upon our vision.

Here, nestling beneath a towering hill,—"Helm Crag,"—is the little village of Grasmere, in whose graveyard the poets Coleridge and Wordsworth lie buried. We linger long over the graves marked by simple tablets. Death has not separated those who were neighbors and friends while living, and who now lie very near to each other in the little graveyard under the hills. A small stream flows gently by their graves, and large trees shade the spot. We think it eminently fitting that Wordsworth, the lover of Nature and her eloquent disciple, should repose now in her bosom—and not in a stately mausoleum—by her murmuring waters, and beneath the green shelter of her wide-spreading trees, where the birds trill their morning song. And Nature, with her numberless voices, chants her vespers over him whose ears were once so ready to catch her faintest whispers. Caverns, lakes, and woods

"Were unto him companionship."

What wonder that an unsurpassed simplicity and

purity should characterize the emanations of a soul born, developed, nurtured, and matured amid such natural beauty and grandeur as surrounded his home! Could there be a "soul so dead," a tongue so mute, that would not be made to blossom into tender sentiment? and if poesy slumbered in its nature, would it not waken to warble with bird-like sweetness when wooed by such irresistible charm as ministered to his senses?

Within the graveyard is the exceedingly quaint old church where Wordsworth worshipped. Over his family pew a white marble tablet is inserted, bearing his chiselled portrait.

Mounting again to the top of the lumbering coach, we start anew, but the prospect soon changes, as we ascend Dunmail Pass, from the lovely and picturesque to the most desolate, wild, and dreary. The ascent is seven hundred feet, and, although from its summit we enjoy the enchanting view obtained by looking back upon the pretty villages of the plain, their bulwarks of hills, sheltered valleys and gleaming lakes, yet surrounded as we now are by dearth and barrenness, we gladly near the terminus of the descent. Derwentwater Lake and the village of Keswick, soon greeting and delighting our eyes, afford us one of the finest views of the long and famous drive.

In Keswick the poet Southey lived from 1803 to 1843, the date of his death. It is a singular fact that

within the radius of half a day's ride, from Windermere
to Keswick, we pass the former homes of four poets,
whose names fame has made as " familiar as household words" to the English-speaking race; a galaxy
of brilliant lights which have illuminated the world's
literature and have brightened hearts and homes. For
through the highest poetic thought and its silvery
speech, the mind is cultured; the sentiment elevated;
the best and finest feelings of the heart developed; a
sweet faith and purity inculcated, and religion exalted;
led as we are through the pure teachings of the true
poet—Nature's own child—to look through " Nature
up to Nature's God."

The soul, to whom poetry, grand in conception, pure
in thought, and exalted in tone, appeals in vain; that
refuses to recognize its beauty and to be influenced
through its charm, is like him " who has no music in
his soul," fit for " treasons, stratagems, and spoils."

At Keswick we sleep and dream of our enjoyment,
which, although but the experience of a day, will, by
the blessed power of memory, prove a " joy forever."

CHAPTER XX.

EDINBURGH—THE TROSACHS—SCOTTISH LAKES —GLASGOW.

EDINBURGH.

EDINBURGH is a queenly city ! From the peculiarity of its situation, being enthroned on three ridges, it affords, from some points, grand and extensive prospects. Like many European cities, it offers the two phases of the old and the new, and, although the modern is the finest and most imposing, yet the old portions of the city, with their narrow streets, crowded buildings, dark, dingy, and uninviting though they be, possess the greater attraction, rich as these localities always are in historic associations.

Alighting from the train, we mount many steps, and suddenly find ourselves in a street, properly named Prince. Broad and fine it is. Here, surrounded on each side by a sloping green, planted with tree and shrub, is the very elegant monument of Sir Walter Scott, "Scotia's darling son." It is of white marble, two hundred feet high. Seated within the arches, he is represented in life-size, with a book in his hand and his loved dog by his side. In the niches are statues of the most prominent characters in his works. The most conspicuous object in this beautiful city is the Castle. It is built upon the summit of a rock upon the central ridge of the city, and occupies, with its works, an area of seven acres, with capacity to accommodate two hundred persons. On the esplanade is to be seen the celebrated gun, "Mons Meg," purported to have been forged in Flanders in 1486. In one apartment of the castle the regalia of Scotland are displayed. They were discovered in 1818 secreted in a chest, which being opened by royal command was found to contain this national treasure. The embroidered velvet, faded and dingy, is yet resplendent with jewels. Another room is shown, in which James VI., afterwards King of England, was born. The castle is a magnificent feature of the beautiful landscape. In every direction it may be seen looming up in its grandeur, as immutable as the rock on which it is built, and as grand as Time, with which it seems coeval. Feeling, after leaving it, irresistibly inclined again and again to turn and gaze upon it, we are reminded of Lot's wife, and think that if in the hapless city of Sodom there had been any such stupendous work of human skill, all the accessories of nature adding to its splendid dignity, we should feel renewed pity for the unhappy consequences of her disobedience.

A visit to Holyrood Palace, in another part of the city, proves very gratifying. It is teeming with associations with the unhappy Mary, Queen of Scots. The apartments most intimately connected with her experience are astonishingly small, and seem sepulchral in gloom. The bedsteads are exceedingly ancient in style, and, being hung and covered with dingy, tattered drapery, look anything but inviting even to the weary traveller. We are shown the room where Rizzio, while at supper with the Queen and several of her ladies, was seized and murdered while clinging to her royal robes for protection, she being impotent to save. The guide, blessed with vision unimpaired or imagination in vivid exercise, insists that he can descry on the wooden boards of the floor the stains of the blood which flowed from the fatal wound of the unfortunate and perhaps guilty man. But, although we call in the artificial aid of glasses, we can detect no traces of the sanguinary deed. As the guide points with the toe of his boot to the fancied spots, we remember the familiar scene in which Lady Macbeth exclaims,—

> " Yet here's a spot;
> *   *   *   *   *   *
> Out, damned spot! out, I say!—one, two."

Passing on to the next apartment, we see more of the faded, moth-eaten hangings, with other ancient relics,

all symbolical of the sadness which pervades the association with the beautiful, amiable, unhappy woman
whose frailties we pity, while we condemn. An object
which holds us long is the little shrine before which
she had been accustomed to kneel. Had she crimes to
confess there, or were her misfortunes due more to
weakness of heart than to depravity of nature? Were
this papistical shrine gifted with language, it might
reveal much that is now enshrouded in the darkness of
suspicion, perhaps removing the cloud which .lowers
over her conjugal relations. Opening into this sleep-
ing-apartment is the smallest of dining-rooms, where
she and her unfortunate husband, Lord Darnley, were
in the habit of dining; a door leading into the boudoir
discovers a close private staircase, which gave him ingress to her apartments. Connected with Holyrood Palace, which for some centuries was occupied by the kings
of Scotland, is the abbey founded by David I. It was
in its chapel that Queen Mary and Lord Darnley were
married. It is now in ruins, only its walls standing.

Holyrood Castle is built upon a low plain, Salis-
bury Crags and Arthur's Seat towering above it to the
south. The Queen's drive, which encircles the two,
offers views such as are rarely enjoyed. The ascent is
gradual, the enthusiasm increasing as the road winds
higher and higher on the elevated slopes. The prospect is not only very extensive, but most picturesquely

varied. We see the sparkling waters of the Firth of Forth in the distance; arable plains stretching out before us, dense woods relieving their monotony; the thickly-populated city in its splendor and glory; church steeples flashing in the sunlight; country residences, with noble lawns; little cottages with rural surroundings; the castle in its majestic strength; and the unpretending Holyrood Palace. The precipitous rocky sides of the crags remind us of the Palisades on our noble Hudson. The drive includes the view of many sites connected with Scott's "Heart of Mid-Lothian." As we begin the ascent our attention is directed to the spot where Jeanie Deans is described as meeting Robertson. Farther on is her humble cottage home, and near to it the Laird's house, where her sister Effie sought counsel before beginning her pilgrimage to London.

A *very* ancient-looking building in the old part of the city is pointed out as having been the home of the old Reformer, John Knox. The house is blackened with age, while the fame of the good man, who once lived and preached in it, grows brighter and purer with time. A bow window on the corner of the house formed on many occasions his pulpit, the audience standing in the street below. The church of St. Giles, said to be about one thousand years old, was the scene of his labors, the old pulpit which he occupied

there, being shown now as a sacred relic in the Royal
Institution.

THE TROSACHS AND SCOTTISH LAKES.

Taking coach at Callender, towards the close of a
damp, murky afternoon, we pass through a region
made classic by Scott's "Lady of the Lake." Arriving at the Fall of Gartchonzie, where the Vennacher, leaping over rocks, rushes down to Coilantogle
Ford, we remember it was here that Roderick Dhu
promised to escort Fitz-James

> "As far as Coilantogle Ford,"

and where, upon arriving, he defied him to a mortal
combat :

> "See, here all vantageless I stand,
>   Armed like thyself with single brand ;
>   For this is Coilantogle Ford,
>   And thou must keep thee with thy sword."

Then comes Loch Vennacher, five miles long and
one and a half miles wide. Farther on is the spot
where the Alpine clan lay concealed until Roderick
Dhu's whistle summoned them :

> "Instant through copse and heath arose
>   Bonnets and spears and bended bows.
>   On right, on left, above, below,
>   Sprung up at once the lurking foe ;

From shingles gray their lances start,
The bracken bush sends forth the dart,
The rushes and the willow wand
Are bristling into axe and brand,
And every tuft of broom gives life
To plaided warrior armed for strife."

Ere long, we see, on the left, Benvenue; and opposite, Ben-An; between them lies the Pass of the Trosachs.

From earliest childhood, when enthusiastically enjoying that inimitable book, the "Lights and Shadows of Scottish Life," our eyes have longed to wander over heathery moors and to look upon a kirk and a manse. The latter word has always seemed redolent with the sweet fragrance of domestic, pious life; simple, perhaps humble, and yet possessing all those elements which help to constitute such a home as man hopes for, woman dreams of, and which is sometimes realized.

As we ride on in the coach, we fall into conversation with its only gentleman passenger, listening with pleasure to his explanations of the scenes through which we are passing, familiar to him, as his home, he remarks, is situated in their midst. He verifies the character of a true Scotchman; intelligent, practical, with that sound good sense which is thought to be a rare quality in the world, but of which the Scotch

character has a full share. Of powerful, brawny
frame, gentlemanly mien, and very plain attire, we
are at a loss with what position or profession to invest
him, his remarks giving us no clue. Chancing, however, to allude to our desire to see a " manse," he
smilingly rejoins, " I can soon gratify your wish, as
my own is now not far distant."

And so it is, that our life-long desire is gratified ; for
peering through the gathering shadows of the twilight
we can see, from amid a cluster of trees, the smoke
curling, showing that a house is nigh. The coach
stops before a pretty, low, rural cottage ; its windows,
festooned with vines, look out upon a small green
lawn, and, as the curtains are drawn, we can see the

> " Ingle blinking bonnily,
> The clean hearthstane, his thriftie wifie's smile ;"

and flocking down the broad pathway towards the gate,
" the expectant wee things ;" and the maids, ready to
give their respectful greeting. Then comes the courteous " good-night" of the blessed man, the closing of
the door, and the dropping of the curtains,—

> " Leaving the world to darkness and to me."

A few moments' rapid driving brings us to the hotel

of the Trosachs, within whose pleasant, hospitable walls we are established for the night.

The next morning, after a short drive through a glen, truly picturesque in the natural wildness of its surroundings, we arrive at the pier, where a small steamboat is waiting to convey us over Loch Katrine. Soon we pass a little wooded island, which is the veritable "Ellen's Isle" of Scott's poem ; and here we will borrow his description of the locality :

> " Where gleaming with the setting sun,
>   One burnished sheet of living gold,
>   Loch Katrine lay beneath him rolled,
>   In all her length far-winding lay,
>   With promontory, creek, and bay ;
>   And islands that empurpled bright
>   Floated amid the livelier light ;
>   And mountains, that like giants stand
>   To sentinel enchanted land.
>   High on the south huge Benvenue
>   Down on the lake in masses threw
>   Crags, knolls, and mounds, confusedly hurled,
>   The fragments of an earlier world ;
>   A wildering forest feathered o'er
>   His ruined sides and summit hoar,
>   While on the north, through middle air,
>   Ben-An heaved high his forehead bare."

Opposite " Ellen's Isle," at the foot of Benvenue, is the opening of the passage that leads to the Goblin's

Cave. This is a large space within the mountain, whose entrance is now closed by fragments of rocks, which have been hurled from above, and by the spontaneous growth of trees and shrubs. It was within this natural shelter that Ellen's father secreted her from Roderick Dhu, and where she warbled her "angel hymn."

Loch Katrine is so far different from Loch Lomond as to forbid any comparison. It is grandly wild and picturesque; hedged in by formidable mountains, towering crags, rocks, and foliage.

Nature, who, like other dames, seems subject to variations of moods, was in her roughest when she breathed rugged life into this region; but we would not have her exempt from the mighty power of her turbulence, for she is most grand when she crowns the landscape with ponderous mountains, and lifts up her forms of praise in the lofty hill-tops, and often most eloquent when she gives expression to her wild whims and erratic fancies, by scattering in great confusion bristling crags, scraggy, precipitous slopes, and deep ravines.

Taking coach again at the terminus of the Loch, we ride five miles to Inversnaid, through an elevated country, barren, dreary, and monotonous. Much of its surface is covered by the modest heather, Scotland's native plant. By the by, what a dreary scene does a Scottish

moor usually present! There is something to the mind
of sensibility inexpressibly depressing in this extensive,
unvaried surface of ground, carpeted with one monotonous color, which appears *en masse* dingy, or, at least,
not bright and gay, as the lively green on our Western prairies, where the pretty grass is relieved by numberless flowers of varied color.

At Inversnaid we hasten to climb to the little bridge
over the pretty, rushing, impetuous waterfall, which is
an enjoyable sight in itself, but is made doubly attractive by being associated with Wordsworth's winsome
creation, "The Highland Girl."

The sky so far, on this memorable day, has been
happily adapted to the scenes through which we have
passed; for rugged aspects, dark gorges, and frowning
cliffs should be viewed through a gloomy, clouded atmosphere, as on stern features and lowering brows a
bright, sunny smile would seem incongruous. Now,
as we are to be introduced to the lovely scenes of Loch
Lomond, the Queen of the Scottish Lakes, the sunlight,
that grand revealer of the milder types of natural
beauty, bursts forth in its glory, illuminating gentle,
grassy slopes, crowning with silvery light the hill-
tops, and beaming on the waters, which return the
smile; brightening, too, the verdant little isles which,
reposing on the ample bosom of the lake, quench their
thirst there, even as the babe, while slumbering on

14

the mother's breast, instinctively imbibes its nourishment.

As the lake broadens more and more, discovering to us extended views of wondrous beauty, infinitely diversified, we cease to exclaim, but are silent through intensity of enjoyment, for oftentimes, when the heart is most affluent in feeling, the tongue is most beggared in expression.

It had occurred to us that this feast of the senses might be followed by a famine, particularly as we had been led to expect meagre entertainment in Glasgow, the next scene of the shifting drama of travel; but on reaching our hotel here, situated on George's Square, we find our first impressions very agreeable ones. This square is embellished by many monuments and statues of great men, and forms a fine promenade. In a most enjoyable ride around and through the city, we find its parks and several of its streets, with those portions of the city affording residences for the wealthy citizens, worthy of *any* city and most satisfying to the stranger.

The splendor of the University, and the remarkable site on which it is built, make it as imposing an edifice and inviting a spot as we have seen anywhere. It occupies an eminence from which an unsurpassed view of the city is obtained, and is for this reason alone well worth a visit. A recent munificent gift from the Marquis of Bute to the University will be devoted to the erection of a grand hall, to be called by his name.

A fine building is the Royal Exchange, in Queen Street, the architectural ornamentation of the sides and the really elegant portico of the front commanding universal admiration.

CHAPTER XXI.

ABBOTSFORD—MELROSE ABBEY—CARLISLE.

ABBOTSFORD.

THERE are certain intellectual shrines to which all cultured persons would gladly make a pilgrimage, and it is not strange that a country as rich as Great Britain in science, poetry, and prose, should possess more than one Mecca where we may pay our worshipful regard. To the enthusiastic lover of literature and science there is great danger of cherishing an idolatrous admiration for the representatives of talent and genius, failing to look beyond these merely *human* mental lights to the *Divine* Luminary whose dim and indistinct reflection all earthly development must be, however grand comparatively.

We are naturally hero-worshippers, and if excuse can be found for such worship 'tis when we strive to crown even the lifeless brows of such bards and men as Homer, Milton, Shakspeare, and the great revealers of natural and mechanical mysteries, as Newton, Fulton, Stephenson, Watt, and others, with the wreath of fame so deservedly won in life.

300

With our mind and heart in full sympathy we seek the haunts of the charming poet and unequalled novelist, Walter Scott. He who through his pen can win the critical appreciation of his readers appeals successfully, at the same time, to their emotional natures, as we owe a debt of gratitude for hours made "rosy-fingered" through the magic of a writer's thought and fancy; life thereby cheated of many a weary moment, sadness and sorrow blunted, and sometimes forgotten even, through the intense interest excited by the graphic portrayal of life's brightest, fairest scenes. 'Tis with eagerness, then, towards the close of a gloomy autumn day, when the skies have been dim and threatening and are still lowering darkly above us, that we ride from Melrose to Abbotsford. The drive is a dreary one, through a desolate-looking country. We alight at the head of a short lane leading to the house which had been the loved home of a man whose mental powers were worthy of a palace and a crown; for kings and queens may be formed of ordinary human mould, but such an intellect as his has few peers, and is only created by Divine will. We look with mournful pleasure upon the fine house which had cost its owner such severe mental labor to secure, remembering those "births of intellect" which were the rich fruit of a mind so prolific that it could without great mental throes, but even with ease, deliver itself of thoughts, fancies, and sentiments which it would seem could only be conceived, if at all, amid conditions of ease and luxurious leisure.   It is indeed only the mind of richest resources and profoundest power that could, with such felicity and rapidity, throw off volume after volume, each hailed by an eager, expectant world with unabated delight.

The muse, so coy and reluctant, and so difficult to win by the ordinary writer, who must court inspiration and seek every inviting means to secure it, was by Walter Scott never summoned in vain, but was always present awaiting his behest.

We enter an open side-door, and find ourselves in an uncarpeted antechamber, where is a huge volume in which visitors are expected to inscribe their names. An inner door presently opens, a small party issues from it, and we are invited by an intelligent woman to wander through the rooms associated with the literary and the home life of the celebrated man.   We follow sadly, the twilight harmonizing with our feelings; the house is dark and gloomy, the rooms deserted; the great and noble spirit that once inhabited them has passed away, and their brightness faded out with his life.   We ascend a flight of steps and enter a room sacred to the memory of the great author, as his *sanctum sanctorum.*   A small room, indeed! too small to have contained a mind whose realm of fancy was world-wide, whose breadth of vision soared infinitely beyond the four walls which enclosed his bodily presence, creating for itself scenes too fascinating to be suggested by aught that met his eye as it roamed over the bounded landscape. One large window supplies the light, looking upon a contracted but pretty flower-garden.

An open fireplace, its glow long since turned to ashes; shelves filled with books; a narrow, circling gallery, with a flight of steps leading to it and to his private chamber; a table in the middle of the room; a very ample leather-covered chair before it, compose the furniture. The chair is worn, and the table shows traces of constant use, seeming the more precious for the signs, as is a beloved face, whose very wrinkles become dear to us. Long and with moistened eyes do we gaze on these relics before following the patient guide into the noble, well-stocked library, which opens from the study. It is said to be enriched with twenty thousand volumes, and among the most interesting are those works which the late owner contributed from his own brain. The ceiling of this room is elaborately carved. The dining-room is very large, its ceiling of carved oak. It contains many pictures, the most remarkable that of the head of Mary, Queen of Scots, in a charger, painted the day after her execution, by Amias Canrood.

A covered case in this room is filled with gifts from crowned heads and others, and with several relics of Scott's brother-poet, Robert Burns. This room, whose broad, low window looks upon the river Tweed, as it flows by at the foot of the lawn, is the one in which Scott died, having, at his request, been brought here that he might rest his dying gaze upon the water he loved so well, his life flowing out peacefully, his weary spirit lulled into sweet repose by the gentle ripple of the ever-gliding stream. So, borne on the waves of time, whose upheavals had agitated and disturbed his later years, his grand spirit was launched upon the Ocean of Eternity, his splendid powers knowing there the fullest fruition.

The drawing-room, furnished in ebony and containing several rich and rare cabinets, adjoins a long, narrow room, filled, as is the hall, with armor and other curious memorials of ancient times; but the objects which draw and rivet attention are in a glass case, which encloses the suit of clothing last worn by the famed author, even his shoes and hat; the accoutrements of a tired soldier, who, after fighting the battle of life manfully and well, had surrendered to the power of death, laying aside the vestiges of his human life to assume the brighter garb of an angel of light.

MELROSE ABBEY.

Three miles from Abbotsford, in the village of Melrose, stand the ruins of the famous abbey of that name. It was founded by David I. in 1136, dedicated to the Virgin Mary, and conferred upon the monks of the Cistercian order. The principal portion of the church remains, but a part only of the roof, and that over the chancel; this is supported by groups of pillars, whose pedestals and capitals exhibit the finest carvings of flowers. The abbey is thought to present the noblest specimen of Gothic architecture and sculpture remaining in Scotland; the east window, facing the entrance, is incomparably fine, a model of architectural skill and beauty. It is fifty-seven feet high and twenty-eight feet broad. Under it, where probably once stood the altar, Alexander II. was buried. A large marble slab covers his tomb. Another slab designates the spot where was interred the great heart of the Scottish patriot, King Robert Bruce. An unsuccessful attempt had been made to carry it to the Holy Land, but it was eminently proper that it should rest in the soil for which it bled and struggled and even died; for his death is said to have resulted from his early hardships and life of toil and exposure. "After life's fitful fever he sleeps well" within these beautiful ruins, with Nature's pennons—the graceful tendrils of green vines—

floating in the summer breeze, while the exquisite window above forms a finer headstone than any modern monument could do.

Patriotism is one of the grandest sentiments of the soul; one of the most liberal of affections; expansive in its sweep; magnanimous and unselfish in its devotion. Demanding as it does an entire ignoring of personal interest, a surrendering of all one's individual good for that of the nation at large, an immolation of self upon the altar of one's country, it must evince a nobility of nature, a depth of soul-power, a grand emotional capacity, and a breadth of mind that give to the world the noblest "assurance of a man."

As long as there is so much of petty meanness, not only floating on the surface of society, but clogging the under-currents of life, so much of intense selfishness apparent, of craving and clamoring for self-aggrandizement, an utter yielding often of the whole moral nature to trickery and corruption in political circles, no *true patriot* will be allowed to go down to his grave

"Unwept, unhonored, and unsung."

We believe the effect of these renowned ruins to be greatly impaired, if not destroyed, by their contiguity to other and very inferior objects. The abbey is enclosed within very high walls, ingress being obtained by personal application to a custodian; but under its very shadow are a hostlery and many insignificant buildings, occupied by the humblest class. We long, by some grand Archimedean lever, to remove bodily these sacred ruins to some spot where, aloof from all surroundings, they may display the grandeur which lies within their splendid columns, picturesque walls, and fragmentary cloisters.

CARLISLE.

Carlisle, although a pleasant old town, fails to tempt the tourist to a prolonged stay, its beautiful cathedral and formidable castle alone rewarding detention. The latter, situated on an elevation which commands an extensive view of the surrounding country, is so truly a vestige of feudal times as to be of great curiosity to visitors from the New World. Its origin dates back so far as to be lost in obscurity, but it is probably a stronghold built by the Romans. Showing no signs of decay, but in its impregnable strength seeming to defy the world, it will probably stand as long as the city of its founders, and when " Rome falls, the world" will fall.

It is now the barracks of the military, and, as we happen to visit it at the hour of drill, we are further edified by a sight which always quickens a timid woman's blood and makes her shrink back, as a martial host with rapid, impetuous tread advances, obeying the orders to "shoulder arms" and "charge bayonets." Gliding past the soldiers' ranks, we climb to the ramparts, from which we enjoy a prospect very pleasing in its wide range of vision. Our minds revert to those troublous times when, during the wars between England and Scotland, this border town and its fortress afforded refuge and security to the affrighted inhabitants of the neighboring country. Mary, Queen of Scots, is said to have stopped here while fleeing from Scotland.

Leaving this grand monument of olden times, we saunter through the sunlit, quiet streets to the majestic cathedral. Entering it through inviting grounds, prettily cultivated, we find ourselves in a vast vestibule, which forms the oldest part of the church, dating back more than a thousand years. The beadle, of imposing figure, with staff of office ostentatiously paraded, pompously conducts us to a seat, as it is the hour of morning service. We form part of a very small audience, but "two or three met together" for the early prayer. Presently the reverend form of the dean, bowed with years, white locks clustering round a noble head, with evidently dimmed vision and with faltering step, enters, leaning on the arm of a young curate. We think, as we observe him in absorbed spiritual exercise, attempting, with the stammering voice of age, to follow the choral service, how soon it must be that his tongue will be unloosed in heaven, joining in the wondrous melody to which the whole nature will be attuned ! How strange a thought that, aged here, bent, decrepit, and trembling with exhausted strength and failing powers, we sink helpless into the arms of death, to awaken instantaneously in another sphere of being, rejuvenated, crowned with perpetual youth, with faculties endowed with heavenly wisdom and perception, soul etherealized, voice of seraphic harmony !

We turn our eyes from the benignant countenance of the aged saint to the younger and less sanctified faces of the minor canons, one of whom conducts the services,—or *leads* them, for the little choristers seem to be the principal officiators. Young, innocent faces most of them have, many of them singing with true unction. As they stand before us in their pure white robes, with uplifted eyes and serious mien, instinctively our thought wanders in imagination to the vast throng of infantile angels around the throne of God, continually chanting praise to Him who said, " Suffer little children to come unto me, and forbid them not, for of such is the kingdom of heaven."

The lofty ceiling of the cathedral is painted in sky-blue, silvery stars dotting its surface. The oriel-window of stained glass over the pulpit is exquisite ; the sun shining through it floods the interior with a gorgeous light, in which are blended the richest colors, beautifying a white marble pulpit, which is placed on one side, as a memorial to Archdeacon Paley, who, having been a native of Carlisle, is buried here.

CHAPTER XXII.

HOMEWARD BOUND—OUR SHIP—THE VOYAGE.

HOMEWARD BOUND.

To the American who has turned his back upon his native land to seek the almost inexhaustible pleasure which is to be found in foreign travel, that variety which meets him at every turn,—and is not human nature constantly clamoring for novelty?—but who at length feels that the feast must end, and home be sought, to him, we say, the words *homeward bound* come with a thrilling sound.

It means return to his native land, which seems to him now, in the light of comparison, more than ever the most desirable of all lands, for although our republican form of government still presents problems which have defied astute intellects to solve, yet he must believe it to contain the grandest elements of national glory. And when time, still riper, shall have burst the shell, throwing off the husk of corruption which has impeded the rich growth, it will reveal a germ which shall contain all the splendor and renown that are possible to a human government.

311

It means, too, a return to a Christian Sabbath. What more refreshing than the rest of that day, the air only broken by the sweet-toned church-bells? What more longed for, while lingering on the Continent, than the calm and quiet of an American Sabbath? What a contrast to the Parisian, where the thud of the hammer falls heavily upon the ear, while the sound of fife and drum penetrates to innermost chambers; scenes of revelry and sounds of mirth constantly offending and jarring upon Christianized sensibilities!

Homeward bound! yes, it means, too, to the satiated traveller, a return to the home, which has no equivalent in the French idiom or experience.

Home! how sad it is to think that he, Payne, who sang so sweetly of its charms, had only *dreamed* of them, and knew them not in the *reality* of his own life! Let us hope that his soul has found a haven, on the heavenly shore, of such blissful rest as he had visions of while on this side of the dark river. Home! which, in its possible happiness, is an emblem of that heavenly retreat where love reigns supreme, and where joy and peace hallow the eternal life!

What enjoyment has not the traveller experienced during his months of absence! What stores of rich facts, what multiplied ideas, what enlarged views, has he not gained! With what quickened perceptions, ennobled sympathies, stimulated intellect, and enkindled enthusiasm has he not returned! What breadth and depth has he not attained, whose arable mind and heart were prepared to receive the good seed which travel sows in all intelligent and receptive natures?

And yet we have met some who, like the Peter Bell of Wordsworth's creation, have

> "Travelled here, and travelled there,
> But not the value of a hair
> Was head or heart the better."

We believe travel to be a great educating power, brightening and developing the intellectual faculties, and affording material for future contemplation and mental digestion. What panoramic views does it afford to pass before the mind in future lonely hours! What dazzling memories to brighten evermore life's gloom! Ever faithful to our mental summons, they shall never die, but fade away in the absorbing glory of Eternity, even as stars cease to twinkle in the crowning light of day!

OUR SHIP.

Those who have not been voyagers on the "deep blue sea" often have the impression that a ship, although grand in its appointments and majestic in its proportions, is a cumbersome, unwieldy, awkward power, and upon their first introduction to one their impressions might be confirmed. But what a change would be wrought in them during the first hours spent on such a gallant steamer as ours, on a bright day, while the brilliant sun is touching with radiant glory the whole surface of the ocean, the fresh breeze making of each wave a "thing of life," and all the influences of the elements surrounding us being peculiarly propitious! With what novel delight do we watch the movements of our beautiful ship, now sinking in the deep embrace of the proud waters, to be tossed aloft like a frolicsome child, then swaying gracefully from side to side, as if to court and then recede from the caress of the dancing waves! How daintily she dips her prow into the crested sea, rising sparkling and dripping with its foam! And when in her graver moods, the elements hushed, how majestically she rides upon the mighty waters!

In the severe gale, "when the waves roar and are troubled" and lash her sides in fury, she sweeps nobly on her course, resisting every assault and outriding every danger. The ocean's mammoth toy, and the ocean's conqueror too, is this noble ship of ours, and when, with proud mien, spread sails, and flag unfurled, she bears us into port, we shall reluctantly bid her adieu.

Go back, mighty ship, to thy enamored spouse, the ocean, safely retracing thy steps through the waves which sport upon its bosom.

THE VOYAGE.

" Ye gods, presiding over lands and seas,
    And you, who raging winds and waves appease,
    Breathe on our swelling sails a prosperous wind,
    And smooth our passage to the port assigned.
    The gentle gales their flagging force renew;
    And now the happy harbor is in view."

Virgil's Æneid.

Sea-sickness differs from most other physical maladies. When under its influence, the poor victim is oblivious to all life's joys and interests; the ties of the heart, even, seem relaxed; the faces of absent children and loved ones may flit before the memory, but for the first time they fail to elicit a smile or to awaken a thrill of tenderness. However amiable the natural disposition, one becomes irritable and captious, wonders that he ever associated pleasure with foreign travel, and, if still acknowledging there be any, thinks it like gaining the gates of Paradise through Hades itself.

That there is no alternative, that the voyage is an inevitable necessity, are facts that give poignancy to his cry, " Ten thousand furlongs of sea for one acre of barren ground." He denounces the man who ever invented food, and the cook, who allows the transmission of its odors to torment his senses, and the waiters, too, who seem to have formed a satanic plot to announce its presence by a deafening clatter of dishes.

Can he ever partake again of home cheer? Will rarest dainties, even, ever again tickle his palate? In a word, shall he *ever eat again?* No, it cannot be; he has forsworn food for evermore!

If Nature in compunctious pity drops the dew of sleep upon the weary eyelids, it is but a short respite: he awakens to wretchedness, for he is to *retch* all day.

The malady is one which, from the time of Noah and his probably suffering companions, no skill has been able to cure or even assuage; indeed, the robust physician in the next state-room may be as completely prostrated as the more delicate frame in our own.

But, as there is no gloom so abiding that time will not dispel it, we find ourselves awaking some bright morning with the familiar old experience of hunger upon us. Can it be that coffee has suddenly resumed its grateful aroma? that broiled steak and baked meats greet once more our olfactories with welcome, savory odors? Yet so it is; the truant appetite has returned, and, what is better, "good digestion waits upon it." We even discover a great impatience for the summons to four meals a day, and make no delicately feminine demands upon the abundance before us. The love of life, too,—that inherent principle,—which really *had* succumbed to the prevailing physical depression of the past several days, has resumed its old sway, and the future, which so lately seemed shrouded in midnight gloom, is now arrayed in all the effulgence of glorious day. Truly, "old things have passed away, and all things have become new."

We believe that nowhere is social pleasure more keenly enjoyed than at sea, after the change has dawned upon all. "A fellow-feeling makes us wondrous kind;" we are a little band separated from the rest of the world, with naught "but a plank between us and eternity;" knit together by the same hopes, the same fears; all bound for the same goal, a port of the New World, yet not knowing but we may be stranded upon the shores of Eternity. There seems to be a universal desire to dispel all depressing thoughts, and to seek in innocent amusement to while the time away. Each contributes his or her share towards the general entertainment, and sweet is the music, droll the pantomime, sparkling the wit, and merry the laughter which enliven the little circle congregated each evening in the cabin. We often look around us and ponder upon the strange scene. We are in mid-ocean; beyond the ken and reach of all humanity; midway between the Old and the New World; floating over a fathomless element, with an unlimited expanse of sky above, the curtains of night concealing its heaven-born light. All is weird-like around us; the dimly-lit cabin, a favorite spot for lurking shadows; the swaying of the lights; the creaking of the ship; the sighing of the

winds, as if deploring their lonely banishment to the
darkness and gloom without; the dash of the waves,
which seem always in restless tumult, their monotonous
music, like a dirge, filling up the intervals of our mirth;
while the sometime roar and shriek of the tempest,
sweeping above and around us, is the powerful requiem
of Nature for the dead, over whom we are sailing.

We look complacently over at the clergyman opposite us, hoping that he, in his spiritual calling, may be
as effective to save as "the ten righteous men" for
whose sake, at Lot's solicitation, the city of Sodom was
to be spared, and, congratulating ourselves that there is
apparently no Jonah on board to endanger our safety,
"we lay us down in peace to sleep," awaking each
morning to fresh enjoyment of the situation.

We find that one's comfort and pleasure on ship-
board are largely dependent upon the character and
bearing of the captain; indeed, all the subordinates seem
to take their cue from him, and as "a little leaven
leaveneth the whole lump," so his graciousness and
uniform politeness seem contagious in the official circle.
We are fortunate in our commander; like him of the
"Nancy Bell," he is a "captain bold," but we trust is
not reserved for a similar fate!

Of "heroic build," Captain H. seems singularly
adapted to the responsible position he has so long filled;
not puffed up, as those often are who are "dressed in

authority," but always sustaining a resolute dignity of manner, which wins our confidence in him as commander, while his intelligence, courtesy, and manliness of character claim our respect and regard.

A chivalric nature is a decided requisite to a captain's social reputation. A bevy of clinging, helpless women hang upon his word of cheer, as a heavy ship drags upon its anchor, and are equally sustained by its inspiring weight. Indeed, so trying is a captain's position made by the wearisome plaints of seasick passengers through demands made upon his assurances of safety by nervous, frightened women, and sometimes by *womanish men*, that we have thought his character should be an epitome of all the virtues which distinguished some of the Biblical saints,—the meekness of Moses, the patience and endurance of Job, with the faith and eloquence of Paul, upon whom was imposed the task of encouraging the crestfallen crew, saying, " I exhort you to be of good cheer : for there shall be no loss of any man's life among you."

A romance at sea being particularly refreshing and exciting, we are glad, after becoming fairly embarked upon our voyage, to discover that we have the germ of one within our midst. All are on the *qui vive*, as the whisper grows rife, and are eager to learn all that can be gleaned from the communicative informant.

To go back a little,—some twenty-five years ago,

a young Englishman, of good family and position, but whose fortunes he must himself expect to carve, full of enterprise and laudable ambition, made his arrangements to sail for America, hoping in its inviting fields to reap a rich crop of wealth.

But there was a drawback ; his heart had been given and his faith plighted to a noble woman. A widowed invalid mother and an aunt claimed, as she thought, her care, and with much suffering, but strong in courage, the lovers parted.

Years passed before the mother died, and soon after the beloved aunt became a bedridden sufferer. The lover in the mean time had planted his energies, as it proved, in a rich soil, and was already harvesting their results. He wrote to his betrothed, urging their marriage, but she, pleading her aunt's dependence, accepted the sacrifice which she felt Providence had imposed upon her. In time her lover married another, and continued to prosper, while the noble English girl plodded on her weary way, performing her duties with a submissive cheerfulness which was rewarded by the grateful love of her afflicted relative.

The aunt died, and after some years a rumor floated to the ear of the woman who had sacrificed her youth to duty, that her quondam lover was now a widower. Had she consulted her mirror and surveyed the effects of time, her heart must have failed her. She would

have seen that the slightness of youth had given place
to an unbecoming rotundity, that all grace of outline
had been lost in unwieldy proportions, the hair tinged
with gray, and that the light of youth had faded from
her eyes through years of watching by a sick-bed.

What, then, must have been her dismay to find that
the lover of her youth was on the ocean, on his way to
see her!

He came. A quarter of a century had failed to obliterate early impressions; Love had successfully defied
Time, that wrecker of beauty and freshness. Was it
an ideal he loved, or did he recognize through the worn
casket the brilliancy and purity of the soul-gem within?
We will not withdraw the veil from those human
hearts; but can we not imagine that their memories
o'erleapt the chasm of years; that they were once
more young and revelling in life's dreams and hopes of
happiness; and that now, purified by suffering and
chastened by the discipline of weary waiting, they are
even the better fitted to be, each to the other, light, joy
and support down the path of life, round which the
evening shadows would soon begin to gather?

Unable to comply with her lover's desire for an
immediate union, she promised to follow him to his
adopted home in America within a few months. Finding it impossible to repeat his absence from a large and
exacting business, with rare delicacy he sent a female

relative to England to act as convoy to his bride-elect,
who is here on the steamer with us! A short, plump
figure, with a good, kind face; short curls dangling on
each side; beaming little eyes, which will soon twinkle
round a good man's hearth; and presenting, altogether,
a most attractive picture of a lovable old maid.

One day, while sitting by our side, she asks if we
think "that one at her time of life can assimilate to
the customs of a new country and succeed in feeling at
home there." "Most certainly," is the answer, for
"if home is where the heart is" the fact is assured.
With a pretty, unaffected shyness she turns towards us,
her eyes luminous with a tearful light, and murmurs,
"*I* think so."

On our arrival at Philadelphia, custom-house officers
are forgotten, politeness, too, we fear, in the universal
desire to see the hero of the drama and to witness the
greeting of the lovers. But curiosity is not fully gratified, for the meeting is consummated, very properly, in
the retirement of a state-room. Presently our hero
appears, and in every respect proves himself worthy of
the character. Tall, nobly formed, with a manner of
great dignity; hair and whiskers quite gray; with a
face so full of benignity and character that we all feel
that our friend may consider her happiness assured in
confiding it to his keeping.

As we drive away we cast back a hurried glance,

which reveals a gentleman bending over the short and ungraceful figure of his *fiancée,* as he assists her into a carriage, her appearance contrasting painfully with that of the distinguished-looking man at her side.

Let them not regret that their youth is past, for the afternoon and twilight of life may be sweeter than its morn and meridian. To be sure, the energies may have somewhat slackened, the blood may course more gently, and the emotions be less vehement in their impulses; but the affections of the heart have struck deeper root and are intensified in their power. There are faces, too, furrowed by time and worn by the friction of life's cares and anxieties, below which the heart beats as freshly as when it throbbed within a youthful breast.

THE END.